Carlos Alvarado

Requests for permission to make copies of any part of this work should be mailed to Permissions Department, Llumina Stars, PO Box 772246, Coral Springs, FL 33077-2246

ISBN: 1-933626-11-9

Printed in the United States of America by Llumina Stars

Library of Congress Control Number: 2006909038

Cry
WaterColors

Dedication

Inspiration is granted on every encounter, but the courage and determination to pursue its guidance comes only from one you admire. Thank you to my mother Berta, my sister Maria, my sister-in-law Marta, and my friends Claudia and Gabriela. Were it not for their encouragement my desire to write would still be in the "if-only-I-could" phase.

Prelude

From atop his daddy's lap, he gripped the steering wheel and stretched to see over the dashboard. Swerving wildly, Mark tried to maneuver the car along the road. His father's hands, spread open like butterfly wings, eased his impetuous turns.

The veins that coursed the back of the hands that guided him were as thick as the shoelace Mark had learned to knot earlier that day. He loosened his hold on the wheel and compared the length of his fingers to those that tenderly held him. There was nowhere he'd rather be than in the lap of the strongest man in all the world.

Mark shifted his weight and looked up to his father's face, then returned the smile that greeted him. Returning his gaze to just above the dashboard, Mark imagined he was driving the car down the road.

◆ ◆ ◆

It was not the recollection of the sun that shone on their Sunday drive around the park that he treasured, nor the wind that whisked through the branches of the willow trees, nor the animal clouds he liked to count as he lay on prickly blades of grass. He cherished the memory of his father's smile, the memory of a world in which he could never be hurt.

If it could always have been Sunday, Mark thought before he slept.

◆ ◆ ◆

It was not Sunday, and he had long since learned to steer a car a straight course. It was night, but even after many years, the emotion still imbued the tempo of his life.

Cloistered in the darkness of the bedroom, his sleep faltered in dreams that yielded to memories that troubled his repose. Awakened after each recollection, litanies of images recalled family he rarely thought about, friends he had long ago lost track of, and characters created for the tales he wrote that were now his sole companions. Distorted by guilt, all glared at him in judgment. Intending resolution, he pieced together the recital.

The dreams told of a distant place and another time, a past that seemed to belong to someone else. Yet among the images, he recognized himself—the cloaked character that gripped his lapels against a cold no one else felt.

Saintly icons, robed in mourning purple, buttressed a church. Worshippers, bent on their knees, prayed in repentance for sins their sufferings had revealed. Self-deprecating penance, dispensed in the isolation of the confessional, guided their psalms. He was cloaked in the purple shroud of Catholic Lent.

Mark had grown up in the ethereal culture of Hispanic Catholicism, where sorrow, guilt, and prayer formed the cornerstones for primal absolution. Through this spiritual purification, one gained God's regard for the dispensation of judgment and granting of rewards.

The ritual of the Catholic universe in the early 1960s was a comfort in the world in which he lived. Were it not for his imagination, this solace might have been his, as well, but fairy tales can displace a child's life.

As real as himself, the angels, stewards of the holy Catholic doctrine, stood in judgment of his every thought and act. Mark feared never doing right; he had no hiding place. At night, while his family slept peacefully, he was often tormented with vivid imaginings of godly disapproval of his daily acts. Crueler than the slap of his parents' hands was the emptiness he felt in his nightly lament. It churned in his gut and bled cold from his sweat glands. In the sphincter of his anus, he felt the pain. This nightly world, suctioned into the hollow of his chest, was the loneliness he feared eternity to be.

At seven, supposedly too young to experience desperation, Mark challenged his confusion. In the silence of his darkened room, he firmly held the point of a knife against his belly. From the pit it made, pressed against his flesh, he felt the warm trickle of blood. Pain turned to anger when he realized it was the promise of eternal reward that allowed God to hold sway over his life. Without eternity, he reasoned, there would be no need for judgment; thus would be resolved his recurrent agony. The knife fell to the floor as he asked God that he be forgiven an eternal existence.

A divine response was delivered that morning by an angel in a police uniform. The messenger's dark skin contrasted the bitter cold of the message given his mother at the front door. Her piercing cry was a siren announcing his father's death in a car accident.

Death had never been as real as eternity, but the silence of his home and the sorrow of his mother told that one was the same as the other. Mark watched from afar, as she cried quietly in her room. He felt her pain, the loneliness of his tormented nights. It was God's punishment for the sacrilege of his petition.

On the cemetery lawn was dug a dark, rectangular hole.
Mark looked away to the black polish of his new stiff shoes.
Brown dirt thumped upon the lid of his father's coffin.
His heels hurt where the shoes rubbed.
Priestly incense sifted through the smoggy air.
The dirt would feel good, if only his feet were bare.
His mother's cry pealed like an offering bell,
And only he knew why his father had died.

When a mound covered the coffin, his mother embraced him and his older brother and sister. Their tears were salty on his lips, but his own face was dry. He tripped on the stiff shoes and fell away from their caresses. Into the dirt, he dug his fingers and screamed in silent prayer. He feared they would know it had been his fault.

Silence extended beyond his prayers, and he retreated into his imagination. In that world, characters harbored thoughts and aspirations he himself feared. Mark became isolated amidst a family that sheltered him with love.

◆◆◆

It was Christmas Eve, Midnight Mass, and Mark was twenty-two years old. Incense filled the hollow of the church. Prayers were sung in solemn tones. Bells chimed like shattered crystals. His heel ached where it rubbed against the leather of his shoe. He had loved his father, but had hoped for dispensation of his guilt. There was none in the penance of the confessional, or in the graces of communion. But the cool marble felt good below his bare feet when Mark left the church.

The rigid order of his Catholicism was displaced by turmoil of identity. He filled conversations with empty sentences, so as not to reveal his lack of social graces. He laughed at jokes that were not funny to conceal his witless humor. He pretended to reciprocate love he felt inadequate to receive. Only to the words that he wrote did he entrust his passion.

That summer, Mark graduated from the University of California at Los Angeles with a degree in literature. No job prospects were handed him with the diploma, so he set out on an introspective trek through the western states. In the abandoned mining towns along the mountain ranges of California and Nevada, he found his muse.

The hissing of the dry gravel below his booted feet was the only sound on the hill above the town of Hamilton, Nevada. Except for the warm breeze, the cemetery was still, as befitted a place of the dead. A single wooden marker drew his attention. Its weathered inscription read, "Mark—1873—Age 22."

Mustard-colored sage covered the flat burial site, as if the ground had never been dug. Motionless, he stood to the side of the grave and stared, as if at the tomb within. In the majesty of the barren hills encircling him was the lure of adventure, an empty canvas on which to paint a life. He breathed the torrid air, whetted with carnal passion not his own. From the wind that howled through the canyons came poetry to refine a soul. From his thoughts, Mark summoned details for a life more complete than his own.

Time passed on Mark's shadow. Were it not for the strengthening of the wind, he would have been more still than the corpse. The breeze stirred him from reflection to read the epitaph once more; it was his own essential truth: dead at the age of twenty-two.

◆ ◆ ◆

Envy generated a will, for on his return from Hamilton, Mark decided to legitimize his imagination through professional writing. For eleven subsequent years, he chronicled others' talents, as a book reviewer for a regional entertainment magazine. At the age of thirty-three, frustrated with the lack of his own creativity, he accepted a position at *Western Ways* magazine in San Jose.

No one questioned his move from Los Angeles. After all, a journalistic position was rare in the esoteric field of his fascination—ghost towns of the Old West. Into the trunk of his car, he fit all his belongings—encumbrances of a past he hoped to leave behind. With the prospect of a new beginning, he surged north on US 101.

Once settled in San Jose, he anticipated the sound of the wind, but in its stead, the gravel of the earth weighed upon him. What time had not changed, distance could only suppress. His history remained buried.

In time, family and friends tired of telephone and greeting card communication. In the absence of conversational pauses and unsolicited laughter, Mark withdrew to the company of the characters in his tales. Complacency in his solitude gave him an emotional balance he feared to disrupt. He would have been happy, were it not for the desires of the flesh.

Susan had been the last romance—whose love he had accepted conditionally. Their relationship became a test of wills, in which his eventually abdicated. Without will, he felt no drive, and so they languished. The separation was formalized by an indictment of his lack of integrity, for which he accepted responsibility; the charge remained uncontested.

That was three years ago, and the pattern of his solitude had been re-established. With it came absolution from judgment, the cruelest of which had been his own. He became the lonely man that everyone considered a pathogen, which no one knew how to react to but his friend Spencer Tate, who simply thought it sad.

Middle age had come upon him as rapidly as desert weeds shadow a storm. A flurry of recurrent chills reminded him of the physical changes age inflicts. He awaited an appointment with his doctor, in hopes of mitigating what he attributed to male menopause.

◆ ◆ ◆

His dreams revealed a life without anticipation, free of remorse, where vulnerability was a theme, not a resource for adventure. He controlled his world through his imagination; the keys of a laptop were his toggles.

Mark sat up on the bed, a cold sweat beading on his flesh. He threw off the blanket and felt his heart heave inside his chest. He watched his naked body tremble, and recognized the loneliness of judgment.

The scar on his abdomen glimmered in the dim moonlight inside the bedroom. Fear turned to anger once he had control.

His body swayed
into a rhythm of pleasure,
until the movement was calmed
with resolution.

Chapter 1

*T*he pen felt like the handshake of an old friend. Mark rolled it between two fingers as if to revive a neglected habit, and then scribbled on a pad the first word that came to mind—love. Such an overused word, he thought, but stared at the paper as if to wish that it be granted.

The trend of flower children during his adolescence was to apply love, in all its conformations, to whatever aspect of behavior was at issue, as if to exert its implicit ideals upon that behavior. Inherent in its use was consequence, a natural progression of pubescent curiosity that he had denied himself at the time, though he had been guilty of the nominal use of the term. Mark leaned back in the desk-chair and wondered how much of what he wrote was of the same hope.

◆◆◆

There had been no warning before the windshield burst into shattered glass and metal crumpled with the sound of thunder. Their world began to tumble, as if in the spin cycle of a wash. With the seat belt strap released, his body jostled against the inside frame of the truck. He turned towards her scream.

In the darkness of the clouded night, amidst the turmoil, he was calmed in her embrace. Time lingered as his thoughts recounted the past.

Not so long ago, his had been a poet's passion, safely bestowed upon the words he wrote. Reality had become a matter of circumstance, not of desire, while vulnerability was a topic for discussion, not a temperament of pride. In his safeguarded emotions, she touched his heart; torrents of pleasure flowed.

Mark retrieved the pen from behind the laptop he was working on and twirled it between his fingers, as if to prime himself for a review. He studied the words he had written, on a topic he had not attempted before, and was baffled by the melodrama. He modified the lines, but he could not get rid of the passion.

Melodrama, he thought, was the exception of our lives, our enigma, not the historical fidelity required for his monthly column. He sat back from the computer screen, as if to clear his thoughts with distance. Melodrama, he considered, was our heightened selves, but it also was the language of his Hispanic culture, through which he had learned to interpret the world in which he had been raised. It was not, though, his style. Mark determined to let the lines remain, for he did not write about himself.

Hunger pangs reminded him that his last meal had been the night before. He saved the unfinished short story into the "Work-in-Progress" folder on his laptop and elected to reconsider the issue later. He set out to the market for groceries.

◆◆◆

A flushed feeling overcame Mark as he lifted the grocery bags from the cash register. It was a sensation he had suffered from sporadically over recent months, but this time it seemed stronger than on previous occasions. As he neared the exit, he felt weak and sensed he was about to faint. He rushed to hide behind a recent delivery of boxed groceries and waited, crouched on the linoleum floor, to recover from the cold sweat that flooded his skin.

"Do you need some help?" asked a store attendant.

Mark looked toward the voice, focusing on the nametag. "No, thank you, Tony. I feel better now."

Tony grabbed at his elbow and supported Mark as he stood. "Are you sure you're all right? You look a little pale."

"Yes—thanks," he answered. "I can take it from here."

He glared into Tony's eyes as he straightened. The young man's face irked him for the sympathy it displayed; it heralded the approach of what he dreaded becoming—an effete older man. His strength regained at the irritation of being discovered, Mark grabbed the cans of vegetables Tony had gathered and headed out the exit door to the parking lot.

He left the windows of the truck closed and sat motionless. He wanted warmth. Mark hoped the glass would magnify the spring sun's heat. With the key gripped in his hand, he stared at his reflection in the rearview mirror. The brown of his irises were constricted. Strands of reddish-brown hair hung loose over his forehead, where wrinkles seemed deeply furrowed by the shadows. He dropped the keys to push back his hair and leaned closer to the mirror. The cold sweat persisted.

Time grants no reward to the lonely, he thought in response to his circumstance.

He jammed the key into the ignition. Were the recurrent chills of the last few weeks a prelude to middle-age deterioration? Mark rejected the thought and let the engine growl his discontent. At forty-two years old, he still felt the deftness of his thirties. It could only be hunger, he concluded, and firmly pressed the accelerator. The tires screeched as he drove onto the boulevard.

◆ ◆ ◆

From a plane, indistinct cul-de-sacs, like alveoli of a choked lung, seemed to embody the suburbs of San Jose. Habit directed him to drive into the one he lived on. The dormant grass in his front yard contrasted the tended lawns of his neighbors. Deep shadows of the waning afternoon stretched across the driveway of the townhouse. An occasional glare of a passing car shone against the front door he closed behind him. Soon the neighbors would all be home from work.

◆ ◆ ◆

3

To develop a character for a story often required distilling personality traits from people he met. It was unusual that he adapted his own. With a scholarly eye, he mused over his perfectly lined groceries stowed in the cupboards and the color-coordinated vegetables he had laid out to cook.

Indulgences were few, but cooking on an impulse was one he occasionally granted himself. On a low flame, he let the mustard broth simmer and tossed in a handful of diced green onions and garlic. He added water and slowly stirred until it was the texture of cream. When the savory aroma had filled his kitchen, he let drop into the gravy two chicken breasts and some sliced potatoes, and sautéed them to a light bronze. He covered the meal and awaited the comforting murmur of the steam against the lid.

The smell of the dinner and the sizzle from the skillet stimulated his saliva. Mark remembered, though, that he had forgotten to buy anything to drink. In all the cupboards, he found only a single bottle of Chandon Brut Cuvee. Mark carried it to the living room, which was sectioned from the kitchen by a serving bar.

Gold aluminum foil sealed the cork; this, and the thick colored glass, gave the bottle a presumption of value. He brushed the dust and recalled his brother's wedding reception. Aglow with love, Joey had embraced his bride and handed Mark the bottle.

"Hope you find the happiness my wife has brought me," he had toasted Mark, and then took a gulp from a second bottle. Champagne foam glistened on his lips when he kissed Marie.

Mark reclined on the sofa and tore at the gold foil. He twisted off the wire hood and gripped at the cork. Happiness was illusory, for it was not long after their wedding night that his brother's wife had sought the company of another. Like thorns on a crown, she left clues that led to the revelation. Were it not for her need to hurt, their marriage would have lasted, for his brother was absorbed with love of her. After a hearty twist, the cork jettisoned across the room, and white champagne suds sprayed into his lap.

"Whoa," Mark shouted, and quickly sat up. "To the happiness we are all in search of." He raised his bottle in salutation, and then pursed his lips over the foaming gullet. After a large gulp of champagne, he looked about the empty walls of his living room and wondered whether being alone was not a better option.

His moist pants clung uncomfortably to his thighs, but when unzipped, they slipped to the carpet. He stood away from them and approached the window. In the darkened windows, he stared at his reflection in the glass. The tails of his shirt covered his skivvies, yet he drew shut the blinds. It wasn't so much for modesty, as it was to secure the boundaries.

On a quick second thought, he turned back and separated two slats of the blinds to glance outside. Against a closed curtain of the bedroom, on the neighbor's side of the fence, the silhouette of a man and a woman appeared at play. He recognized their shadows, but he had not met the couple since they moved in three years ago. It was obvious their world required no intervention, he thought. They seemed content with each other. The slats crashed shut with the quick release of his fingers. Mark returned to the kitchen with the champagne bottle cradled firmly to his chest, as if for fellowship.

A loud gurgle from the covered pan called his attention. He leaned over to remove the lid, and the released steam clouded his vision and filled his nostrils with an appetizing aroma. At the dinner table, he set the meal with a glass of champagne.

Mark was a social drinker, but on this occasion, every forkful of food seemed to require a sip of drink. It was not so much to augment the meal, but for the effect of the alcohol. He wished to displace his envy of the playful couple next door.

When he was writing, silence was a condition he liked for its contrast. That was what Mark considered when the empty champagne bottle rolled off the table and thumped to the carpeted floor. The sound it made seemed to reverberate through the house. He staggered to the adjoining living room and tuned the radio to a soft rock station.

Sunday drives around the park and all the loves he had left behind were in the melodies of the music. Mark danced instead of cried, until his lonely shadow slowed and dropped onto the sofa.

◆ ◆ ◆

The phone's ring awakened him. "Mark?" a familiar voice asked from the other end. "Is that you, buddy?"

To remove the stale taste in his mouth, he cleared his throat before he answered. "Yeah."

"Are you all right? You sound drunk."

"Maybe—I—am," he said slowly, and pulled his crusted eyelids open. To test himself, he moved his eyes around the room, noticing no waver in his vision.

"This is Spencer Tate. Are you still asleep?"

"Spencer!" Mark noticed the filtered sunlight in the living room. "What time is it?"

"About ten."

"What? I've slept all night." Mark jumped off the sofa and, distracted by a full bladder, walked on to the bathroom with the cordless phone held to his ear.

"Just called to see if you want to go on a commando mission tonight."

"Yeah, that sounds good." Embarrassed to display a body function, Mark sat to urinate, so the stream would not echo into the conversation. "How's Kathy?"

"She took the kids to visit her mother. She'll be gone for the rest of the week. How about I meet you at headquarters at seven?"

"Sounds good—I mean, roger." He shut off the cordless phone.

A frustrated soldier of fortune, Spencer lived his military fantasies vicariously, through the war games he programmed for a living. His distinction was air combat, but it was through his research of gun battles in the Old West that they had first met. Mark had introduced him to ghost town sites of especially gory battles, from which Spencer had drawn inspiration for a computer game. There had been a lot of make-believe and not much else in common, but one had needed the other, and so, during the few years since, they had become good friends.

Mark could not recall their last time out together, but "commando mission" was Spencer's euphemism for a boys' night on the town. More often than not, it was simply going to a bar to get drunk. The shiver on emptying his bladder reminded Mark of last night's binge, and he dreaded repeating it.

The blinds were still drawn when he entered the bedroom and stood at the foot of his disheveled bed. The rumpled bed-spread was slung to the left of the double mattress. He stared at his body's stains, camouflaged by the colored sheets, and reckoned that his personal habits were no better than what Spencer suspected. What difference would one more night of drinking make? Manly fellowship was why they needed each other.

◆ ◆ ◆

Discipline was what a writer struggled to maintain, but Mark was surprised at how much easier anticipation had made it. Neither the stops at the store and bank, nor the calls to his editor had interfered with a full day of writing. It was exactly seven when he walked into the bar.

The Seoul Lounge was their commando headquarters, not so much for all the drinking they had done there, but for its intriguing foreign atmosphere. Without much imagination, one could conjure exotic and clandestine schemes in the dragon-decorated bar. As much as Mark could tell, the decor was appropriately Korean.

Randy Durocher tended at the bar, as he had on Mark's previous visits. With his sandy blond hair clipped military style, he didn't appear the fifty-something years he must have been—for all the Vietnam War stories he liked to tell.

"Sue Ye," Randy shouted toward the back door. "We've got a customer."

With one foot propped on two boxes of beer, Randy continued a conversation with two men at the far corner of the bar. Cigarette smoke spiraled from a communal ashtray. All were turned toward two players at the pool table. Mark sat on a stool at the middle of the bar.

"What will it be, honey?" Sue Ye asked in a heavily accented voice as she wiped the counter.

"I'm waiting for a friend." Mark pulled away from the edge to give her room and was sure she did not recognize him. "He shouldn't be long. I think I'll wait 'til he gets here."

Sue Ye turned toward the single door in the back. She was attractive, and without a strand of white in her black hair, she seemed fifteen years younger than her husband, Randy. Mark preferred her hair loose, draped over one shoulder like a silk veil upon her breast, rather than tied back in a bun as it was now. He glanced back to Randy and wondered what the attraction was, beyond sexual, that bound one to the other.

"Colonel Tate," Randy shouted toward the front door.

"Sergeant Durocher," Spencer responded from the doorway. His chest broadened, as if to scan the room with his breath, rather than sight. He focused on Mark. "Commander Balcon, I'm glad you kept our rendezvous."

Spencer approached Mark, who stood up to stretch out his hand. Spencer grasped it firmly and led it to an embrace. The whiskers of his groomed beard brushed against Mark's neck.

"It's been a while," Mark said, and hastily stepped back.

"Come yonder." Spencer continued on to the empty seat next to the corner man and reached out to Randy for a handshake. His rotund belly seemed to support him as he leaned over the bar. "You remember Mark," he added.

"Sure. How you doing?" Randy glanced at Mark, but quickly turned back to Spencer. "Hey, I have a great new beer for you." He pulled open the flap of the box he had been resting his foot on. "This is best served warm." He poured the beer into a frosted glass.

Spencer took a large gulp. "Oh, man!" He contorted his face in an exaggerated grimace. "This tastes like elephant piss."

"How did you know?" Randy bellowed in laughter.

"Hey, give my buddy one," Spencer said. To Mark, he added, "This is some shit. It'll straighten your pubic hairs."

"That's a good one," said the corner man, who faced Spencer. "That'll make it easier to reach for my prick. You never know when you're in for a quick one."

"Hey, man, mine's always on the alert. They don't call me Dick for nothing," said the man whose back leaned against Spencer.

The group laughing, Spencer moved away from his stool. He held the bottle at the neck and walked across the lounge. "Hey, Randy, we're going to a table. Your company is too vulgar for my sensitive ears."

"Ooh," the chorus responded.

"Send Sue Ye over. I think we'll order some of your dog meat," he said, and motioned his head for Mark to follow.

"If I was a man who cared, I might be offended by that," Randy replied. "It's the Vietnamese who serve dog. We only have roaches." Laughter muffled Randy's call for Sue Ye.

◆ ◆ ◆

"Mr. Tate," Sue Ye said, and handed them the menu. Mark recalled she couldn't pronounce Spencer. "How you been?"

"Just fine," he said. "You look as lovely as I remember."

"Oh, honey! You talk a lady good."

"I do a woman better." Spencer stared at her breasts when Sue Ye leaned forward to lay out the silverware.

"Oh, honey, you so nasty." She smiled and asked, "You want more beer?"

"Mark, finish that down." He grabbed his own bottle and gulped what remained. "Bring us some Korean poison."

"Oh, honey, I'm the poison you want." Sue Ye cackled on her walk back to the kitchen.

Mark scowled, as if to force every swallow. He hoped to displace the bitter taste of the elephant piss, but was relieved of the chore by the emptied bottle. His focus blurred by the liquor, he stared at the elephant on the label and the "12.5% alcohol by volume." Was that legal?

The second beer was smooth, without the alcoholic kick of the first. He gargled it to cleanse the taste of elephant feet in his mouth, then ordered his dinner.

"All I've been doing is working," Mark continued their conversation. "There's always a deadline, but thank goodness there are readers interested on my articles."

"Are you still getting up to the ghost towns?"

"Not as often as when we worked on your program. By the way, I like how that game came out."

"Thanks, but it hasn't sold well."

"Oh, no. I suppose I should have bought a copy."

"Thanks for nothing, man."

Mark sat back into the chair for Sue Ye to set their plates before them. "I think I'll be driving up to Tahoe soon."

"Oh, yeah?" Spencer said. "Going up with a chick?"

"No. I think I'll go alone. Just want to get away."

"Ah. How sad." It was Spencer's favorite term for Mark's supposed run of bad luck with women. He dug the chopsticks into a mound of white rice and asked, "Are you seeing anyone?"

It felt like forever since he had last been with a woman. "Not now," he said, staring at the chopsticks he gripped between his fingers; he maneuvered the tips to test their grasp.

"Man, you need a woman." Spencer filled his mouth with a portion of the peppered beef. A morsel slipped from his lips and smudged the white hairs of his beard. "What I would do to be single again." Spencer rolled his eyes and arched one eyebrow. He searched about the lounge. "Hey, Sue Ye. Come here."

"You need beer?" she asked and approached their table.

"Yeah, bring us some more. But wait a minute." He held her arm to stop the turn. "You got a lady for my friend?"

"How long?" she asked Mark.

"What?" He lost his grasp of the kimchee cabbage.

"No, no, Sue Ye. Not like that," Spencer interjected. "He needs a real girlfriend."

"You got no lady?" she asked, not looking away from Mark.

"No." He tried to recover the cabbage from the table where it had fallen.

"Why not?"

"No one loves me." Mark pretended sorrow to distract the focus of their intention. To Spencer, he shrugged.

"Why not? You handsome and got job. Right?"

He looked at Sue Ye with a smile. "Well, I don't know about handsome."

"You like boys?"

"Oh, god." Mark felt a flush on his face.

"Sue Ye! He needs a girlfriend, not an insult," Spencer said.

"I got girl for you." She walked away, but soon returned with beer.

Sue Ye had left a count of her returned visits by the pack of empty bottles on their table. When their heads wobbled just above these, she noisily cleared them to the side to get their attention. A young Korean lady stood behind her.

"Honey," she said to Mark. "This Rose May. She quiet, but beautiful. She give you good love."

Mark pushed himself back from the table. His head lagged, but stopped with a snap. He appealed to Spencer. "Is she serious?" His palms sweated and his chest quivered.

"Go on," Spencer answered. His body still drooped above the table, but his stare remained on Rose May. "Go on now. Don't let me forget that I'm a married man."

◆ ◆ ◆

Up a narrow stairwell, a little beyond the restaurant bathrooms, he felt his shoulders scrape the textured concrete walls as he swayed between them. The red lamp at the top of the stairs guided his unwary steps. A pine-scented cleanser permeated the air he breathed.

Her hand, smooth as silk, led him tenderly. In her white chiffon dress against the dim light ahead of them, she seemed like a swan. Her long black hair, held at the nape of her neck by a wide ribbon, framed her face as she looked back to ensure he followed. Her eyes were all the temptation he needed.

In the room at the top of the stairs was a narrow mattress raised on a wooden frame. He stood before it and wondered whether they would fit, but relaxed at thoughts of the physical contortions that would permit them to share it.

On the opposite wall was a single window, curtained by a purple sheet. A small washbasin stood in a corner by the door. An overhead red light was reflected on the linoleum floor.

Mark turned to where she stood waiting at the door and stretched out his arm for her to approach. With her hands upon his chest, he closed his eyes and yielded to her fingers loosening the buttons of his shirt. Her body pressed against his as she unzipped his pants. His clothes glided off him as he reclined onto the mattress.

She stood before him, her arms reaching behind to unbutton her dress, which then dropped to the floor. The fullness of her breasts drew his stare, which he then let drift to the curves of her hips. She unfastened the ribbon that bound her hair, and like the flare of a fan, its black strands fell away from her shoulders. Mark remained silent and lay back on the bed.

It was the weight of her body, the feel of her flesh. It was the firmness of her nipples, her moisture, and her scent. It was motion, and it was rhythm. It was consummate.

The squeal of the bed and the joy of his cry trailed into silence. They lay motionless, one upon the other. Mark stared away to the red light. She did not speak English; as far as he could tell, she did not speak at all.

◆◆◆

Besides an occasional neon sign, the strip-mall's parking lot was unlit. The one light above the Seoul Lounge seemed to glare on his dull stare. Muddled, Mark worked to focus. The firmness of his truck's cargo floor slowly got his attention. He sat up.

There was no traffic on the boulevard and no one else on the lot. Mark scurried to the far corner of the building, his step echoing as he approached. Braced against the wall with one arm, he leaned into it and unzipped his pants. The cold air that stroked his bare skin caused his body to quiver. He mused at the steam rising from his urine's trail on the wall.

His shadow was thrown before him when a floodlight shone on him from behind. "Put your hands above your head," commanded an amplified voice.

Mark stood still, unable to halt the flow of urine. "Oh, shit," he mumbled to himself.

"Put your hands up, now."

The elastic band of his briefs snapped back as he yielded. Moist warmth streamed down the inside of his leg.

"Keep them above your head and turn around."

Mark stared at the ground, where a small pool steamed at his feet. Footsteps approached.

"Look up," thundered the voice behind him.

His antagonist's outline was sharply sketched in the flood-light. Mark balked and stared at his feet.

"Hey. Don't I know you?" the voice asked.

Mark raised his hand to a visor, and his eyes strained against the light.

The silhouette turned and added, "Sam, cut the light."

The warmth faded when the light was turned off, yet sweat formed on his face. The officer's red hair, Mark thought, should help his recollection, but memory failed him. "I don't know," he replied.

"Hey, Sam, guess what? This guy lives next door to me. Nancy and me always wondered what he was up to—now I know. He's a Seoul Man."

Mark stammered, "What do you mean?"

"At least he's got taste," said Sam. "They do have the best women in town."

He aborted the protest and searched his empty pant pockets. Mark tried to recall when he spent the money, but he could think only of Rose May and the feel of her flesh.

"Well, Fredrickson, should we take him in?" Sam moved be-hind Mark.

"Nah. We've got nothing on him." In a softer voice, Fredrickson advised Mark, "Stay out of that scene, man. Don't be bringing no germs to the neighborhood."

◆ ◆ ◆

Mark shut the truck door quietly behind him. A distant dog's bark was the only sound. He stood motionless as a gust of wind carried the reek of urine from his pants to his nose. In the approaching dawn, Mark surveyed the homes of his neighbors; he was the germ Fredrickson had warned against. He was a lonely man.

Inside the townhouse, he prepared to shower, but he wished Rose May's fingers were there to undress him. Naked, he slipped between the bed sheets, but it was the warmth of her flesh he wanted to comfort him. He embraced his pillow and recalled her scent. With his eyes closed, loneliness didn't matter. In the morning, he would write the tale Rose May would have told him.

Chapter 2

*R*ose May had once carted granite tailings from deep within the mines in the hills about the town. Calluses on her hands reminded her it hadn't been so long ago. The stones she had stacked into a pyramid, as if in testament to the dream that had lured her west. Yet from the wood planks of the boardwalk upon which she now stood, they seemed an obelisk, a memorial to the lives surrendered in a shared illusion. With a steadfast gaze, she pondered on her shattered dreams and the body of her fiancée, buried in a cave-in.

Footsteps on the wood planks roused her. A town lady stopped short of the step-off and grabbed at her skirt. She continued onto the road, her dress guarded against the mud. Rose followed, prodding the stem of her umbrella into the mire, as if to measure its depth. From her other hand, an embroidered cotton purse swung loosely, brushing her dress, which draped to mid-leg. Colorful pantaloons warmed her legs to the fur trim of her boots.

It was silver she now mined, from the hearts of lonely men. Like the delusions that had brought them to the mines, so they came to her *for love. It was not upon stone they set their dreams, but fleeting pleasure that she enjoyed giving.*

With no more dreams to harvest, only tasks to accomplish, Rose had much business for that afternoon.

"No, no. That's all wrong," Mark shouted to himself and selected the Save command of the program. *Rose May is Korean,* he admonished, then shut the laptop. *She doesn't even speak English.*

The water kettle screamed from the kitchen and called him away from the den. He waited for the shrill to intensify and watched the steam erupt through its hood. "Go ahead and holler," he shouted, as if to prod it on; its wail became his own.

Mark drank a cup of coffee at the dining table and pushed aside the mustard-stained plate. With his legs stretched out below the table, he felt the champagne bottle roll away. Reclined in the chair, he focused his stare on the damped light from the adjoining living room. He searched his thoughts for the voice of Rose May, but found only bitter recollections. These consumed his attention, and if brains really could fry, it was how he felt.

Ah—how sad, Spencer had said about his plans to travel alone to Lake Tahoe.

Don't bring no germs to the neighborhood, had been the cop's advice.

With his eyes closed, he took a deep sigh to stop his body's tremor, and then rushed to the living room window, as if needing fresh air. Cautiously, he parted two slats of the closed blinds and stared between them to the neighbors'. Their bedroom curtain was open, but the shadows inside and the silence of the yard told him no one was home.

Bent with the weight of his back against them, the blinds cracked with the dissonance of a guitar out of tune. His knees weakened, and his body slid to the floor. He committed to making the trip to Lake Tahoe.

◆◆◆

From the beaches along the central California coast, gentle hills rose to a mountain range that settled to the east in the San Joaquin Valley. In early spring, these hills were carpeted with seasonal green vegetation that turned gold in the summer months. Yet in the valley, an incessant winter fog shrouded farms and funneled Mark's thoughts to tales such as *The Grapes of Wrath* and *Tortilla Flats*. He liked to imagine himself on an adventure in Steinbeck's country.

A lighted sign abruptly shined through the fog and prompted his inspection of the gas meter, which faltered on empty. He drove the truck into the gas station and stopped at the single island of pumps. The wooden building a few yards back, supposedly a coffee shop, was weathered. Red paint on the trim panels had peeled heavily. An adjoining empty garage stood in darkness with a degree or two of slant. On the front panels, a winged horse was shaded by overlaid white paint. Mark thought the station had long ago been abandoned.

The screen door from the coffee shop swung open, and an old man in his seventies stepped out. His visor was turned to the reverse side. He stretched his arm into a stained jacket. The light from inside lit his path toward the pump. "Howdy, son. Want'er filled?"

"Yes, sir, but isn't it self-serve?" Mark stepped up to the premium pump.

"Only the interstate guys have enough pumps." He reached for the nozzle.

"Is it far from here?" Mark asked and backed toward his truck's opened door.

"Don't worry. You won't get it cheaper. Fill'er up?" he asked again, the nozzle held with his gloved hand.

Mark hesitated and searched for the unit price. It was reasonable. "Yeah, fill it up."

The old man was intent while fitting the nozzle into the tank of the truck. A distant mechanical clamor from the direction of the fog-shrouded fields distracted Mark. He sat back in his seat to listen, and envisioned barren soil in the wake of a tractor being prepared for spring seeds, probably cotton. It would be summer when its crop, white as winter snow, was harvested. The fog would be a reprieve from the stifling 115-degree heat.

"That'll be twenty-five bucks," the old man said, and returned the nozzle to its hilt.

"Sure is cold." Mark stood up from the truck and handed him the credit card.

"We've got hot coffee," the old man answered and carried the card toward the coffee shop. Mark followed, more to recover the card than for the offer of warmth.

At the wall opposite the entry door, a wood stove heated the small dining area. A single fluorescent bulb illuminated the cafe. Four empty tables were arranged to one side, and a Formica counter lined the other. Mark sat at the counter while the old man searched under it from the serving side.

"I knew I had it here," he said. Small metal slab in hand, he straightened, then worked the lever to imprint the card. "Shit. I bent it. Don't no one use money anymore?"

"Sorry," Mark replied. "I don't have enough—that is, until I get to an ATM."

"Well, how're you going to pay for breakfast?"

"Breakfast?"

"You look hungry, boy. I'll just add it on the gas bill." The old man removed the jacket and turned to the stove behind him. "Eggs and bacon?"

"Just two eggs, over easy."

"You must be from the city. Here you get them whichever way they turn."

Mark smiled at the old man. "Whichever way they turned" was exactly how he appeared to live his life. The pictures on the wall seemed without reason. They were front covers from magazines—photos and greeting cards from distant lands and different times. Pens and pencils tied with rubber bands stood clumped inside porcelain cups at the end of the counter. An old ledger was left open, stains of grease on its white pages.

"Where you heading?" he asked, pouring coffee into a cup.

"Lake Tahoe." Mark reclined against the backrest and unzipped his light jacket. The coffee was strong, but it fulfilled the old man's promise of warmth.

"Ain't you taking a long way about?" He was turned to the stove and seemed to speak to the eggs he tended.

"I suppose I am," Mark answered, reading the John Deere label on the reversed front of the man's hat.

"Never been there myself, but some folk say it's heaven. I got a picture of it somewheres here." He flipped the eggs over.

Mark noticed a yolk broke. "Yeah, I think it is heaven. I have a cabin there."

"I thought you come from the city," he said, and stuffed the toaster with bread.

"I do, but I like to get away."

"I thought you said you ain't got no cash." The old man scraped the eggs from the flat of the stove and dropped them on a plate. "How come you got two homes?"

"Well, I don't have any cash now, but I can get some at an ATM." Mark sat up on the chair.

"If you ask me, rich folk ought to carry cash all the time, not a silly gold card that bends when poor folk grabs at it."

Mark noticed a teasing glint in the old man's eyes as he set the eggs and toast before him. His banter was a prod for conversation.

"I'm not rich, just lucky with a book I got published. It's just that I left kind of in a hurry," Mark said, more to stoke the old man's hankering than to provide any reasoning.

"People are always in a hurry. Even out here. They take the interstate and pump their own gas." He poured himself a cup of coffee. "Now take me, for instance. I was blown out here in a dust storm from the panhandle of Texas when I was just a boy. My folk are all gone, but I stick around. Never been nowhere farther than half a tank would take me. But I gots all the time in the world to know here well."

Mark was intrigued as to what elements of *here* were satisfying to get to know *well.* He looked about the cafe and saw only a past. "Where are your children?"

"Got none. Never married." The old man held the cup with both hands and sat on a stool behind the cash register.

"Did you ever want to get married?"

Mark ate the eggs sandwiched with the bread and sipped the hot coffee. The old man's eyes stared at him, pleased that he liked the food.

"I fell in love once. That was a long time ago. I suppose she never worried how far her tank would take her, 'cause she took a trip and never came back."

"Did you ever hear from her again?"

"Yeah, she wrote a few times. One of these picture cards is from LA." Toward the cluttered wall, he waved his index finger, like a wand granting a wish. "She wanted me to come, and I almost did, but I just couldn't leave where my folk wanted me to be."

The old man stood to clean the flat of the stove. His stare seemed transposed in time. Silence bears its own vigor, and that which followed troubled Mark. The old man's reminiscences mirrored his own pain. He continued with breakfast, surreptitiously watching the burned oil being scraped away.

"Well, that was good," Mark said to disrupt the quiet. He sat back and padded his belly, to highlight his satisfaction.

"I'm glad you liked it." He cleared the plate away. "More coffee?"

"No, thanks. I better be getting on."

"That's right; you're in a hurry."

The old man's hand trembled as he wrote the credit card's number on the imprint of the bill. Mark felt a chill when he signed the receipt.

"Take this." The old man handed him a yellowed business card. "I need a new picture from Lake Tahoe."

"Trapper Garza," Mark read. "Boy, that's a name with some story."

"Stop by, next time you're in the area, and I'll tell it." He followed Mark to the door. "Drive safely. They say it's going to rain like a cow pisses on a flat rock."

20

Mark laughed at the image and zipped up his jacket. He wondered if it ever did rain inside the heavy fog he drove into. Trapper Garza's figure faded from his rear-view mirror.

◆◆◆

The fog remained dense. Like driving in a mineshaft, nothing was visible beyond a few feet. His thoughts seemed cast on the windshield before him. With images of elephants pissing in beer bottles and cows on flat rocks, he drove the valley road, wishing for a smile. *Maybe Trapper Garza was right*, he thought, *to build his world within the confines of half-a-tank of gas.*

Mark did not notice his ascent of the eastern side of the valley until sunlight abruptly broke his trance. He pulled into a vista turnoff.

Adorned with clouds, as if with a vestment of cotton, and bejeweled by the high-noon sun, the vast San Joaquin basin appeared transfigured. Atop a granite boulder, with the wind sweeping from the valley floor below, Mark imagined himself in flight above it all.

◆◆◆

On the western slope of the Sierra Nevada Range, he continued a steep ascent. Rocky banks formed the walls of the canyon. Heavy packed snow covered the crest. With the sky still clear, it would be no problem to make it over the summit. On four-wheel drive, he forged over the pass at 8,700 feet. Descent on the eastern slope was rapid, and Mark was surprised to still see sunlight when he reached the high desert floor.

He continued north, skirting the Sierra Nevada. These mountains had baited men and women with gold and silver. Abandoned towns, where dreams begot despair, had become their tombstones. Mark loved to explore them, making their stories his gold.

To the west, colors of the sunset ebbed from the crest of the mountains. Shades of salmon pink upon scattered clouds braced the salvia blue sky of approaching night, but darkness prevailed upon his arrival at the lakeshore route. On the Nevada side, he headed north toward the corona of lights on the shores of Lake Tahoe.

Red lights flashed from a bend on the road. Like a flashback, the reflection of the lights in the forest hinted of stains on a linoleum floor. Mark was startled by the image of Rose May. It took him a moment to register the stalled car on the embankment. He slowed, and then stopped when he glimpsed the driver standing in the beam of the inside headlamp.

Pine scent from the forest drifted through the opened side window. "Need some help?"

Her gloved hands gripped the lapels of her long wool coat, as if to shield herself against the cold. The black of her pupils stared back warily. She hesitated, tossing a quick glance to the back of his truck. "Yes, thank you." She approached the window. "I think I ran out of gas."

"Do you want me to check the engine?" It was an empty offer, since he only knew where the battery was, and he could tell that was not the problem. All the car's lights were on.

"I'm sure it's just the gas. I've watched the pointer sit on empty for about twenty miles." Her short black hair flared when she turned to look at the stalled Mercedes-Benz. "This has never happened before."

"I guess it wasn't a half-tank trip?" he said, and smiled to himself.

"What?" She gazed probingly at him.

"Nothing. How about I drive you into town and get some gas? I'll bring you right back."

"Thanks. But how about if you drop me off at home? I'll get my neighbor to help me in the morning."

"It'll be no problem," he said.

"I'm too tired. I drove up from Palo Alto, and I just didn't need this." She stomped her foot on the gravel.

"Come on in, then." He reached across and opened the passenger door.

"Let me turn off the lights." She stopped midway to her car and turned to him. "Do you mind if I bring the groceries?"

Mark stepped out and helped with the bags in the trunk; they seemed full of cans.

Once back on the road, Mark glanced toward her. The folds of her upper eyelids were full, with a gentle slope. Probably Japanese, he thought. She continued to clutch at the lapels of her coat, so he turned up the heat. "Cold?"

"No, its fine. Thanks for stopping," she said to his reflection on the windshield.

"Are you from Palo Alto?"

"No. I was just visiting my fiancée."

"A long-distance relationship?" Wasn't that an oxymoron? Doesn't passion become encumbered by time and distance? It was what he had thought when he parted with Susan three years earlier. *What did it matter,* he thought, *if others considered it an excuse?*

"It's not that far." She looked briefly toward Mark. "He comes up most weekends."

The thump of a jostled grocery bag interrupted their silence. "Planning a romantic dinner?" he asked.

"No way." She returned Mark's gaze with a wispy smile. "You can't be romantic when your hands smell of garlic. He has to take me out for that. But I've been with him too long not to know not to let him get hungry. Plenty of cans in those bags for him to fix himself a meal."

"How long have the two of you been together?" Mark imagined cans of dog food, and her fiancée barking, but then thought of Susan, who had enjoyed cooking his meals.

"Nine years." She loosened her grip on the lapels and rested her hands on her lap. "Since senior year in high school."

He had stayed with Susan for eight months, and by then she was talking of marriage. "Shouldn't you be married by now?" he asked although he feared he was being intrusive. He glanced toward the lake, as the road was just above shore level. *Should marriage always be the end result of love?*

A welcome sign greeted them at the city limits of Incline Village. Her stare remained fixed on the road ahead. "I suppose there aren't any *shoulds* in our life," she answered nonchalantly, "only *wants*. I guess neither of us has wanted to be married."

To *want* he had not known with Susan, but it was what she asked of him in bed and everything else she had arranged for them. He had fashioned a relationship of *shoulds*.

Snow banks encrusted with black dirt lined the sides of the street. Traffic in town was sparse, yet a signal light guarded the main intersection. He stopped at the red light. In the corner gas station, Mark watched a man pumping gas and the mist that formed with each breath he took. Winter still lingered.

"What do you do?" he asked, and on the green light continued forth into the intersection.

She sat forward, with hands braced on the dashboard. "Turn right two blocks down. I'm a writer."

"Oh, seriously? What do you write?"

"Haiku."

"In Japanese?"

"No, I write only in English."

"I've read some, but I get lost in the subtleties. My poetic insight doesn't go beyond the concrete imagery of cowboy poetry. I'd love to read some of your writings, though."

"It's the second house down." She leaned back onto the seat and jingled keys in her coat pocket. "You can just leave me at the curb."

Shoulds were still much of his character, and so he drove up the driveway to a new, wood-paneled townhouse. He carried the grocery bags to the front door, where she insisted, with gratitude, they be left. It was only when he reversed the truck out of the driveway that he saw her open the door. He supposed she was too guarded a writer to ever offer to share her poems.

◆ ◆ ◆

It was a beacon, the desk lamp at the window, first house at the bottom of the wooded hill. For as long as he had owned his cabin at the summit, the light had always tendered a welcome upon his arrival. Mark leaned forward and looked up to its beam. The shadow of its owner stood behind it. He felt the weariness of the long drive dissipate.

24

Ten hours was usual for the journey, but the clock on the dashboard marked twelve hours since his departure. It didn't matter. He drove through the slush that remained on the road and ascended the hill to his home.

◆◆◆

Comfort is where one hung his hat, a seventies Motown song on the radio enticed him to think. But given no hat, bed had made a difference. He was well rested after a prolonged sleep.

It was late morning when he sat at the dining table, a warm cup of instant coffee at hand. He sipped it slowly. His hands were wrapped about the porcelain, feeling the warmth from within, but his thoughts were of Susan, with whom he had last shared this vista.

Celestine blue faded to the color of mist at each horizon. Shadowed mountains were sketched upon the sky; ribbons of white purled their crest. Evergreens shaded the snow. Streams of pearls formed clouds above the water, and a sapphire glaze mirrored it all. It was a divine palette, which made him feel as if it were Sunday.

Front-row, center, was his view of Paradise. After a signing a generous book-writing contract, it had seduced him to purchase the cabin the first time he laid eyes upon it. After seven years, it still bestowed on him the same spell.

Mark made a mental note to send Trapper Garza a picture post-card.

Chapter 3

$\mathcal{E}$xhaust fumes clouded the main intersection, where traffic was heavy, as it tended to be on Fridays. These were the locals with errands to run before the swell of the weekend tourists with skis and snowboards loaded on the roofs of their ATVs. Mark waited for the signal to turn and looked above the vapors, where the cloudless sky seemed free of defilement. He wondered if the Haiku poet had written an interpretive lyric for the vexing hubbub.

Mark was on a mission directed by the growl in his belly. It had been more than twenty-four hours since his last full meal, and he had found the cupboards empty.

◆◆◆

The Maidu had been a regional native tribe, long displaced from their habitat and eventually, from distinction. Off the main road through town was his favorite coffee shop, which bore their name. When its ancestral association eluded his queries, he had simply submitted to enjoying its character and food.

Slabs of redwood formed the structure, which was not quite a log cabin. It seemed original to the area, from a time when the town forest was fodder for its lumber industry, rather than a backdrop for trophy homes. Though updated for environmental regulations, the beamed ceiling harbored an ancient fragrance of burnt wood. This scent had charmed him most on entry.

Maidu Cafe was more crowded than usual, but he didn't often

come at lunch. There were two open tables, while diners in noisy conversation occupied the others. Only one seat remained at the counter. Two bulky men, contractors, he supposed, held their ground while he forged between them. Mark sneaked a view of the headlines in the newspapers that each held at arm's length. "Continued violence in Sacramento," warned both. He shifted his gaze to the menu.

"Well, stranger. Welcome back."

Her hazel eyes were barely visible above the serrated edges of the papers. "Emilia," he said, with hesitation. They had chit-chatted previously, but Mark was not sure of her name. He attempted to glance at her tag.

"Come on, guys, give me some room," Emilia said, looking at his neighbors. Each swiveled on their stool, opening a view of her between their papers. She reached with a coffee pot and filled Mark's cup. "Cream and one sugar. Right?"

"That's right."

"Why bother with the menu? I already know what you're ordering." She scribbled on the order pad.

"How do you know?"

"I'm the Maidu oracle." Emilia flicked her eyebrows and turned. Her brunette ponytail swung with her, as if in punctuation. She clipped the order to the kitchen window.

He watched her dart about the restaurant, taking orders and delivering food. She was athletic and moved with swiftness and efficiency, but her smile was engaging. The diners she tended seemed likewise impressed.

Emilia was tall and lean, but her leg, which showed from the side slit of her peach polyester dress, defined her musculature. Her skin was olive, but darker than his, probably a tan from high-altitude skiing in the winter sun. Mark wondered why he had not previously paid her much attention.

Outdoor sports were favorite pastimes for the locals, particularly the young. Skiing, snowboarding, and mountain biking were the most popular. He glanced at Emilia, crouched at a table in conversation with an infant, and tried to guess her age. He turned his gaze to his neighbor's newspaper. She couldn't be more than thirty.

"Why so glum?" she asked, on her return with his breakfast. "Here you are—two eggs over easy, home fries, and whole wheat toasts."

"You are amazing." He felt the contagion of her smile.

"So, you won't doubt me again?"

"No, I don't think I will." He dipped the toast into the soft yolk, and hoped for another opportunity to test her skills.

Emilia returned to refill his neighbors' coffee, but held the pot above Mark's cup to ask, "More?" Demurely, she cleared her throat, and he returned her gaze. "Or more about me?"

As if on cue, the newspapers crackled, and folded away, fully exposing him and the flush on his face. He gulped a swallow of the coffee, but knew the warm sweat on his forehead was not from its steam. Mark was relieved when Emilia was called to the service window, but baffled by her apparent overture.

The din of a crowd at the front door caused him to notice that there was no empty table. Emilia was busy with the rapid turnover of the diners. He stared at his breakfast, as if to justify his seat, but a smudge of egg was all that remained on the dish. He wanted to stay, but was daunted when the dishes were cleared away. Mark waited until she was at the cash register.

"I'll be skiing at Diamond Peak tomorrow," she said, and collected his money.

"Maybe I'll see you there," was his reply, and instantly regretted its noncommittal nature. He gripped the change and walked out, mindless of the crowd. Behind him, the screen door closed with a clap.

Falling snow dusted the way to his truck, but he could have been walking on clouds for the lightness of his step. While the engine warmed, he sat inside, as if in a trance, and repeated, *or more about me?* Mark recited her words as if they would betray a secret. He fumbled with the coins she had given him and hoped he had left a good tip.

◆ ◆ ◆

Winter's quiet on spring's debut, flakes of snow continued to fall. Whorls of white dust formed in the wake of his truck as he drove up the hill. Laden with powder, pine branches leaned onto his path. Mark felt at play on a carpet of white, driving on un-tracked snow. The muted sounds of the tires echoed the truck's glide and, at each turn of the road, he let the wheels slide, as if to a waltz. He watched the rear of his truck skirt snow banks to either side.

On his drive up the hill, he solidified plans to ski in the morn-ing. He was still gripping the pocketed coins when he entered the house. In the picture window of the living room, mist con-cealed the view of the lake, but Mark leaned onto the glass to watch the vapors of his breath dance as he repeated her ques-tion. *Coffee? Or more about me?*

On the ledge of the cold fireplace, he sat to open the laptop. He typed in her question, and searched for a correlative file in his word processor. There was no comparable text. It had not been his creation; she had asked it. Her words, enhanced by her smile, tempted his imagination, but he slammed shut the laptop. He would not transpose his emotion.

The rhythmic tap of his restless feet on the parquet floor mimicked that of his heart. Anticipation, so much resembling in-decision, fueled his restlessness. Mark thought to call Spencer Tate, but "How sad" was not the scale on which he would permit his feelings to be tested. Mark could find no other option but to parry his agitated energy with a hard workout at the gym.

◆ ◆ ◆

In writing, transitioning an abstraction to what is tangible is difficult, more so when the reader's mind is in his heart. Mark realized this en route to the health club, at the opposite side of town from the Maidu Cafe and halfway to the slopes. Both were in his mind; Emilia was in his heart. He was puzzled that such a fleeting encounter would fire so much emotion.

◆ ◆ ◆

Mark had maintained a diligent exercise program. It was the "executive plan," to keep the forty-something gut from sprouting over the belt. It was also a commitment: to be as muscularly fit in his forties as he had been in his thirties.

Age had not been part of the program twenty years before. But when the body parts of his peers began to drip like prayer candles, he continued with fervor. He hoped to forestall time's folly on his own physique. With its success, he became animated by the routine.

Mirrored walls encircled the weight room, in which Mark examined his image. A white T-shirt outlined his muscles, and shorts revealed the definition of his thighs. To accent his reflection he squinted his eyes and gritted his teeth, then flexed his biceps against the gripped weights he held. At forty-two, he thought his appendages persevered with dignity. *How old is Emilia?* was a thoughtful interruption to his fancy.

"Are you done with the bench?" asked a young man whose garments fit like skin. Bulges extended from each joint of his limbs. His torso seemed garnered by a sheath of muscle.

"I have two more sets," Mark responded and forced his focus to the barbells on the floor. "But you can work in."

"Thanks, man, but I'll come back." He worked the standing curl bar at the post beside Mark, who continued his exercise.

"You're swinging your body," the young man said into the mirror, and continued with his curls. "You'll do better to decrease the weight and maintain good form."

"Thanks. I guess I am." *And your diaper needs changing.* Mark took lighter barbells from the rack and, without swing, finished the third set of lifts. He proceeded to a station on the opposite side of the room.

An older woman worked the thigh adductors, while Mark used the adjacent quadriceps machine. The roam of their eyes met on the fronting mirror. "Hi. It's amazing what we have to go through to fight off age," she said.

After an indulgent snicker, he replied, "Yeah." It, though, was not age he struggled against, but an ache in his thighs on extending his knees. "Hmm." He lifted the weight.

"What muscles are you working?" he asked, curious about the sensuous exercises she did. Mark studied the wrinkles on her face and thought she was in good shape for her age. In black leotards, though, she seemed from a time long past, and not very attractive.

31

"Thigh adductors and the pubococcygeal muscles," she said, and separated her legs to push on the weight.

"What do they do?"

"Heighten sexual arousal."

Mark looked to his thigh muscles in contraction and quietly cleared his throat. "Oh. That sounds interesting."

The woman stopped mid-motion; the apparatus kept her thighs wide. "Have you ever heard of Tantric Sex?" she asked, as if offering an investment opportunity.

He looked at her reflection in the mirror and shrugged. "No. Is that something like tawdry sex?"

"Quite the contrary." She released herself from the contraption and stood to look at Mark. "You might consider it experiential divinity through the practice of physical intimacy."

"I suppose you're not Catholic."

She chuckled and released the bun that held her long zebra-patterned hair. She squatted briefly to stretch her legs, and reached into her bag. "Here is my card. If you are interested, my husband and I have an introductory workshop every week."

"Thanks." He read from an unadorned white card, *Carol & Andrew Weber, Tantra and the Art of Intimacy.*

"He is not the music man," she added, then went into the ladies' dressing room.

Mark stared at the print on the card as if further explanation was coming. Susan's complaint had been that their relationship had lacked intimacy. Had he known it was as simple to learn as flexing his pubococcygeal muscles, he might have acted on her demand.

"Hey, man." The body builder interrupted his thoughts with a tap on the shoulder. "Can you spot me?"

"Sure." Mark followed to the bench press and safeguarded the card in his pocket. He wondered where divinity factored into intimacy, and whether it was why he had fallen into hell on the breakup with Susan.

"Give me a boost. I'll do about three reps."

Mark glanced at the weights at either end of the bar. There were more than he would lift the entire year. He approached the head of the bench and looked about the gym, but there was no one to replace him.

Flat on the bench, the young man hyperventilated in preparation to lift, then groaned to a count of three. On the third repetition, his powerful chest strained raising the bar; he bellowed under the bulk. Mark lightly assisted and prodded, "Push it, man; it's all you."

His face flushed by the effort, the bodybuilder sat up. "Hey, thanks for the spot," then stretched out his hand. "I'm Shannon."

"Sure. I'm Mark." He grasped the hand and noticed Shannon's heartfelt smile, the afterglow of testosterone. "I'll be around if you need another spot."

◆◆◆

With the melody of spring rain, water dripped from the melted snow on the overhang of his roof. Patiently, in the shade of the deck, icicle melt cascaded like a silent waterfall. A warm sun animated the spoils of the brief storm.

Mark sat on the perch to the fireplace, next to the laptop, and lifted its hood. He stared into the empty screen as his fingers played over the keyboard to type in her words—*Coffee? Or more about me?*

His fingers stopped over the keys; he could take it no further. His imagination stopped at her words. He lifted the laptop, feeling its weight and texture. It was scratch-resistant, like the treasures concealed inside. It was black, like a casket, for the tales of emotion buried within.

Not this time, he shouted in his mind and selected DELETE.

◆◆◆

It was colder than the sunlight would have one think, but Mark could find no logs for a fire. He dug deep in his pants' pockets to warm his hands and felt the card on tantric sex. He withdrew it and mused at its inscription: *Tantra and the Art of Intimacy.* Would his read, *Mark Balcon and the Lack Thereof?*

The backrest of the sofa was draped with a lap warmer his mother had knitted for Susan, her would-be daughter-in-law. Mark reclined and spread the warmer over himself.

Chapter 4

*D*arkness slipped through the windows during the two hours he napped. The blackness caused Mark to wonder if his eyes were fully open. In the sky, there was no moon; starlight profiled the scattered clouds. Night, he thought, reflected his circumstance, isolation affirmed by the shadows.

But shadows, he thought, bear no bars, and circumstances can be conditioned by the will. He took the card Carol had given him on tantric sex and intimacy, and knew he had failed Susan, but his failure was a lack of courage to try to understand.

Mark jumped from the couch, and flung the coverlet over his laptop, as if to rip open the bars that isolated him. His thighs ached from the earlier exercise, but it only seemed to propel his momentum, to defy the essence of his solitude.

Beyond the window, through the beclouded forest, casino lights at the edge of the lake sparkled. Brighter than the stars, they lured his attention. Gambling had once been a pleasurable pastime, and he thought it a good place to begin the night.

◆◆◆

A steamy shower soothed his muscles, but not his disquiet. At the vanity mirror, Mark stared at the reflected image of his naked body. Drops of water dripped from his hair and glistened on his flesh. A red hue tinged the skin of his chest. Startled by his arousal, he quickly dried himself.

He wrapped the towel around his waist and wiped the steam from the mirror to review his reflection. Salt-and-pepper whiskers shadowed the sharp angles of his jaw, the hairline receded from the edge of his temples, and wrinkles showed where he had not felt smiles. He was a timepiece, with every stroke of an hour featured on his face.

Fashion is a tease, Mark considered, when he realized the wore-me-downs he kept in storage were all he had available. It is a promise of vanity, that our faults should be concealed. He tried on a pair of olive slacks, a pale beige shirt, and an ultramarine wool sweater. In colors from the divine palette, he took a second glance at himself. The wrinkles that crossed his face were smiles once shared and tears restrained. Age was, after all, the wake of circumstances, on which the *will* set its course.

Mark shaved the whiskers and combed the hair to fill in the margins. He brushed the flat of the black sneakers against his calves, contented with their dull shine. As if to settle a bargain, he sprayed himself with the only cologne he found.

◆◆◆

The Hyatt Hotel/Casino parking lot was located within a grove of tall ponderosa pine. By the truck, Mark gathered himself against the cold, bundled in the woolen sweater Susan had given him. He recalled the Christmas three years prior. On the card that came with it, she had expressed her love for him, but bid farewell. He had felt numb at her departure, but so had he been in their relationship. He assumed the blame and never responded. The sweater had remained under the tinseled tree, in its colorful wrap, until the dried pine needles became a fire hazard.

With a deep sigh, Mark took a whiff of pine scent, which warmed him more than the wool fibers of the sweater. He had not loved Susan, but he had cherished the affection she gave him. He looked above the canopy of the forest, as if to pray, and asked Susan for forgiveness, hoping that life had since gone her way.

Together with the smell of tobacco and alcohol, a rush of warm wind brushed against his face when he pushed open the glass door. It was like daylight inside the hotel lobby with all the lights that greeted him. The decorum was plain, the focus of attention a central rock fireplace in which tall flames roared from a gas log. There was much activity: guests with clumsy postures toted skis and luggage, while others greeted friends with shouts of delight. From the cheers, it appeared their weekend parties had already begun.

Waves of shouts and laughter from the adjoining casino distracted the newly arrived. One-armed bandits, dispersed throughout the spacious gambling floor, whistled forthcoming rewards—the metal clang of generously dispensed coins soon followed, beckoning stragglers into the dimmed casino. Overhead neon lights illuminated aisles formed by opposing blackjack tables. Enthralled, Mark entered the casino.

It was busier than he had hoped, but there remained one table with no other players. Mark sat at the end stool and counted out on the velour top his fifty dollars. He looked at the dealer; he seemed familiar. He appeared to be in his thirties.

"How are ya?" the dealer asked and gathered the single deck of cards that was splayed in a semi-arc, face up, on the tabletop. "Haven't seen ya here for a few months."

"Hope these empty chairs aren't a sign of your skill," Mark said. He was surprised at being remembered, and glanced at the nametag to respond, "I was here last month—and even won. I missed you then. Hope you'll be as generous tonight, Tom."

"Well, let's see what we can do." After he exchanged Mark's money into five-dollar chips, Tom shuffled the cards. "Where's your lady?"

"I'm here alone." He shifted on the stool. Tom had confused him with another player. "It might have been someone I met here."

"Yeah, this is a good place to meet chicks." Tom handed him the cutting card.

"I feel the luck," Mark said, inserting the plastic card into the middle of the deck.

"Well, let me dish it out to you, then." Tom began to deal. "First card up is a queen of hearts. A very good sign. It means you're in luck for romance."

"I'll settle for that." Mark leaned forward and picked up his two cards. "A perfect blackjack," he cried out and turned the spades for display. "Is this an omen, or what?"

"I guess the queen of hearts foretells all good fortune. After all, it costs money to seduce a fine woman."

"I'll settle for the money if you keep dealing the same hand." It was for male bravado that he chuckled, but on the prospect of romance that he placed his aspiration. Mark gathered his winnings and let his eyes roam the room. "There are some beautiful ladies here tonight."

"Yes, sir. I'm like a hummingbird in a field of roses." Mark noticed the gleam in Tom's blue eyes as he continued, "I have to admit, though, the best nectar is always at home."

"Well, Tom, it's pretty dry in my home garden." He picked up two face cards to the dealer's six up card; but the tease of a winning hand did not generate its requited excitement. Mark stared through the table, and wondered which germs the dealer would warn him against.

"Man, that's only temporary." Tom dealt himself a breaking card. "I have a feeling your fortune will change tonight. That's what these cards are telling me. Want a drink?"

"Sure." He needed an elixir of courage to accept his promised fate, but remembered his stagger up the stairs behind Rose May.

Tom raised his hand, and as quickly, a hostess approached Mark from his right. "Would you like something from the bar?" She stood sidelong, her flank rested against the cushioned border of the table. On the palm of her right hand, leveled to her bosom, she held a tray. Her breasts were cradled snugly in an uplifting, low-cut dress.

"I'll have a beer." Mark felt the warmth of embarrassment when he realized his stare was directed elsewhere than her face. With ballistic motion, he turned his attention to the table, but it was too late to retract his impetuous splitting of two face cards.

"What kind of beer would you like?" She reached for an empty glass to the left of Mark and lightly brushed his arm with her breast.

Beads of sweat formed above his eyebrow and threatened to drip. He wiped his forehead with the palm of his hand, but his stare remained resolute on the cards. "Bud Lite would be fine."

"That comes on tap—or would you prefer a bottle?" If preferences were options, he would rather the earth swallow him.

"Bottle," he answered with finality. Mark listened for her departure as he watched Tom deal a six onto his first face card and a three on the second. Too worn out to struggle, he stayed on both hands.

"Man-o-man, she caught you with your eyes down her dress. You looked like she had you by the balls," Tom said as he dealt himself five small cards that broke the dealer's hand. "Yes, sir! The brown of your eyes are truly white. My man, you are in definite need of a good lay." Tom paid both hands. "And I'm happy to contribute to that cause."

Mark's laugh flourished into a howl and his play of cards into camaraderie with Tom. He affirmed the bond with a dealer's bet, and the cards continued in his favor.

"All right, man. I think we have something here," Tom happily stacked the winnings from the dealer's bet.

The hostess reappeared and assumed the previous pose. She set the bottle of Bud Lite against the cushioned rim of the table. The warmth of her breast brushed his arm. In tandem, Tom and Mark glanced at each other. The hostess seemed puzzled by their snickers. Mark noticed she was about his age. Her dark brown eyes brightened when he dropped a tip onto the tray.

"Thanks," she said, and walked away.

A second dealer tapped Tom from behind. "Thanks for the bets," Tom said to Mark and splayed out the deck of cards on the table. Waving his hands to the security cameras in the ceiling, he added, "It's that time. The home nectar awaits me."

"Thanks for the fortune telling." Mark pushed some dollar chips toward him.

"Hey, good luck, man." Tom clapped his hands over the table and retrieved the chips. "Remember, the queen of hearts reins over romance, and she ain't going to let your balls get swelled up." He winked and stepped away. Mark watched him drop the chips at a repository, then pat the back of a floor supervisor, with whom he shared some laughs. Tom continued, with pep in his stride, to the home garden.

"Are you making a bet?" the new dealer commanded, more than inquired. She shuffled the cards and held them with both hands crowded to her chest. With a glare directed at the table where his bet should have been, she appeared like the jack of spades seeking justice. So prompted, he placed a bet where directed by her stare, and held back a chuckle he wanted Tom to share.

"Are you lucky tonight?" Mark asked.

"I don't know. I'm just beginning my shift." She dealt herself an ace card up. "Insurance?" she asked, and finished with the rest of the hand, unaffected by the intimidation of her card.

He took a gulp of the beer to lubricate his throat and prepare for a financial fall. He peeked at his down turned cards—a thirteen was not much to insure. He retreated to the cushion of the backrest. "Do you feel lucky?" he asked.

"If I could feel luck, I wouldn't be standing here," she replied and turned over her down card as an exclamation. "Blackjack."

"Suzanne from Kansas," he read from her nametag, as if to call out his nemesis. She may have jabbed the first blow, but Mark was intent on battle. The beer was an elixir for courage, but the cards were his dagger. He stared at her hands as she restarted the match.

Suzanne was lean and tall, and appeared to have once been attractive. The shriveled skin of her face was that of a nervous smoker. Her white-blond hair was a product of overindulgence in bleach. The only thing Kansas about her was the old maid twist in which she held her hair. She gripped the card deck with authority and seemed determined to devastate Mark's treasure. If it weren't for the beer so generously dispensed, he would have sought battle elsewhere. It was with relief he welcomed another player.

The young woman, probably in her mid-twenties, sat on the stool opposite Mark. With her left hand held close to her body at the level of her waist, she guarded a roll of one-dollar chips. With her other hand, she brushed back sandy brown strands of hair to glance briefly at Mark. She then focused intently on the cards Suzanne prepared to deal.

"Place a bet," Suzanne directed, without a welcoming tone.

"I'm sorry." The newcomer appeared startled as she gathered two chips to place on the table marker.

Mark and Suzanne simultaneously turned to the placard at the end of the table, and acceded to its edict of a two-dollar minimum bet. Suzanne began to deal. After a few hands, it was clear the new player had shifted the luck to Mark's benefit, but not her own. With sympathy, he watched her discard the losing hands.

Her emerald eyes drew his stare; they seemed to shimmer on the cascade of cards Suzanne had dealt before her. His face imitated hers when she cried out, "Twenty one!" Her smile of triumph gradually ebbed into a conspiratorial grin. She turned to Mark, as if to an accomplice.

"Congratulations," he responded, and felt himself surrender to whatever plot she was scheming.

"It looks like you're doing well." She glanced at his chips, which were stacked against the cushioned border of the table.

"Suzanne is ripping me apart, but you've brought good luck."

While the dealer continued, undaunted, Mark watched the young woman's hands. Folded on the green velour, they seemed to guard her chips from Suzanne's resolve. Her long, manicured nails mirrored the neon lights in their gloss of clear polish. She wore no ring, neither of commitment, nor for embellishment. He was seduced by her lack of ostentation.

"Would you like another card?" Suzanne asked.

Mark was jolted from his musing and straightened in his chair. When he reached for the dealt cards, his hand lightly slapped the glass. A ripple of the beer spilled onto the table. "Oops, sorry about that. I'll stay."

Suzanne wiped the table clean, but as if to avenge his effort, she turned an ace upon her exposed queen of hearts. "Blackjack," she said nonchalantly.

"Oh, no!" his co-conspirator screamed. "I worked hard for those cards. Suzanne, how could you do that to me?"

Mark counted out an unnatural twenty-one as Suzanne, as deftly as she had cleansed the spilled beer, swept away the losing cards. The young woman stared with disbelief at the spot where her cards had once been.

Mark considered an overture to console her and was startled when she spoke, "Can you imagine? Losing that hand with a twenty-one?"

"I told you she was mean," he said, and sipped his beer. "Let me buy you a drink to alleviate the pain."

She smiled. An attractive dimple formed on her cheek. "That's quite generous; a kind offer like that cannot be refused," she responded in play, to the house-complimentary drink.

While Suzanne shuffled the deck, Mark called out to the hostess attending the adjacent table. "Suzanne has left a bad taste in our mouths. Please, a round of drinks for everyone," he said, with a grandiose motion of his hand.

The hostess approached and assumed her pose. "What will the lady have?" she asked, only partly turned toward her.

"Tomato juice, please."

"As in Bloody Mary?" the hostess asked.

"As in plain."

The hostess brushed his arm on her turn. "Rather attentive, isn't she?" he said after her departure. "Driving home tonight?"

"No. I'm staying at the hotel. I'm just not much of a drinker." She held the cutting card Suzanne had handed her and measured it against the deck. With whimsical determination, she forced it in at the selected depth. "There. The luck will now be on our side of the table."

"Good cut," he said, to wish her a good hand. "You don't drink alcohol?"

She picked up the newly dealt cards. "It's not that I don't drink. It depends on the occasion." She glanced away to a decorative neon light on the ceiling. Looking bemused, she bit her lower lip, as if to restrain a recent memory. "There's nothing like a pre-dinner chardonnay to set a romantic mood."

"Sir, are you playing this hand? And don't knock the beer." Suzanne interrupted his fantasy of a white-clothed dinner table sprinkled with candlelight, and the dimple of her smile refracted through the crystal of a wine glass.

"Oh, I'm sorry again." He rushed to look at his cards. "I think I've had too much beer, and I need a big card." Suzanne dispensed a nine card to match the concealed twelve. "Perfect," he responded, but felt penitent when he noticed the young lady's losing hand.

She glanced at his winnings. "That certainly could buy you a nice, romantic dinner."

The hostess returned with the tomato juice, which she left by the dollar chips. Mark gulped what beer remained and took the glass the hostess handed him. Her breasts brushed his arm on her turn to another table.

"How romantic can a dinner for one be?"

"In the spirit of romance, cherished thoughts keep our company," she replied without sympathy.

"Then let's drink to wine and romance." He raised his glass, watching that the beer did not spill.

"And to all things we share." She raised hers in response.

"Excuse me for interrupting the poetry," Suzanne interjected, "but aren't we here to play blackjack?"

They broke out in laughter.

Suzanne continued to deal. From the stage beyond the slot machines, a band started playing soft rock music. The cards dealt to her were more agreeable than her previous hands, but his own were fickle. The enthusiasm with which she relished her wins was infectious. Mark could not help but tap his feet to the music.

With a flick of her hand, she turned her first card. "Give me a ten," she shouted at the displayed ace, as if volume influenced luck. "Yes!" she greeted her second card. The dimple of her smile punctuated the pleasure she was having. "Finally—a blackjack."

"That's the way to do it," he said, trying to mimic the energy in her tone.

He listened to the music, which was mostly from the eighties, music he liked. With the rhythm usurping his body's movements, Mark felt temptation whenever she offered her attention. He wondered whether it was Tom's queen of hearts working on his behalf, or the sorcery of his elixir.

"Hi, lady and gent. I'm Oscar, and I've been sent to take your money." Mark had not noticed Suzanne step back and the new dealer step in. He was average looking, a college-type bundled with charisma. His black hair gleamed almost purple in the neon light. "And what are your names?" he asked.

"Belinda," she answered, her eyes focused on Oscar's hands while he shuffled the cards.

"And a beautiful Southern belle ye be. There aren't too many Belindas in Nevada."

"I be from Louisiana, with a mortgaged sugar-beet planta-tion, and if you be a gentleman, only the best of cards you'll give to me."

"Whoa, my lady. A top order that would be, but for the spar-kle in your eye, my soul I would give. To do your part, though, take this magical card and split the block." He handed her the cutting card, which she inserted into the deck. Her eyes did not waver from his stare. "Consider your wish granted," he said, and raised the deck of cards to his heart.

Oscar dealt Mark the first card. "Are you Miss Belinda's fortu-nate escort or the evil banker seeking her fortune?"

Dumbfounded by their interplay, Mark felt witless. "Neither. I think I'm lost in space."

"That's good, I think," Oscar said, and feigned seriousness with a frown. "'Tis better to have been lost in space, than never to have loved at all."

"Oh, my god, you're a riot," Belinda laughed.

Snubbed by their rapport and eventually by the cards, Mark decided to play his last chip. A queen of hearts was accompa-nied by a jack of spades. Not enough of a hand for the unnatural twenty-one Oscar dealt himself.

◆◆◆

Mark walked the aisle heavy-footed, toward the casino's exit. Periodic shrills affirmed gamblers' claims to luck, and drew his attention. The cacophony of dispensed coins into metal bins tempted him to other treasures. Bewitched by the luster of the neon lights, he pondered one more play.

Mark wondered what tortured him more, being spurned by luck or Belinda's attention. He shoved his hands deep in his pockets and gripped tight the coins Emilia had given him. Assured that the queen of hearts would inevitably prevail, he walked out of the casino.

Chapter 5

*S*plintered sunshine sprayed his uncovered body. Beyond the closed blinds, a symphony of droplets from melting snow mocked his idle repose. Mark ruminated over the motivational prompt he had contrived to scroll across the computer screen—"Success requires creativity and activity," but it lacked the inspiration to move him off the bed. Writer's block, though, was not what troubled him.

Startled by the ring of the phone on the bedside table, spurred by anticipation, as much as reflex, he quickly sat up to answer. "Hello!"

"Marco?" a heavily accented voice called from the other end of the line.

"Hola, Mami." Comforted by his childhood greeting, Mark rested back on the pillow.

In melodramatic Spanish, his mother continued, "I've been calling you every day. I've been so worried. I thought something had happened." The English translation depended on the emotional inflection of each syllable.

He listened to her conversation, envious at the passion she inflicted on the mundane. The love apparent in her admonitions offered solace. He wished to tell her what he felt and why he had come to the lake, but could only muster single-word responses that left him feeling empty.

"*Te quiero*," was her goodbye, which contrasted painfully with the silence that followed.

His body trembled, as he did during the nightly lament of his childhood. To regain the resoluteness with which he had held the knife against his belly, Mark gripped the desire Emilia's eyes had tempted. He stood up and raised the blinds. It seemed a perfect day to ski.

◆◆◆

A slip on the ice in the parking lot of the ski resort reminded Mark that middle age joints have their limits. The bulky gear he wore offered protection, but cost him the energy he'd need to climb onto the first lift. It had been a few months since he had last skied, and a few more seemed the wiser option.

Middle age was not all physical encumbrances. The occasion to ski at will, rather than cope with holiday crowds, was a prerequisite of accumulated capital. Trapper Garza may have considered him "rich folk," but Mark knew it to be true grit; it comes with time and effort.

The slopes seemed unencumbered, and the lift lines short. Mark passed the singles queue with defiance—no one would care he was alone—and waited in the doubles line.

"How's it going?" welcomed the lift attendant, who continued to shovel the snow from the ramp.

Mark scuttled to position and nearly tripped on his crossed ski tips. With his balanced regained, he flexed forward, his buttocks projected to the oncoming chair. "Looks like a great day for skiing," he said to the attendant.

"Watch the chair to your left," the attendant cautioned Mark, who was prepared to receive it from the right. At that moment, the rim of the seat crashed against the back of his thighs and propelled them forward. He fell, slumped into the chair, and was lifted above the incline of the slope. He glared at the chasm below his skis, and struggled to an upright posture.

But for the gentle breeze, there was pleasant silence at the summit. No other skier followed him off the lift. Mark stood at the edge of the mountain, as if from a platform above the world, and glanced east toward the Carson Valley. The panorama was boundless. The valley was an earthen basin, hemmed by jagged desert mountains, sparsely adorned by chaparral. Above it was the celestine blue of a cloudless sky. To the west, gentle streams of snow flowed into the thicket of the pine forest. Beyond the canopy of green was Lake Tahoe, a shimmer of silver from the late morning sun.

On the gentle downhill glide, his muscles and joints loosened. Prudence, an imposition of mortgages and credit card debt, as much as inflexible body parts, guided Mark on the ski run toward the forest. A black diamond sign halted his stride.

From the ledge of the hill where he rested, the expert run seemed a vertical drop. Before he had overcome his caution, the swishing sound of a skier approached from behind. He stared at her form as she continued without pause down the slope.

Like a hummingbird's wing, her bright green jacket was fanned out by the wind. The ski pants fit snug on the curves of her hips, which swiveled deftly on each of her turns. Like a dancer, poles held at arm's length, she kept rhythm with the motion of her body. Her weight shifted from hip to downhill hip as she took each mogul at its crest. She seemed to fly just above the snow.

Her triumphant roar at the bottom of the run stirred Mark to follow. As if dragged by the poles that trailed him, his arms floundered, and the skis sounded gritty as they scraped the face of each mogul. Where she had grace, he looked for survival. But he imagined a dance in her wake, and it was all that mattered.

At the base of the hill, a small crowd had lined up for their turn on the chair lift. To the side of the roped area, three skiers were joined in jovial conversation. The one facing away was the skier in green. Her companions were cliché ski-jocks. Both were tall and brawny, with sun-bleached brunette hair. On their snow-tanned faces, they wore dark sunglasses. With red ski-patrol jackets, they could have been twins.

Mark strained to hear her voice, but the skier in green remained turned away from him. He positioned himself to snoop on the conversation but was rattled by their laughter. He shifted his focus on the couple ahead of him, embraced in a perpetual kiss. Mark scuttled to the singles line.

"Are you single?" he was asked from behind, caught with his skis tangled on the rope between the queue lines.

Mark turned to face his questioner and recognized Emilia, the skier wearing green. "Oh, my—It's you," he answered.

"Mark! I had hoped you would come. Can I ride up with you?" She skated to his side.

"By all means." He struggled to free the trapped ski, and then scooted to make room. He glanced behind her and was delighted the twins had not followed. "I was behind you down that last run, but I couldn't keep up. You're a great skier."

"Thanks. Did you take 'Diamond Back'?" she asked and moved forward in line.

"Yeah, but not with the grace you did."

"I love those six-foot moguls. I've been skiing them all morning."

Emilia brushed her lips with a chap stick, and the glove she removed fell to his feet. Mark reached for it, and as he did, the skis slid into those of the couple still in an embrace. "Oops, sorry," he said, but the couple didn't seem to notice.

"Thanks." Emilia took the glove and smirked toward the undisturbed couple. She added, "I didn't see you on the slope."

"Of course not. You blew me off at the top of the hill."

"I'm sorry. I suppose I can be that way. I get so focused when I'm having a great time, and it's such a beautiful day." Joy showed on her face.

The couple ahead remained embraced, even as they continued to the platform. The attendant finally got them to separate and board the on-coming chair.

"Maybe they're just trying to keep warm," Mark said as he and Emilia took their positions.

"Make sure to take the chair to the left," the attendant cautioned Mark. Then to Emilia he asked, "How was the run?"

"It was great. Have you been on it today, Jerry?" she asked and positioned herself into the moving chair.

"As soon as I get off work," he answered and held the chair for Mark.

"It seems everyone knows you around here." Mark settled himself comfortably in the chair as it lifted them above the trees.

"I sometimes work the ski-patrol, so I've gotten to know most of the regulars. Did you go into Maidu for breakfast?"

"No, I had cereal at home," he said, and lifted his sunglasses off his face. He hoped she would do likewise.

She turned and, through her glasses, glanced at him. "I'm really glad you came up today."

"So am I." *Have I said enough?* he wondered, but then heard only silence.

The lift ascended just above the crown of the inclined forest. He shivered with the cold of a gentle breeze. "How long has it been since you were that deeply in love?" Mark directed her attention to the couple ahead, again secured in an embrace.

"You mean lust. Probably when I was their age, in high school," she answered. "How about you?"

Emilia's gaze had wondered off to the runs on the slope, considering which next to take. Mark hesitated. He could not think of an answer. Lust was a fountain of conflict that carried plots for all unwritten novels, but it was not something he could recall having felt.

"Probably then, as well," he said to his feet.

"Do you mean lust or love?" she asked and lifted her glasses to look at Mark.

He understood what it meant to melt when the hazel of her eyes bore down on him. "Lust, I suppose. Love is too complex."

"Love is no more complex than we are; lust is what we learn to become," she said, and nothing else.

Had he lost her?

The lift's summit station was at the crest. The trees, bent leeward, seemed stunted at the higher altitude. Vestiges of a recent storm were evident; dark pine stalks were embossed white with fury-blown snow, and a chill wind swept the ice crystals that molded themselves to the pine.

"I'm taking one more run before lunch. Follow me," she said. They glided off the lift to where he had earlier stood.

"The whole world at a single glance." Emilia's outstretched hand spanned the view from the Carson Valley to the lake. "Here we can become who we are."

Mark re-strapped his boots and straightened to follow her on a stream of snow into the thicket of the forest. He listened for the music Emilia's body swayed to, and heard it in the wind that opened her wings and brushed against his face. With the poles gripped at the handles, he led them forth and danced on the moguls. He roared in triumph when he came up to Emilia at the bottom of the run. He sprayed a rooster-tail of snow at her legs on his rapid stop.

"Freedom feels good." She turned away from the flying snow. "But hunger doesn't; let's go for lunch."

A narrow path led them below overhang tree branches. Chunks of snow fell when their shoulders brushed against them. She stopped at the lodge and waited for Mark, who followed far behind. "What? You fell? You've got snow all over you."

"No. You just blew it all on me."

"I did not. Did I?" she laughed and swept the snow from his shoulders. "I guess I got even. Are you hungry?"

Before he answered, Emilia had unstrapped her skis and spiked them into a snow bank. Her boots sounded harsh on the grated floor as she stepped into the lodge. Mark rushed to keep up and jumped the two steps to the deck, but slipped when he landed. His arms flailed to catch the rail.

"Good move!" she shouted from the door.

"You liked that, heh? Just my way to get you to stop. I didn't want to be left in the cold." He continued into the lodge, inspired by her laughter.

Two patrons sat at a long bar opposite from where Mark and Emilia had entered. Beer bottles at the ready, they were in a spirited conversation with a female attendant.

"Emilia!" the attendant called out.

"Norma!" Emilia responded from the door.

Mark followed across the wooden floor and pivoted around empty log tables. Off the end of the bar was a large stucco fireplace, above the mantle of which were two nine-point antlers. A strong odor of spilled beer supplemented the absence of sunlight.

"Let's eat outside," he whispered to Emilia as they approached the bar.

"Well, girl! I was just telling these guys about you." Norma motioned to the two at the table. They leaned to their side and over the counter to gaze on the subject. They gripped their bottles like gearshifts. Their loose plaid shirts gave them away as snowboarders.

"What about? My Maidu oracle skills?" she asked, and winked her eye at Mark.

"These guys are engineer students at Berkeley. I was telling them about you going there for Native American prayers."

"Well, it's not for the prayers that I go," she answered. In a more casual tone, she added, "But we're hungry. I'll take a Swiss cheese sandwich," then pointed to the display refrigerator, "and that fruity punch."

"I'll have the same," Mark added and reached for the clipped dollar bills in the inside breast pocket of his jacket. He stooped to the floor to pick up a glove he dropped. While he collected himself, Emilia paid for her order.

"No, no. Let me."

"Let's make it some other time," she said. With her food gathered in her forearm, she headed for the side door.

"Are we on for 'Steamers' tomorrow?" Norma called before Emilia had walked out. "You know Victor will be there."

"I'm planning on it."

The deck jutted out above an escarpment of boulders, and the forest enfolded its periphery. With the shadow of trees parted as if on curtain call, a central vista of the lake was on display. The diners turned to the sun, like marigolds on a prairie. Many of the men had bared their chests, and women wore bikini tops.

"Do you mind if we share your table?" Mark asked the single diner at the only open table. She moved to the opposite end in response.

Even before he was settled on the bench, Emilia had begun to eat her sandwich. "I'm so hungry. I was shaky there for a while. They say the last run is always the most dangerous, and I can see why."

"Well, you seemed in pretty good control." He removed his sunglasses, as his back was to the sun, and enjoyed the sheen of natural light on her face.

"Thanks for offering to pay; but I was heading here anyway. It wouldn't be fair."

"No problem, but I'm in debt for your showing me the way. I'll take you up on that some-other-time request," he said and bit into the sandwich.

With an impish smile she asked, "Will it be breakfast?"

"Why?" He leaned forward, his elbows rested on the table, and he copied the curious movement of her eyebrows.

"It's all I've ever seen you eat."

"Not quite." He bit into the sandwich. "This is lunch. What other of my idiosyncrasies can I dispel?" He felt a flush on his forehead with thoughts of the germs the cop had warned him against.

"You always order the same breakfast."

"So, your powers as an oracle are based solely on probability." Pretending indignation, he added, "I'm feeling a little self-conscious."

"Don't be. I've enjoyed watching you, especially when the yolk drips from your toast. It's cute how you dip the tip of the napkin into the water glass to wipe it off your shirt."

"Oh, god!" He straightened to look away, and with a quick swipe of his hand, swept the crumbs off his mustache.

He noticed a red-coated twin emerge from the lodge. Emilia touched the hand gripping the corner of the table, as if to respond to the sudden gloom on his face. "I'm only kidding."

Mark hoped the exhaled air of a deep sigh would blow away the intruder, but instead, it seemed to lead him to them.

"Emilia," the twin cried out.

She loosened her hold of his hand and turned back. She hesitated prior to a response. "Victor."

"Why didn't you tell me you were coming to lunch?" he asked, with a brusque Boston accent. The twin maneuvered himself to the edge of the bench on which Mark sat, their shoulders buffeted against each other. Mark scooted to make room. The lone diner stared away, but her ears were piqued in their direction.

"I thought you and Bob were taking a patrol run," she replied. Then to Mark she offered, "This is Victor Celeste."

"Pleasure to meet you." Mark tightened his handshake against the lie. "I'm Mark Balcon."

The lone diner left the table stealthily, and Mark wondered whether he should follow. He looked across to Emilia. Her sunglasses were perched on her forehead. Her eyes pleaded for him to stay.

"Bob was called away to the infirmary. Someone twisted an ankle or something like that. I thought I would take a run. I was hoping to catch up with you." Victor's gaze was as intent upon Emilia as he was on his chatter. "Maybe we could go down the Gulch later. Bob went down it today and said this was the best he's seen it."

The Gulch was exactly that, a monstrous ravine that ate neophytes. Large boulders terraced its fall. When covered with snow, they formed shoots to propel undaunted skiers into flight. The fearless attempted helicopter spins or eagle spreads during the two-hundred-foot drop. Those who missed a turn survived on a castigating rear slide, a prayer of contrition their only thought. Mark preferred to recall it in springtime, a tranquil waterfall by which to have a picnic.

"I think I'll pass it up, Victor," Emilia answered. "I had a bad spill on it last month. You were there when it happened."

"Yeah, but the snow was bad, too icy. Bob also took a spill then, worse than yours. He says now it's the best he's seen it. Let's do it later today. There aren't going to be any more storms before the season is done. This is the best it'll get. All right?"

"I'll pass it up, Victor. I don't want to spend the spring in crutches." Emilia alternated her glance between them, as Victor controlled the conversation.

History was communal, but not necessarily universal. Mark could not think of a shared experience or any other way to join the discussion. He brushed vigorously at imaginary crumbs on his lap, but surprised himself when he stood up. "I guess I better go," he said, to cover for the disruption.

"Don't, Mark," she responded. "I didn't mean to ignore you."

"You didn't. I just have some errands I need to get done." He felt committed to the rash decision, though her eyes beckoned to him once again.

"Will I see you tomorrow at breakfast?" she asked, with a smile that seemed determined to develop a history between them.

He looked at Victor, still focused on Emilia, and wished him more than crumbs on his lap. "Yes, I'll be there," he answered.

"Nice meeting you," added Victor, as if the last comment was required.

At the front of the lodge, Mark found Emilia's skis planted into the snow bank. He mused at their colors: turquoise banded the back, lavender on the front, and a stripe of gold parted them. The palette of colors was that in which Native Americans of the Southwest painted their imagery. *What prayers does Emilia invoke on her trips to Berkeley?* he wondered. His were a supplication to the queen of hearts. Mark touched the skis as if to ask for a response.

In the wind, he found the music to continue Emilia's dance. He skied the slopes without effort, down to the base lodge. Dissuaded by his pretext for the quick departure, he resisted the temptation for more runs and proceeded to the parking lot.

Chapter 6

*S*ki runs traversed the mountain like white strips of decorative ribbon; but the rear view from his car was not so benevolent. Mark regretted the impulse to leave Emilia and, as the distance grew between them, he wondered at its effect.

Mark tried to forget, the defensive medicine to which he was accustomed. But forgetting does not mean forgiving, nor does it recover a lost opportunity. Regret was a compulsion to anticipate, and like the touch of her hand, he felt magic in wanting to see her again.

◆ ◆ ◆

Solace from the trees, or the colors of the skies, was understandable. That traffic at the town's main intersection offered likewise was serendipitous at best. Mark was distracted from his compunction. In its stead, he considered the Haiku poet and the outcome of the canned meal she planned for her fiancé.

Loose association was a writer's technique he enjoyed using. It allowed his fictional characters adventures beyond his own experiences. That it would also influence his life became evident when he realized he had not yet shopped for groceries.

A wide aisle led from the market's entry to the wine section, where Mark valued the chardonnay by the thickness of its glass. Raised at eye-level, the bottle refracted the light into a spectrum of blush. He recalled the toast to "cherished thoughts that kept our company," and retracted that salutation. Alone, he decided, would not be enough.

No light peeked through the porcelain bottle of Sake he found among the exotic drinks. Adorning the label was a heron, its colorful plumage fanned in boastful display. He considered the Haiku poet, grabbing at her lapels against trust, and then writing interpretive subtleties to secure her emotional ambivalence. *How much of what he judged was himself?*

At the cash register, he reviewed the items in his shopping cart—the rudiments of health: fresh fruit and vegetables, bread and sandwich items, milk, and orange juice. He had left the chardonnay on the shelf, much as Trapper Garza had let his lover's card hang on the wall.

"Hold my cart to the side," he directed the cashier, and ran the aisle to the wine section. In his life, hope was an illusion, a refracted light in the spectrum of blush, but at that moment, it was all he had. He cradled the heavy glass bottle and carried the chardonnay to the cart.

◆◆◆

The casino was a short drive from the market, which he made as if by habit. Inside, multicolored neon lights were the only respite from darkness. It seemed an abstract garden, in which there never had been day. Among flowers that did not bloom, a sparse crowd sat hunched over game tables, feasting on melancholy. Like a potion of their bewitched state, clear yellow drinks were set at hand's reach. Their attention was on the dealt cards before them. One-arm bandits dropped silver into tin plates and preached the sermon that cajoled gamblers to further play.

A gentle breeze greeted him in the parking lot. Dusk rested on the canopy of the forest. He had no view of the mountain, but a luminous ribbon of white hinted at the trails on which Emilia had been. He felt for his untapped gambling budget inside his pocket and smiled at the jingle of the coins she had given him for change. Time swayed with the colors of the sky. From his deck, the night seemed brushed with strokes of carbon while clusters of stars rendered its dimension eternal.

Appetite was a curious drive, he thought, insatiable even when gratified. A want or a need always seemed to linger. The tasteless turkey sandwich he prepared failed to substitute for the chicken breast, wrapped with bacon strips and baked in a mushroom sauce, which tempted his thoughts. He felt his fingers, nimble and ready to type, but it was with Emilia he wished to spend the night. He dimmed the light so as not to dull the outside view and gently stroked the laptop's keyboard. As if to listen for music, he felt the compulsion to write.

From the Incomplete Folder, he withdrew a tale he had let linger. He could not recall when he last visited this world, and so he reread the lives of the character suspended in their vocation. Like a god wielding a mighty sword, he pecked with his fingers at the keyboard and dispatched further details for their lives. Winds of a pending storm were abated, and forlorn characters appeased.

Punctuation was a dictum, and on the last promulgation, Mark reclined, to read the world he had created. He laughed at his divine powers and wondered if he could part the waters, as well. In romance, he was better off trusting the queen of hearts.

◆ ◆ ◆

He awakened in the morning, well rested and feeling the active tense in which he had written his characters. Outside the bedroom window, a band of gold breached the eastern crest of the mountains while scattered clouds muted the glow. A crystalline lace of icicles clung from the banister, as if to forewarn him of the cold. He put a ski jacket on over a sweater and hoped it would suffice. His gloves were stowed into a pocket.

The road through town was quiet; only two cars were parked in the lot at Maidu, each with an overnight blanket of ice. He parked adjacent to the one closest to the entrance, and wondered whether he had misjudged the time. Mark snooped through the frosted side window for Emilia's colors of the southwest, but halted, thinking he would raise suspicion.

The screen door squealed, and the wooden door gave way to a push. He was relieved the cafe was open. A gray-haired man sat at the counter with a newspaper held open in one hand, and a cup of coffee in the other. No one else was visible.

He closed the door behind him as a waitress appeared from the kitchen. She brushed away a smoke-gray curl that dangled over her forehead. Crow's feet sharpened the corner of her eyes. There was no color to her skin except the magenta of her lips. "Would you like a table?" she asked.

"No, thank you. I'll just eat at the counter." He hung the jacket at the entryway and continued to the second stool from the gray-haired man, whose stare remained fixed on the paper. There was no noise from the kitchen.

"G'morning," said the man, with a quick side-glance.

"Morning," Mark replied and skimmed the headlines of the business section the man was reading. "How's the world of money?"

"Good." His eyes did not waver from the print. He set the cup on the saucer and turned the page to the stock prices. "I think the market is getting too pricey, though." He folded the paper and set it on the stool between them. "Laura, how about some more coffee?"

The woman wiped her hands on her apron as she returned from the kitchen. "I'm sorry, Warren. I'm by myself this morning. Just trying to catch up on some of the preparations." From the back counter, she grabbed the coffee pot and approached the man. "How was breakfast?"

"Good," he answered, in the same tone with which he had reflected on the world of business.

"Having coffee this morning?" she asked Mark.

"Yes, please." He turned the cup over to receive it. Level to the brim, she poured the coffee, and steadily raised the pot. A pigmented froth quickened the steam to carry the aroma.

"Are you ready to order?"

"Didn't spill a drop. That's pretty good," he said. "Let me have a minute to look at the menu."

"I'll take the bill," Warren said, and placed five dollars from his wallet on the check. "I've got to get going. Tell Emilia I missed her."

"Sure will. She'll open tomorrow." Laura pocketed the money and gathered the dishes, then returned into the kitchen.

60

Mark looked away from the menu to the front window. His focus was blurred by the silence. The rattle of glass in the kitchen fixed his stare beyond the window to the parked car. The sun had scaled the mountain rim and the sheet of ice on the windshield dripped lucent beads of water. Remorse overwhelmed him as he imagined Emilia with Victor.

"Have you made up your mind?" Laura asked from the kitchen door.

"I'll have an egg-bagel sandwich." He did not look away from the window, but he was no longer hungry.

It wasn't long before Laura returned with the sandwich; but in his trance of regrets, time was not a factor. "Everything okay?" Laura asked and refilled the cup.

"Yeah, I think so." He turned back to the meal and raised his arms behind his head, as if to hold back his thoughts. "You didn't pour from up high this time."

"I didn't think you were paying attention. You seem kind of out of it."

"It's too early in the morning. I'm just tired," he said, and reached for the newspaper.

"Tell me about it. I switched shifts today, so I had to open." Laura wiped the counter where Warren had eaten. "Honey, it's sure hard to wake up when it's darker outside than when you went to sleep." Laura returned to the kitchen.

He was glad not to have to think of a response and reached for the business section Warren had left. The first article predicted an inevitable market correction; but equally convincing was a second pundit in a later section discussing the economic parameters that would maintain the bull market. *What greater value had an expert's opinion than a rabbit's foot?* he thought. Their odds were those of Trapper Garza, *Whichever way they turn*. Forget did not forgive, but he was grateful for the distraction.

Mark took the bill to the cash register and waited for Laura. Two diners were at the table by the window, but he had not noticed their arrival. The parked car beyond the window had not been moved, and the ice had melted.

Laura took the money. "How was breakfast?" she asked, but did not look up from the cash drawer.

"Good." He mimicked Warren's assessment to pretend nonchalance. At the counter, he left two dollars. "Is Emilia working later today?"

"She better be here soon. People are starting to come in," Laura replied, then crossed the room to the new diners.

He zipped the jacket and tucked his hands deep into its pockets to thwart the cold. Behind him, the screen door clapped shut as he put on the gloves. The inside view of the first car was no longer smeared by ice, but he instead stooped towards the door of his truck. With gloved hands, he fumbled with the keys.

An older model car drove up to the front of the coffee shop. Mark gazed through the window of his door and saw Emilia step out from the passenger side. Turned back to the car, she continued a conversation with the driver. A concluding chuckle was all Mark could understand.

Crouched below the level of the roof of his truck, he felt inconspicuous as he turned to canvas the car when it drove by. An androgynous silhouette of the driver was all he discerned.

"Mark?" Emilia called from the cafe entrance. "Is that you?"

The keys dropped from his hand and clinked on the gravel. He straightened as if commanded. "Hi." He cleared his throat.

"Coming in for breakfast?" She leaned to the jamb, and held the screen door partly open. Indoor light shadowed her smile.

"I just finished." He bit his lower lip, but could not think of how to withdraw the rash comment. *Was it a sickness he was catching?*

"You got here earlier than usual, but then I'm late." She opened the door wider and motioned toward the inside. Her smile faded. "I better go. Laura is probably upset."

As soon as the door closed behind her, she reopened it. "I'm meeting some friends at Steamers tonight, about seven. I would like it if you could come," she said.

Emilia recognized his assent, seeming to mirror the smile he felt on his face.

Chapter 7

A sundial records time by the shadows. Mark felt time through the span of warmth across his forehead while bent over the laptop. The cool of evening roused him.

Writing fiction was his binary entertainment, imprinted digitally, and failing an outcome. He straightened in his chair and, into the Incomplete Folder, saved a second short story he had long neglected—a catalogue of imagined lives whose fate awaited his disposition.

Fate is, he considered, as he prepared to meet Emilia at Steamer's, *the sum of personal turns of events, and divinity its ultimate source.* In that his childhood challenge of this order had placed him where he stood, Mark was satisfied to let the night be "whichever way it turned."

◆ ◆ ◆

There were only a few cars in the restaurant's lot. None that he recognized—and not the older model Emilia had gotten out of that morning. The androgynous silhouette, as well, remained uncast.

At the entryway to Steamer's, Mark brushed the flat tops of his sneakers against his calves. Failing a shine, he continued on to the foyer.

"Table for one?" greeted the hostess.

"No," he replied almost defensively. "I'm waiting for some people."

"Maybe they are already here. What party are you with?" She turned to scout the almost empty dining area.

He creased the pleats of his pants. "I don't think they have arrived." He didn't know what name to ask for and stared away from the hostess to the lounge.

"You can wait for them in there," she said, "or here," and pointed to a wooden chair at a corner of the foyer. She returned to behind the podium and resumed her paperwork.

From the wooden chair, he had a good look at the dim lounge. A lonely bartender washed drinking glasses that he hung on an overhead track at the bar. The muted sound of disco music floated from the room.

Lighting in the dining area was likewise dim. Large upholstered chairs engulfed the few diners who sat on them. Whispers, Mark thought, would make a better name for the restaurant. It was all he could make of the conversations.

Lint on his blue woolen sweater was as conspicuous as he felt himself to be, sitting alone in the foyer corner. His only distraction was to pick at the fuzz.

Two couples, chattering jovially, entered from the front and proceeded to the lounge. Mark recognized Laura, the Maidu waitress, but he felt too shy to approach the group. Lacking an introduction, he decided to return when Emilia could do so.

Half an hour was all he needed to walk the commercial area of town, but it was an endless journey for the many thoughts that tempted him to continue home. The memory of Emilia's eyes beckoned him back.

"You're here," the hostess said when he re-entered the foyer. "What party were you waiting for?"

There were many more diners than prior to his departure, but he noted Emilia among the earlier group, still in the lounge. "I see them," he responded. "Thanks."

Emilia had joined the two couples at a table across the lounge. She faced the entrance but was distracted by spirited conversation. Mark recognized the ski-lodge cafe attendant with them. He stopped at the first table inside the lounge and pulled the chair into the shadow, aiming to establish a balance against self-doubt.

In the isolation of his thoughts, Mark shut his eyes and imagined her smile. He let his body sway to the soft rock music that filled the room with the rhythm Emilia had danced on the moguls.

"Falling asleep?"

Startled that his imagination could be so vivid, he opened his eyes and gripped the sides of the table to straighten in the chair. Emilia stood across from him.

"Oh—gee—no," he stammered. "I was just thinking—I'm sorry. I didn't mean to take you away from your friends."

"I was afraid you wouldn't join us. Besides, I see them almost every day." She rested her hand on top of the opposite chair. "Would you mind?"

"Oh, please do," he said and rushed to the chair she held. He hesitated to draw it out; his hand partly covered hers. "If you rather, we can go over to your friends."

"Let's just sit here for a while." She gripped tighter and prompted him to pull the chair for her to sit.

"I was working myself up to go meet your friends." Mark pulled his chair closer to the table. "But this is better."

"You know Laura from Maidu?" Emilia was turned to better point out from across the room, her friends, who continued in animated conversation. "John, next to her, is her husband. He is a delivery guy in town. Bob, you may have seen, is ski patrol, and Barbara is his most recent girlfriend. She is a receptionist at the Hyatt. Norma you met at the lodge, remember?"

Mark had casually listened, but he was most interested in the emotions on her face. With each introduction, she revealed a history that he envied. He quickly glanced toward her friends when she turned to him.

"Yes," he answered, wondering whether Bob was Victor's twin. "Now there's no reason to be intimidated by them. We don't have to stay in the shadows, if you don't want."

"I'm glad we are alone," she replied.

Her words seemed to enclose them as if into a cocoon. Mark returned her gaze; she was all he cared to know about. In Trapper Garza's words, he thought, *and I gots all the time in the world to know here well.*

"Are they all friends?" he asked.

"Yes, except for Barbara. I just met her tonight. The others I've known since I moved to Tahoe." Her fingers gently touched the cardboard doily on the table. Her glance remained on him.

"Let me get you something from the bar," he suggested, hoping to provide an element for a metamorphosis—his, preferably. She already possessed the splendor of a butterfly. "Chardonnay?"

"That would be nice."

Mark crossed the lounge to the bar, enthralled in the spotlight of her gaze. The overhead lights seemed dim in comparison. On the return, he cradled a bottle in the crook of his left arm. With tender fingers, he gripped the stem of two crystal glasses. On the polished dance floor, he shuffled to the music, and returned to her like a moth to a lantern.

"Now if I only had some candles," Mark said and placed the glass before her, "the mood would be set."

"We can create our own mood," she responded, and gazed at her glass.

"That may be true, but I've been out of the scene for a while and need some props, at least 'til I get some confidence." Mark poured the wine into each of their glasses and sat in his chair.

"Props are good," she said, and looked at him with a smile. "We could all use reassurance."

"Let me make a toast."

She raised her glass to meet his. "Please do."

"To romance and spring snow." The light of the room, refracted through the crystal, sprinkled across the table at the turn of her glass.

"It sounds like something from a poem," she said.

"It's just an off-the-cuff salutation you inspired."

"Is there meaning to it, besides being a prop?" she asked.

"Ah, let's see. How about, 'as with winter, so with romance, each adversity heralds a springtime bloom.'" Mark raised one eyebrow and grimaced in anticipation of her response.

There was a pause, during which she appeared pensive. "I think there is poetic potential there."

"I'll work on it," he offered, and took a second drink. He glanced through the crystal at her smile. "Where are you originally from?" he asked and leaned forward.

"From Georgia." She held the glass to her lips.

"A Georgia peach," he embellished.

"Without the fuzz," she interjected. "I'm just a simple Cherokee."

"So that's why Norma said you go to Berkeley for prayers with Native Americans."

"You don't have to be Native American for prayers." She sipped at the wine, and a drop spilled to her chin. Emilia wiped at it with the napkin Mark handed across the table.

"Oh, I know, but I'd wondered about it when Norma mentioned it at the lodge." He leaned back on the chair. "You may think badly of me, but I don't know much about the history of the Indians—I mean, Native Americans—even though I write a magazine column based on the history of the Old West."

"Don't worry about it. People satisfy their interests." Emilia leaned forward. Her fingers encircled the base of the glass, which she had set on the table, "You're not local, are you?"

"A native Californian," he answered, glad for the change in subject. "A direct descendant of a Spanish Conquistador." Mark felt a cool sweat form at the back of his neck when he realized their discordant ancestry. He looked to the darkness that enclosed the dance floor, as if to the screen of a confessional, and blurted, "I'm sure he was just a journalist, keeping an account of their adventures. That's where I got my writing talent, you know."

Her chuckle welcomed back his regard. "If we had to answer for our fathers' sins, earth would truly be hell," she said.

The music was livelier and louder. More conversation sounded from the other tables. Mark looked away and noticed two others had joined Emilia's friends. He was glad her back was turned, since Victor was among them.

To hold her attention, Mark added, "Tahoe is where I feel most at home. My paradise."

"Lake Tahoe is definitely a corner of heaven."

"What brought you from Georgia?" he asked.

"I wanted to take time off after college and experience some of the things I had read about." She sipped the wine and paused. "I've spent time in other parts of the country, but I felt a spiritualism here that is magnetic."

"I think I know what you mean, but I've never put it in such terms."

"Actually, I don't know why I've stayed. It's like a tempo, created by my senses, that simply directs my life."

The introspective stare that followed seemed to search beyond the confines of the room. He wanted her back. "What did you study in college?"

"Religious studies." She returned her gaze to Mark.

"Really?" He restrained the surprise in his inflection. "What are you doing as a waitress?"

"What does anyone do with work but pay for a livelihood."

" I mean, shouldn't you be working in a church, or some job requiring a ministry?" He smiled to accentuate the intended humor. "I mean, judging a guy who drips egg yolk on his shirt doesn't require a degree. Maybe it does. What do I know?"

"I wanted the historical perspective." Her hazel eyes held a distant, but delighted gaze. "I figured life could be more fulfilling and engaging if I knew how things came to be."

Emilia brushed back a beckoning curl. "Actually, being a waitress has been quite good." She leaned forward, her elbows on the table, and rested her chin on the back of her folded hands. "Think of all the rewards—dripping yolk and all the breakfast gore."

He wanted to feel the soft flesh of her face and the curl of her hair between his fingers. There were a million thoughts he wanted to share. Instead, he laughed.

"And what is your reason?" she asked.

"I'm sorry—reason for what?" Did he missed something she said, or had she read his mind?

"Why are you in Lake Tahoe?" she asked.

"Wait a minute. We weren't finished with your story." He felt the energy of the music, as well as his desire. Mark leaned forward and mirrored her pose. "Would you like to dance?"

"I would love to."

He held her hand in the palm of his and led her to the center of the empty dance floor. Mark recognized Gordon Lightfoot's "Early Morning Rain." Its tune was a bit hillbilly, but infectious. He watched Emilia prance about with a country western foot movement popular in northern Nevada. After tripping clumsily over his sneakers a few times, he abandoned his attempt to mimic her steps.

The curls of her hair danced on her shoulders, each brunette fiber silhouetted against the ceiling lights. Her rouged lips, thinly parted, formed a smile that highlighted the whiteness of her teeth. The coral rose of her cardigan flattered her skin, and its embroidery broadened the fullness of her breasts. Turquoise trousers hung from her slim waist, contouring the curve of her hips. The trouser legs fit snugly into the tops of worn leather boots. Mark thought Emilia was more than the Maidu oracle; she was a Cherokee princess. To the whirlwind of sound, she pirouetted on the axis of her body. Mark was drawn in by the contagion of her joy. He reached for her outstretched hand.

The music slowed to Chris Isaak's "Two Hearts." Mark raised their clasped hands and drew her near. With one arm around her waist, he guided her movement. They glided across the length of the wooden floor. Her legs brushed the inside of his at each of their turns.

Emilia swayed gently to "When I Fall in Love," by Rick Astley, and pressed her body to his. Mark felt the moisture of her hand when it slipped away to embrace him. She rested her head in the cradle of his shoulder. Silk, he imagined, was no softer than the feel of her hair on his cheek.

> Caterpillars spin into a shelter of delicate fibers
> and dance in circles of an impassioned universe.
> Closed eyes see desire;
> in these shadows is a different world.
> They are the earth and the moon,
> intertwined in an embrace.

Mark felt only pleasure.

The melody shifted to rock & roll, and their trance was disrupted. Three couples took to the dance floor and displaced them. Mark held her hand, and they returned to the table. From her purse, she withdrew a tissue and wiped the beads of sweat on her forehead. "Would you like one?"

He smelled her fragrance on him. "I'm fine. Thanks."

"You dance well," she said, and sat on the chair.

"I'm only as good as my partner." Mark was hesitant to sit. Emilia's friends had joined the dance. Victor was paired with Norma and appeared to be whispering in her ear. Victor's nod in their direction had fazed him.

"I'm sorry I missed you at breakfast today," she said, "but I'm very glad you came tonight. I was afraid you wouldn't."

"It was all I could think of," he replied, and scurried to his chair so she would not turn to the group on the dance floor. "Breakfast was not as good as usual," and in the same breath, added, "Do you come here often?"

Emilia turned when a finger tapped on her shoulder. "Norma!" She noticed her friends beyond. "You guys are partying! Norma, this is Mark."

Half-turned to Mark, Norma responded, "Hi," and without pause, returned to Emilia. "Why don't you join us? Victor is here."

It was a singular *you* Mark heard in Norma's suggestion. Emilia grimaced in response and extended the invitation. "Would you like to join them?" she asked Mark.

No was selfish, *yes* a lie. "You go ahead. I have work to do, anyway." Mark dropped back in his chair.

"You've used work as an excuse before." Emilia touched his hand, which clutched the edge of the table. "I want you to stay."

Butterfly wings unfurl from the cocoon and rainbow colors are revealed. Magic was in the touch of her hand. "You're right. Tonight, I'm yours," he replied, with a smile that touched every wrinkle on his face.

Mark refilled his wine glass. *In life*, he thought, *there are no guarantees*. What he wanted, however, was reassurance that he would prevail over his solitude. So, as if to draw on the potion promised by the queen of hearts, he drank the wine in a single gulp. With the bottle clasped against his chest and the wine teetering in her glass, which he held at arm's length, he followed Emilia and Norma across the room.

They joined the group and danced to a tune that mocked the passion Emilia and Mark had shared. Frivolous body movements foiled pair dancing. Laura's grasp frequented her husband's, John. Bob's seductive glance was fixed on Barbara. Emilia and Norma twirled among Victor, Ray, and Mark.

They continued a non-stop session of dance. Mark was first to tire and withdrew to the single table that served as base, a trestle for their drinks. Leaning forward on a chair, his elbows on the table, cupped hands under his chin, Mark stared at an empty bottle. To disrupt his introspection, he looked up to Emilia, who was still dancing.

"Well, old man, did you get your fill?" Ray punctuated his question with a slap to Mark's back as he accompanied Norma to the table. Ray was a local contractor and father of three, but who was separated from his wife. He had come with Victor.

"I think I did," Mark replied, "but you don't look in any better shape."

The two couples converged at the table. Bob and Barbara stood to the side, where the light was most dim. He kissed her on the lips, and then bent his head to lick the sweat from her neck.

Laura sat at the table and wiped her face with a handkerchief. John searched the bottles, and with a single gulp, emptied the one left with beer. They were both middle-aged, but Mark thought they were older than he was.

"Bob seems a bit thirsty," John said about the enthralled couple. "But I think he would do better to drink some beer."

"I don't know about that, John," answered Ray, who sat across from Norma. "I wouldn't mind some of what he's getting."

"If you ask me, you get too much of it outside your home," Laura interjected.

"Ouch, Laura," Ray said, his folded hands gripped tight between his thighs. "It's been a while since I've had any, though. I think Marge will take me back. She knows they meant nothing."

"She's a good woman. I think she'll forgive you," added Norma, staring at Emilia and Victor on the dance floor. "Don't they seem a good couple?"

The conversation had been like lint on his sweater, a good distraction from Emilia and Victor on the dance floor. Norma's reference, though, shattered that screen. Mark looked up and could not help but agree; they did appear a good couple.

Before the music had finished, Emilia walked toward their table. Victor followed two feet behind her, his arm partly wrapped about her waist. He leaned to her to whisper, and Mark could only look away.

With a swift brush of Mark's hair, Emilia nudged him to move his chair. She took the seat next to his and sipped what remained of the wine from his glass. An impression of her lips rimmed the crystal when she returned it to the table. Mark stared at the imprint and revered its tacit intimacy, more details for their shared history.

Laura tugged at John's hand toward the front door. Bob placed the jacket over Barbara's shoulders and embraced her from behind. Norma searched in her purse and retrieved a silver ring from which hung one million keys. Ray stood away from the table, toward the exit, and jingled coins in his pants' pocket. Victor sat deep in his chair staring calmly at Emilia, who tightened the belt of her overcoat.

"Would you like a ride home?" Victor asked her.

"I'm going back with Norma. Thanks," she replied, and glanced at Mark, who had stepped away from the group.

He lagged behind in the foyer, where each bade the other a good night. Emilia stepped back before they went through the door and turned to Mark.

"I had a very good time," she said and cupped his chin in her hand to lower his lips to hers.

To the taste of her rouge, he replied, "I'm glad I stayed." For reassurance, he whisked his lips with his tongue, for the sense of her on him.

Emilia rejoined the group in the parking lot before Mark recovered. He smiled from the doorway to notice her driving away in Norma's old model car.

The sound of paper crinkled in the grip of his hand, but he waited for the last of Emilia's friends to drive out of the parking lot. As if revealing a treasure map, he unraveled the folded paper at each of its wrinkles. It was a note on which Emilia had written her telephone number.

The night was cold, but he was warm in his wool. He stood alone on the asphalt, but the taste of her lipstick persisted, and kept him company.

Chapter 8

Monarch butterflies migrate north in spring and return that fall, traveling hundreds of miles on their journey. Nature is patient; Mark was not. He tossed and turned in his sleep, and often sought for a hint of daylight through the open blinds of his bedroom.

Paper crinkled on his step out of bed. It was Emilia's note, fallen from the nightstand. "Call me tomorrow," he read. The flourishes in her handwriting bespoke her invitation.

Mark returned the note to the table and placed it over the pyramid of coins. It was too early to call; she would still be at work.

Out of the shower, he struggled with the towel around his waist as droplets of water fell from his hair. At every glance in the mirror, a reflection of the phone appeared. It was too early to call.

Minutes did not cooperate. *Time*, he decided, *would be swifter if left unattended*. He would expend anticipation in a tour of the neighborhood.

A red-tail hawk flew over the road he walked and into the forest that he rarely visited. Its distant squall reminded Mark of the poetry in the forest, poetry he thought Emilia would enjoy and he wanted to share. Returned home, he considered the poetic potential Emilia had commented on upon hearing his salutation and thought to further develop it into a serenade.

After staring at her note so many times, he had committed the telephone number to memory. To dial it was simple. To wait out the rings was unnerving. A male voice took the call, but Mark hung up before its message was completed. He redialed slowly, and matched each number to the note. The same monotone voice answered, but Mark did not heed the mechanical request to leave a message.

On the third dial, a female voice not Emilia's answered, "Hello?"

"Hi, Emilia?" he asked.

"No, but just a minute. I'll get her."

"Hi, Mark?" Emilia asked.

"How did you know it was me?"

"I'm the Maidu Oracle, remember? Actually, Laura thought it was you." There was a brief conversation away from the phone. She continued, "We just got in from grocery shopping."

"I'll call later if you want. I know you're busy."

"No, no. Laura is on her way out. She just ran in to use the bathroom." He heard Emilia tell Laura to call later, and then returned to the line, "I'm sorry. It gets hectic on shopping days. I try not to do it too often, but I suppose I have to eat."

"Maybe I could cook dinner for you one day." Mark lay back on the bed, a rolled pillow propped beneath his head. "It might save you time next time you shop."

"Well, that would be nice," she replied. He heard the sound of cans into cabinets.

"You're not vegetarian, are you?" he asked.

"Oh, no. But I'll only eat what Walt Disney has not made a movie of." They laughed.

"I guess I better get to a video store," he added, "to make the shopping list."

"Let's watch 'Bambi' after dinner," she suggested.

"Hey, whatever you want. It'll be your day."

"I'll hold you to it," she said.

"I'm sure you'll be impressed with my cooking."

"At least we won't have much cleaning to do," she mocked. "You certainly leave those breakfast dishes clean. A dog would starve waiting for your leftovers."

"I'm getting self-conscious here. Do I eat that poorly?"

"I'm only kidding." He heard her sigh, after which she continued, "I have enjoyed watching you eat. For the last two years, it's all you've shared with me."

Mark felt heavy in the bed. To share, he thought, is not something he's had to do, for all the years he's been alone.

Her distant voice came from the handset that had slipped from his ear, "Hello? Mark?"

"I'm sorry. I dropped the phone." He hesitated, then added, "More the reason to have you over for dinner. There is no excuse but tunnel vision to have ignored you." *And going as far a half a tank would take me*, he thought.

"There is no need for an excuse," she replied. "But I would love to have dinner."

"When?" he asked.

"Not today. Laura and I ate all the unwrapped items we bought at the market, and now I'm stuffed."

"Today is only Tuesday. Let's make it on Friday," he said.

"It's a date." After a pause, she added, "It's so beautiful outside, and I really need to walk off some of this weight. Would you like to join me on a hike in the forest?"

Mark turned to the window. The mound of snow on his deck continued to drip in a stream of water; a thin layer of mist above it splayed the sunlight into a rainbow of colors. It was springtime, and the poetry in the forest he wanted to share had more to do about themselves than birds and trees. "I would love to," he responded.

◆◆◆

The park was a heavily wooded peninsula that jutted into the lake at the southern end of town. Heavy snow isolated it, in what Mark considered nature's repose. Granite boulders formed a rampart at the water's edge.

Double tire marks tracked through the frozen snow into the park. He maneuvered the truck along them to the solitary jeep parked in a grotto of evergreens.

The seclusion of the park was the tranquility of a relentless winter. Snow still blanketed the summer trails, and tall drifts lingered in the shadows of the redwoods. Like arrows of light, beams of sun flashed through the canopy and thinned the snow.

"You made it here quickly," Emilia welcomed him from the trail that led away from the snow-covered lot. She held gloves in one hand, and with the other, she waved at Mark to follow. She wore the green ski jacket, and a blue nylon shell covered her trousers and was strapped over the collars of leather snow boots.

"It's cold out here," he said, and walked to where she stood.

"I suppose you weren't expecting much snow." She glanced at what he was wearing as he followed her stare. His hands, raw beyond the cuff of the knitted sweater, were stowed deep into the pockets of his linen pants, which hung loose over his sneakers.

"I guess I should wear my jacket." He shivered at a cold gust of wind and returned to his truck.

"We'll stay around the beach," she suggested when Mark began to follow. "The snow has pretty much melted there."

The trail was hewn out of knee-deep frozen snow and wended its way through a stretch of forest. The muffled sound of their shoes on frozen ground harmonized with the gentle stream of melting snow. A woodpecker added percussion high above their march. Footprints of deer, like melodious notes, trailed between the trees.

"Do you think we'll see Bambi?" Mark asked.

She laughed. "I was just thinking the same thing."

The dense forest opened to an expansive panorama of the lake. Turquoise waters at the shoreline unfurled to a royal blue at the center of the lake. The mountain rim against the cloudless sky was mirrored upon the water.

Gentle waves lapped at the pebble beach on which they walked. The afternoon sun warmed his skin, but the chill in his feet distracted him. The socks were soaked and his feet squeaked inside the sneakers.

"It might be better if you take your shoes and socks off," Emilia said. "I think it's warm enough for them to dry."

Embarrassed that she heard the squish, Mark did as she suggested. He rolled the legs of his pants to his knees, relishing the feel of the warm sun on his moist feet.

"All right, I'm ready," he said. The socks hung loosely from inside the sneakers that he gripped with one hand.

In a timeless promenade to the lake, behemoth stones were banked one upon the other. The trail ended at the granite face of the boulders. Emilia stopped, the crest of the rampart well above her head. A gentle wind sifted through her hair as she gauged the best route to take.

On the beach, where it felt warmest, a few feet from where she searched, Mark laid out his shoes and socks to dry.

"Mark, come up here," Emilia called from atop the last boulder to the lake, several feet above the water. "It's nice and warm up here." Her face was illuminated by direct sun, her hair blown back at the temples.

From where he stood on the beach, the rampart's facade seemed vertical to the summit. Toward the lake, the pebbled beach sank into the frigid water. Beyond the beach, into the forest, deep virgin snow filled the precipice. There seemed no option; Mark confronted the rock wall, as he thought she must have done. Her shadow above him tendered a dare, and he groped for a secure handhold. Taking the challenge, he thought, was adventure; weakness was to ask for her direction.

A small promontory jutted out from the granite wall at the level of his hip. He jammed the toes of one foot onto it and lifted himself. With one hand, he reached a crevice at arms' length above his head and his body became flushed against the rock. The fall below and the climb ahead were equidistant. Mark committed to the climb.

With his free foot, he felt the craggy surface for a second hold. A chink on the rock was the toe's prop, on which Mark heaved his body's weight. He reached with his hand for the crest that loomed above his head. Both arms were stretched overhead to grip the rocky cornice, when his foot slipped from its toehold. The right knee scraped the rock as Mark hung suspended from the capstone. He dug his fingers into the granite and, with a burst of strength, lifted himself onto the ledge.

"Are you all right?" Emilia responded to his groan, and then added, "It would have been easier around this end."

He turned away from the view of the fall he would have taken to the stepping-stone approach where she pointed.

"My way was more adventurous," he answered and covered with his hand the blood that trickled from his right knee. When her gaze turned to the lake, he lifted the cuff of the rolled pants and inspected the wound. It didn't appear deep, he thought, and quickly unraveled the pants' legs to conceal the injury.

"Is it nature or nurture?" she asked.

He sat next to her and stared into the lake, where he thought her focus was. "What do you mean?" He tried to erase the guilt from the tone of his voice.

"Why are men like boys?" she asked. "There always has to be some personal challenge in everything."

The warm moisture at his knee felt as if it was expanding. He pressed his hand more firmly against it, but joined her in laughter, more to suppress his fear at being revealed.

"Would you rather it one way over the other?" he asked.

"I like it the way it is." She paused, her gaze on his.

A strengthened breeze fanned a strand of hair across her face and stole away her gaze. With gentle fingers, she brushed back the wanton curls.

"You know, nature is our nurture," she said, as if to answer her thoughts. "I look at everything here—the boulder we sit on, the lake so deep, the mountain that changes colors with the weather. Do we, like everything else, become only what is destined?"

"Is that what you were referring to last night?" he asked without looking away from where she stared. "I mean, about this place having magnetic spiritualism."

"Oh, that's just the beginning. There is so much beauty here." She looked at the water and her reflection. A curl dropped to her forehead, and she brushed it back. "I feel beautiful just being here."

He wished to touch her. "You are beautiful."

"And that is what I mean, nature is our nurture. Your thinking I am beautiful makes you want more." She glanced at him.

"You probably also feel you need more," she said and raised the energy in her voice. "So, do we make our destiny, or do we become what we are destined?"

"Which one do you think?"

"A question is never an answer." Emilia turned her body to him. With her knees flexed, she wrapped her arms around her legs. "Which would make you happiest?"

"These are questions never asked in my catechism class." He looked away and thought he did not understand. "Are these the questions you go to Berkeley to pray for or inquiries for your religious studies?"

"I don't know." She hesitated with a sigh, and brushed back a wave of his hair, which undulated with the breeze over his forehead. "I did pray to be here with you."

"Why? Because I drip egg yolk on my shirt?"

"Yes," she answered and looked into his eyes.

"Oh, so you prefer the clumsy type." He didn't understand, but he hoped it didn't show in his eyes. It was the pleasure of the moment he cared to enjoy, but the red halo encircling his hand on the knee stole his attention. He pressed harder to stop the flow.

Was the vanity of his clumsy adventure a *germ* she would renounce? There was no further deliberation; an impulse consumed him as he ran the stepping-stones into the lake.

"Mark, where are you going?" she called from behind him.

"Into these spiritual waters." To mock old-time prayer revivals, he flapped his hands above his head and walked into the frigid water. "I will not be destined to eternal clumsiness."

"Come out of there," she yelled to him from where the water lapped her feet. "I promise I won't talk in allegories."

He waited for the red stain at his knee to be cleansed and the trickle of blood halted by the cold water. "It's not your allegories I don't understand," he said as he lumbered from the waist-deep water. "I just don't want to disappoint you."

Emilia smiled and wrapped her arms around his neck when he came to the water's edge. "The opportunity to be disappointed is the chance for love," she said.

Raising her on her tiptoes, he firmly embraced her and held her in a kiss. The warmth of her breath was inside him and his frozen toes, still in the water, were thawed.

She slipped her hands to his chest and gently pushed away. Gradually, the heels of her feet dropped to the pebbles on the beach, and they separated from the kiss.

"We better get you dry and warmed up," she said. His dusky lips quivered with the muscles of his jaw as she scanned him from head to toe. "I only live a mile down the road."

The wet pants clung to him and dripped water from the unraveled cuffs. His toes were blanched, but he walked onto the beach without hesitation. His socks were almost dry, but water seeped through the canvas when he forced the sneakers back on.

"I'm ready. Lead me to your home," he commanded, with an impish smile frozen on his face.

Chapter 9

In the melody of the forest was a new track, that of a single man marching towards deliverance. His sneakers squished and pants swished, but it was difficult to run with a straight knee. Mark didn't want to fall farther behind. His frozen smile warmed in anticipation when he returned to the parking lot.

"Follow me," she shouted from her truck's door.

Once inside the truck, he set the heater at full blast and turned the vent to his feet. Afraid he would not be able to slip back into his shoes, he left them on, and pressed the accelerator with his heel. He wiggled his toes to speed their recovery, awaiting the pain of their thaw.

Going south, away from town and up a hill into a thicker forest, he followed Emilia. Blackened snow bordered the road, and the lake was lost among interpolated stalks of redwood pine.

In the early evening, the forest's canopy was sketched deep green against the indigo blue of the skyline. To the west, the sunset waned into bands of golden clouds, woven with strings of lavender. This celestial canvas inspired his imagination.

Words are like the colors of passion, he thought, *and I'll make these the watercolors for her poem.*

He retraced the feel of her lips with his tongue, and felt the warmth of her breath still inside of him. The sharp red lights of her brakes broke his romantic trance. He screeched to a stop at the point she had made her turn.

"Ouch! Damn it," he said to the pain of half-thawed toes jamming against the brake pedal.

He followed a side road deeper into the forest, past granite outcrops, into a narrow valley. The dirt road continued to a small rock-faced house. Its mallard-green roof was camouflaged under the overhang of the forest. Vaults of snow clung to the eaves. From the truck, he strolled to the house along a walkway carved into hardened snow. At the entryway, like an inverted crystalline pyramid, a wind chime hung frozen within an icicle, drops of water its only melody. Emilia waited at the door.

"Welcome to Hansel and Gretel's cabin," she said, then entered the house.

To silence his clothes, he walked stiffly. "You must be Gretel," he said from inside the door. "I hope Hansel is out at play with the three bears."

"You've confused the fairy tales. But no, Hansel is up there." Emilia pointed to a large mohair effigy of Bullwinkle that hung over the fireplace mantle in the front corner of the living room. Its head was crowned with a Georgia Tech cap. "He's pretty good company, particularly on long winter nights."

"If I took his place on those nights, is that where I would have to hang?" Mark approached the mantle, but sidestepped the Middle Eastern rug on the wooden floor. "I know someone who might look good affixed to that mantle, though."

In the center of the small room, Emilia sat on a love seat that faced the cold hearth. She draped the jacket over the armrest. "Who's that?"

"What's that guy's name?" He pretended indignation.

She stood up to the bar table on the opposite wall that separated the living room from a tidy kitchen. Emilia set her car keys on the counter. "What guy is that?"

"That guy who tried to take you home last night."

Filtered sunlight from a small window on the third wall dimly illuminated the room. Emilia walked to a side table at the far end of the sofa and turned on a Tiffany replica of a Dragonfly lamp. He felt his shadow thrown to the wall and expected a slap.

"Mark, you're not serious?" The polychrome glow from the lampshade shadowed her face. "He's just a good friend."

"I'm sorry if I misjudged," he replied, and hesitated before adding, "but there was more than friendship in his eyes."

"Well, I won't argue that. He does have the cutest bedroom eyes." A slap would have been less painful then the abrupt end to the discussion.

From ceiling to floor, shelves laden with books lined the fourth wall. Peripheral to the book cabinet was an opened door, through which Emilia exited. A light was switched on where she entered, and he heard the zap of a zipper.

"Make yourself comfortable," she called back to him.

Like the ripple of moonlight on lake water, the light from her room was scattered over seams of the floorboards. Mark remained at the carpet's edge, restrained by the stiffness of his wet pants.

"This is a nice house," he said to prod an invitation to where she had gone.

"I love it here. It used to be the home of the lands-keeper for a wealthy estate." She returned to the living room wearing a thin cotton pullover sweater, draped loosely to the hips of snug-fitting blue jeans. He envied her feet, warm in woolen socks. "The main house at the lakefront burned down in the '60s, and all the property was given up to the National Park Service. Now I rent this cabin from them."

"How did you find it?"

"Victor found it for me. You know—that guy with the bedroom eyes you would like hung over the mantle." From a wicker scuttle, Emilia grabbed two split wood logs and knelt by the fireplace. She looked up at Mark. "You don't have to stand there. Have a seat."

"My pants are still wet."

"Well, for god's sake, take them off."

Mark hesitated at the command and watched her gather splinters of wood from the scuttle. She set a match to the hand-fisted mound and their stares fixed on a thin stream of smoke that rose in a spiral from the fledgling fire into the flue.

His clothes felt like a cast, and it was good to get out of them. He sat on the floor to pull at his socks, but the shock of the cold wood to his buttocks did not stun him as her scream that followed.

"Mark," she shouted from the fireplace. "You cut your knee."

"It's fine." In reflex, he placed his hand firmly over the laceration, as if to conceal it. "It'll heal without any bother. The lake water cleaned it well."

"You've been hiding it since then?"

Emilia dropped the logs over the mound of splinters and scooted over to Mark. She inspected the wound.

"It looks like it needs stitches." She looked up at him. "We better go to a doctor."

"It's okay." He forced confidence into his voice.

"It must be hard being a man," she said. "What would it take to make you cry?" She probed the wound with her fingers to calculate how wide the gap would open and determined that the edges came together at an even plane.

"Ai," he said faintly. With gritted teeth and mist in his eyes, Mark then added, "How about some Cherokee shaman healing prayers, instead?"

"Don't have much experience with that," Emilia replied. "When I was seven, though, I did watch my grandmother deliver a neighbor's child. I could pretend to be a nurse, as I did then."

There was more than passion in the smile she gave him, and the words he used to describe her in his mind were endowed with color. He watched her walk to the bedroom and return with an armful of implements. "What have you got there?" he asked.

"Go take a shower and clean the wound with this soap." She handed him an antiseptic solution, along with a bathrobe and towel. "Make sure you clean it well."

The shirttail draped over his briefs on the way to the bathroom; he planned a cold shower to chill the excitement he feared obvious.

Distraction was a defensive mechanism he had mastered, and a method he employed to brave the gush of cold water. He sniffed the two hair products that hung from the shower spout inside a metal basket; but no implicit function was revealed by their scent. He read the labels, as an anthropologist does hiero-glyphics: a jojoba conditioner promised a desert star's sheen, while the mango conditioner the gloss of a tropical rain.

The white ruffles of a fabric body scrub, like camellia petals in bloom, were flared open on a porcelain basin. He lathered her soap on his skin and fitted her shower cap snuggly. Nothing but her hair, though, carried the fragrance he remembered.

A rose-colored froth foamed from his wound when he brushed at the knee. Mark watched it trickle down his leg and twirl away into the drain. "Damn it. I stirred up the bleeding."

The wound appeared to require a few stitches; but the thought of a long wait at an emergency room was not how he wanted to spend the time. Emilia's nursing, he decided, would do him more good than medical attention. He grabbed a face cloth from outside the shower door and fashioned a tourniquet, which he applied to the knee. He tested the impromptu ban-dage, which held firm on a stiff knee, effectively controlling the seepage of blood.

Naked but for the washcloth, he dab-dried, so as not to stretch the skin, then covered up with the cotton bathrobe Emilia had handed him. It was a man's robe with the smell of a recent wash. "Emilia," he called out from her room. "You really don't think Victor had an ulterior motive last night?"

"What?" Her voice returned.

He sat on the corner of her bed and hesitated to reply. Fa-miliarity is a lonely man's crystal; it must be handled gently, for its allure tempts the bounds. "Whose bathrobe?" he dared.

"I don't know." Emilia's tone carried a tease. "I've had so many men go through here. It could well be Victor's. Do you want more reason to hang him over the mantle?"

Mark studied the framed photographs that decorated the walls of her bedroom, depicting Emilia's family and friends. Vic-tor did not appear among them.

"Well, no," he answered. "I was just wondering."

"Just don't fill gaps in knowledge with jealousy," she sug-gested. "What's taking you so long in there?"

"I'm just looking at your photos." Mark focused on a series of them in which she was among a group in folkloric dress. In the center was an older woman. "What do you mean, *filling the gaps with jealousy*?"

"Only that," she said, but after a pause added, "Victor is a sweet man and a good friend. His problem is in his intentions."

He gathered his clothes while searching for the gist of her aphorism. "I don't understand," he concluded.

The crackle of firewood in the hearth was the only sound he heard on his return to the living room. Emilia sat on the floor with a poker at hand to incite the flames. Beauty creates its own desire, he thought, and the image of her by the fireplace was just that for him.

"Let me put it this way," she continued the discussion in a softer voice. "Love with Victor is love without grace."

Solving riddles was not his forte, but neither was it for him to disrupt an abstraction with his ignorance. He clutched the crumpled clothes against his chest and wondered what "love without grace" would necessitate. Would spilled egg yolk on a lapel suffice, or would it require the desire he felt for her?

"I've missed you," she said, and turned to him. "I was afraid you had run off into the forest."

Her silhouette glimmered against the flames in the hearth; a shadow was shrouded over her back. Mark remained at the far end of the sofa.

"I'm sorry. I was nosing through your photographs."

"They are the tangible memories of my family and friends that I keep for company. Actually, they're a journal of my life."

Photography was to Mark the betrayal of failed hopes and the cruelty of time. His own, he kept stored in a neglected closet, inside an empty shoebox. He envied the tone of her contented nostalgia.

"Lay your clothes out on the sofa." She had set the sneakers to dry, raised on their heels and leaning against the rock platform of the fireplace. "And sit down by the fire, so I can bandage your knee."

"Why is Bullwinkle grinning at me?" He wrapped the robe around himself, ensured the front flaps overlapped, and then tightened the sash. The fire felt warm from the carpet where he sat. His covered legs were stretched toward her.

"Does Hansel make you insecure?" She sat up, her legs flexed under her, and threw open the garment over his knees.

"What's this?" she asked, and removed the washcloth. "You're still bleeding."

"It had stopped with the washcloth." Blood oozed from the wound where she prodded. Mark grimaced in anticipation of the pain her fingers threatened to cause.

"I don't know about this." She rose to her knees and bent over his leg. "I think we should go see a doctor."

"I trust you more than I would a doctor," he replied.

"Even if I'm just a pretend nurse?"

"What is being vulnerable without trust?" Mark asked.

"Just what I didn't want to hear."

Emilia let a solution drip into the wound that fizzled to pink foam; she then dried its trickle with a swift swipe of gauze. Mark watched with the trust of a child in a parent. With the impunity of a lover, he wished for her touch. With the impatience of desire, he filled the gaps of who he knew she was and imagined her the attendant child at a parturition:

> *Water boiled inside a black kettle, over the fire of a wood stove. Against a log wall, she sat in a far corner of the partly lit room. Quietly, her feet dangled above the earthen floor as her fingers gripped the raw wood of the seat. Her pale skirt was unfurled to below her knees, and a thin leather ribbon bound her black hair from her face. Her hazel eyes were frightened and averted from the subdued cries of a woman giving birth. In the middle of the room, her grandmother knelt on a woven rug and with outstretched arms, coaxed an infant from her mother's womb.*

He recalled her warning, *Don't fill gaps in knowledge with jealousy*, but felt no guilt for the imagined tableau. All he wished was to paint her history.

"There. Now don't be suing me if it becomes infected." Emilia capped the bottles of solution she had used to clean the wound.

"Is that your grandmother in the photo?" he asked.

"Which photo?"

"The old lady with the group in folkloric dress."

"The old lady?" She accented her objection to the description by applying pressure on drying the wound.

"Ouch," he said. "So much for trust and vulnerability."

"I just can't see her as 'the old lady.'" She smiled. "But yes, that's my grandmother."

"Was that taken in Georgia?"

"No. It was actually taken at the reservation in Oklahoma."

"Aren't you from Georgia?"

"What's with all the personal questions?" Emilia sat back on the heels of her feet and grabbed for the rolled up bandage.

"Just wanted to fill gaps in knowledge," he answered.

"What, you're feeling jealous?"

"Yes, of your life before I met you."

"If it would be any solace, I am now what I was then."

"I can see the influence of your religious studies in some of your comments." He leaned back onto his outstretched arms and watched her approximate the wound edges. "But tell me all about you, in the simple English of infidels."

"Infidels?" She added a snicker for the irony. "That was the catchword for missionaries to ensnare aborigines in reservations. We're originally from Oklahoma. We only moved to Georgia after my mother's death."

"I'm sorry," he said, to her mother's death, as much as to the historical lapse in his choice of words. "And who are *we*?"

"My father, grandmother, and older brother." With two fingers, she held the skin edges taut and began to wrap the bandage around his knee. "To answer your next question, my father believed my mother's spirit would await him in our ancestral lands."

"And that is in Georgia?"

"Yes, the southern Appalachians."

Emilia was on her knees, bent above his leg. The hair draped her outside shoulder. On each turn of the bandage, her hand brushed the inside of his opposite thigh. She knotted the bandage, but did not withdraw her hands, resting them lightly on his knee. He straightened to touch them and watched the crimson flames dance from the logs to sparkle in her eyes. Mark felt pleasure swell in him.

"You are beautiful," he heard himself say.

"And beauty makes you want more," she said, as if to repeat an invitation.

He followed the lure of her gaze and reached to touch her face. Like magnets on a string, she leaned to him as he to her. In their kiss, he smelled her fragrance and tasted the moisture on her lips. The warmth of her breath inside of him he wished to make his own.

They rested on the carpet and as if she were an orchid in the palm of his hand, he held her close. A cool breeze flushed his skin as the loosened sash fell from around his waist. The hairs of his flesh reached, as if for her fingers, which worked to slip off the robe. Mark felt the muscles of his naked body become firm.

Turned, so that Emilia lay flat, he straddled her and helped her lift the wool sweater above her head. He watched the suppleness of her breasts glisten with her sweat as she brushed back the strands of hair the sweater had carried to her face.

The flames flickered with their shadows, but for a moment, they remained motionless. Each fiber of her hair flared among the flowers of the carpet. Her lips glimmered with silent joy as the sheen of her flesh cascaded down the gentle curves of her body, and spiraled to her navel. He waited for her breath as he would his own, drawn from the fullness of her chest; nature's nurture was as much in the desire as its gratification. It was why thinking her beautiful made him want more.

From the slope of her nose to the dimple of her chin, he tasted the skin of her face. Gold, a bead of sweat gleamed in the cleavage of her breasts. Mark tenderly caressed them and felt their softness with his lips. Her nipples hardened on the tease of his tongue. Arched to him, her moan of delight excited him, as did the brush of her fingers in his hair.

With the patience of deprivation in the midst of temptation, he snapped open her zipper but needed her assistance to pull off her jeans. His body slipped between the smoothness of her thighs that circled his waist. Mark felt himself a man between her legs.

Their sweaty bodies undulated to a shared rhythm. He laid his face on her breast and groaned with pleasure. With his arms wrapped around her waist, Mark moved inside of her.

It was not envy or jealousy that made him want to paint her history, but the desire to comprehend what gave him so much rapture. In his mind, he searched words to give it color:

> *Emilia's sigh was a subdued cry,*
> *that of a mother in post-labor.*
> *A frightened child sat alone,*
> *in the dark of a bedroom.*
>
> *What defenses has a child,*
> *but prayer against a threat?*
> *Dark angels with painful tidings.*
> *grants one vulnerable*
> *bearing a trust.*

Like a tightened noose, a shudder of fear rushed his muscles, and Mark felt himself become flaccid. There was no explanation—simply the dismissal of his lust. In desperate motion, Mark thrust his pelvis against hers but felt trapped between her legs. Demurely, he stroked himself to no avail and slipped away from her hand, which searched to please.

But for her shallow breaths, the room was silent. In the fireplace, coals glowed hotly. Mark looked away from her and noticed her nipples were still erect. He slid off her and knelt between her legs. With the stroke of his tongue and the touch of his hand, he tasted her flesh. The rhythmic pant of her breathing was in concert to the pressure of her fingers in his hair. Emilia's thighs folded about his head, and her muscles became taut on her burst of joy.

Naked, they slept in a loose embrace. Jolted awake, Mark opened his eyes. *Love without grace*, he thought, and focused on Bullwinkle's grin. *He knows the answer to the riddle, and it's why he grins at me*. Gingerly, he removed his arm from under her head, but despite his care, Emilia awakened.

Mark stood away to the sofa to watch the cinders burned in the fireplace. He was comforted by the dark.

"I think my clothes are dry," he answered the question he only felt her ask.

"You don't have to go," she said. "Your clothes will be drier in the morning."

"I better go." He tucked his shirt into his pants. "I have a lot to get done in the morning."

"Will you be at Maidu's for breakfast?" She covered up with the bathrobe.

Mark hesitated at the front door. Without light, shame was easier to hide. He was glad only an overcast moon reflected on the snow.

"I'll try to make it." He walked on to the truck and did not look back.

Chapter 10

Hindsight was not an option, only the regret of having left Emilia motionless at her door. Can one surrender what has not been granted, he thought, and could she dispense with his affection when what he had offered was only a tease? At a turn on the road, Mark watched her disappear and hoped that he, too, would likewise banish.

It seemed he drove into a tunnel, for the forest appeared colorless. A single star sparkled in the overcast sky, but whatever its light, it was blurred by the moisture in his eyes. His heart pounded in the void inside his chest, and *I hurt her* was the pulse.

Darkness would no longer hide his shame. He felt it with Emilia's quizzical stare. The muscles of his throat tightened. His lips quivered, like worms from the tomb of the man whose soul he'd borrowed.

Water would ease the throat,
and water would drown the worms,
but he wanted to cleanse the sorrow,
stored since his father died

and he let tears flow
that no clenched fist
could wipe away.

If forget does not forgive, time allowed for neglect. In the morning, swollen eyes were all that remained of the night before.

He prepared to return to San Jose.

Shades were closed and blinds were pulled, but there was light enough to see her note on the nightstand. He folded the paper in four and stowed it in his shirt pocket.

It was late morning when he drove out; it had been difficult to get out of bed. Without clouds, the sun was bright. He wore sunglasses. The snow in Maidu's lot had melted. No need for the jacket. There were more tracks through the sludge into the park. Spring crowds were coming. The road south ascended into a thick forest. Side roads should be better marked.

She's better off without me, he thought.

◆◆◆

HWY 50 heading east was not his intended direction, but it was where the road passing the caretaker's cottage took him. With no other cause to keep him from home, he continued unfettered down the mountain to the desert.

On HWY 375 south, at the California border, a Nevada casino jutted out from a barren hill to overlook the solitude of the high desert. Filling a saltine bed in the valley was Topaz Lake, more of a mirage than a placid stretch of water. Mark stopped to indulge in the isolation, as well as satisfy his hunger.

The wooden walls in the small casino reeked with years of cigarette smoke and beer. An attendant stood at the single open game table. Except for the clang of silver coins being dropped into a slot, there were no other gamblers. He continued to the coffee shop beyond the casino.

"Good morning," said a waitress wiping down the glass counter. "Sit wherever you like, honey."

The dining area was bright. Large windows faced the lake and surrounding desert. Only one couple, in their late fifties, dined in the room. They sat across from each other at a table by the central window. Mark sat two tables from them.

The waitress from the counter carried a meal to the couple's table. "Let's see, you had the omelet, and she was steak and eggs."

"You got it," the man said. He sipped from a glass of beer and took a drag of the cigarette. He raised his arms as if to surrender, and the meal was set before him. On his thin arm, below the rolled cuff of his T-shirt, was a tattoo of a bare-chested hula dancer.

Except for the longer hair and leather vest, the woman was his mirror image. "Thanks," she said to the waitress, a cloud of smoke released with her words.

"Do you want lunch or breakfast?" the waitress asked Mark.

"Breakfast." He continued to stare at the couple.

"Honey, your face looks as long as I am wide." She laughed and handed him the breakfast menu.

She was rotund, in her sixties, with a grandmother's smile. Her facial skin was fissured by wrinkles, the result of years of cigarette smoke.

"I was just thinking of how far I still have to go."

"Coffee?"

"Yes, please—Mildred," he read her nametag.

She went off to the service station by the glass counter.

The couple ate in silence. Smoke curled from the cigarettes they kept wedged between two fingers. *What keeps them entertained?* Mark wondered.

"Where are you going?" Mildred asked on her return and poured the coffee.

"San Jose."

"No wonder the long face. You're lost."

"No, I know. Just wanted to take a roundabout."

"Honey, this isn't a roundabout. You're lost. What are you having?" She pulled out the order check from the apron's pocket.

"I'll take the scrambled eggs."

"Yup, scrambled." She chuckled and tucked the order check into the pocket, then carried the coffee pot into the kitchen.

"I think we'll make Las Vegas by sunset," Mark heard the man say.

"Shit. We stopping somewhere before then? My ass ain't going to last on the back of that bike," she said.

"Wish I had the Harley. Those Jap asses aren't as wide as what we got."

"Shit, your ass is no wider than my baby finger," she replied.

"It ain't my baby finger that makes you howl like a whore."

Mark laughed at their banter and wondered if love could be that simple.

"Here you are," Mildred announced. "Scrambled eggs for a scrambled mind."

"Hey, wait a minute," he said, although he agreed with her observation. "Give me some credit; I made it here for you."

"Like I said, scrambled mind." She laughed back to the counter.

The couple left. Mark drank three coffee refills. He paid the waitress at the counter.

"If it ain't a woman that's got you frazzled, it ain't worth the bother," Mildred added with the change.

"Thanks," he replied.

The game tables were covered and all was quiet. The dealer had left and only he remained in the casino. Mark continued on his roundabout journey.

◆◆◆

As a granite wall canyon closed in on the desert, he began a slow ascent of the Sierra Nevada. Staggered boulders, one on top of the other, formed ledges that made the palisades seem a jigsaw puzzle.

The brush of the valley gave way to Jeffrey pine that reminded him of the peninsular park. One tree attracted his attention—solitary, rooted into a crevice high on the granite wall.

Do we become what we are destined? he asked, and as if to look for the answer, stopped into a turnoff below it. Were it not for the limit of his wounded knee, the climb to the tree was easy.

Such a precarious perch, he thought as he reached into the crevice to gauge the distance the roots traveled for nutrients. Destiny had offered the seedling a slim chance for survival, yet it had matured. *What had made the difference?* He feared he lacked the answer.

Mark withdrew his hand from the crevice, staring at the dark soil wedged into the cleft of his fingernail. *We become what we are destined*, he thought, *as much as a metaphor defines a poem*. Passion, desire, and tenacity nourish each stanza.

He closed his eyes to the scent of the pine needles and listened to the river deep inside the canyon. Destiny may be what we are given, Mark concluded, but love is the reward.

◆ ◆ ◆

Central San Jose was a distant cluster of lights when he arrived at the suburb of his home. A big red pickup was parked in his neighbor's driveway with a dealer's placard that filled the space for the license plates. The cop's new toy, he thought. Nothing else appeared changed.

The mailbox was stuffed with junk mail, which he discarded into the empty garbage can at the curb. A greeting card from his mother, an envelope from his publisher, and a reminder note from his doctor were carried into the house.

A foul smell from inside greeted him at the door—the remnants of the chicken meal he had prepared two nights before his departure. He took the trash to the curb, fanned the room with open windows, and sprayed the house with a potpourri freshener.

A family of cats stared from his mother's card. With a few Spanish words, she expressed her unconditional love. The check in the publisher's envelope was payment for the previous month's article and royalties for his most recent book. It hadn't sold as well as he had hoped, but it reminded him that he was behind on his next article. He would visit Arren in the morning for an extension.

Mark could not recall why he had made a doctor's appointment, but it was timely to have the wound checked in four days.

The den was where he spent most of his time, and the clutter on his desk was a tiered accounting of what he had accomplished. Moving a few levels to the side allowed him to set the laptop on a level surface.

On the opposite wall hung a single framed photograph, at which he stared, as if for the first time. He did not recall the occasion for which he had posed with his mother, brother, and sister, but it had been a few years since he had visited.

Photographs family and friends had sent he kept in a shoe-box. It was on the floor, in a corner of the room. With the box on his lap, he sifted through the contents and decided to arrange a journal of his life. He glanced at the empty walls and realized there was plenty of space to display it.

◆◆◆

Unlike the technology firms that blossomed in the suburbs of San Jose, American Publishing resided in a downtown, two-story brick building, as it had since founded in 1918. To prevent further demolition of the area, the city council had designated the building a historical landmark. With its spirit of a bygone era intact, Mark enjoyed his visits as time-warped adventures.

The firm had achieved moderate success in the publication of educational books and magazines on esoteric subjects. Such was Western Ways.

"Mark, how are you?" Betty shouted from across the editor's reception area. She watered the window plants and added, "I called you a number of times and left messages. I was worried about you."

"Thanks for the worry. I went up to the lake for a few days." Betty, about thirty, was the editor's secretary. He often informed her of his whereabouts. "How are you? You look nice in red."

"Thanks." She wore a red dot-print shirtdress that flattered her figure. "Arren has been wanting to talk to you."

"Oh, oh. What haven't I done?"

"I don't know what it was about, but I don't think it was critical. I can tell by his voice when it is." Betty was behind her desk and fingered a scheduler, then looked up and added, "You seem different. Is everything okay?"

"I suppose I haven't been looking my best. A woman at a coffee shop said I was frazzled." He sat on the sofa.

"Let me know if there's anything I can do. I'll get Arren." She reached for the phone, but stopped when Arren walked in from the front.

"Mark, where have you been? Have you been talking to Betty?" Arren did not stop until at the door to his office. "Isn't she wonderful? Come on in. I've been wanting to chat with you."

Mark walked toward the door but winked to Betty, who shrugged in response. Arren rested his hand on Mark's shoulder and closed the door behind them.

They sat across the desk from each other, student to instructor. Twenty-two years prior, Mark had taken Arren's literature course at UCLA, and had not transcended that relationship. Arren intimidated him.

"What do you think of Betty?" Arren asked. He leaned forward, as if to disclose a secret, and added, "How would you like to go on a date with her?" He lifted a single bushy eyebrow and fell back to his chair. The power was his to grant the wish.

Mark looked for a hyphen or exclamation point to extend the pause before he answered. "What are you saying?"

Arren folded his hands on the edge of the desk and sat deeper in the chair. He would have to negotiate. "You know my wife, Susan, the matchmaker. She found out Betty was not dating, so they went out for lunch a few days ago. You know—preliminary compatibility review. Anyway, to cut the fat, it turns out Betty wants you."

The Ansel Adams photograph of the Half Dome behind Arren was hypnotic. It was awhile before Mark moved his stare from it.

"I'm old enough to be her father," he said in a quiet tone.

"Just an older brother," he replied. "She's twenty-eight."

"She is a sweet woman."

"And quite a good looker." The gleam in Arren's eyes assured no mistaking of the fact.

"What would Susan say if she knew about your lust?"

"After forty-one years and three sons, she knows I'm a window-shopper." Arren paused, and in a more sober tone said, "But look at you, Mark. You're middle age. What is it now, forty-two?-You're successful, and you are a good man. But you don't enjoy life. You wear blinders all the time."

It was not the first time Arren had plotted to fix Mark up on a date. It was the first time, however, that his tone carried a sense of urgency. "You're right," Mark replied.

"I don't mean to get down on you, but cut yourself some slack." He stood up from the chair and walked to Mark, who had stood as well. "Heck, what's the use of being Jewish if I can't be a yenta?"

"Thanks for the concern." They shook hands.

"Did you bring in the article for next month's issue?" Arren asked at the door, his tone that of a professor at the podium.

"Not yet, but soon." Arren closed the door behind him.

***

"Did you get it all?" Mark asked. Betty was seated on her chair behind the desk, bent forward. She appeared to pick at something on the floor.

"I spilled my money." The purse rested upright on her lap. "I was just counting it out to go get some yogurt for lunch. The phone rang, and I dropped the purse. I think I got it all." She took a second look around the floor below the desk.

"Don't worry about it. Let me take you to lunch."

"Are you sure?" she asked. "You don't have to. I'm sure I have enough." She opened the palm of her hand and revealed four quarters.

◆ ◆ ◆

It was sunny and warm on the walk to the restaurant, one block from the publishing firm. Betty carried a sweater straddled on her forearm, and Mark thought of the mound of snow he left on his deck.

"How was the weather at the lake?" she asked.

"A storm dumped a lot of snow just before I arrived, but it was like this most of the time."

"It must be beautiful," she said, and stepped through the door he held open.

"Can we sit outside?" Mark asked the hostess who greeted them. "Do you mind?" he asked Betty.

"Not at all." They followed the hostess to an outside table. She grabbed her hair, which drifted with a gentle breeze, and secured it with a clip. "It's beautiful today."

"Is that a butterfly?" he asked, indicating her hair clip.

"Yes," she answered, and then added, "You should've let us know you were going to the lake. I thought you'd gotten lost in some ghost town."

"Or kidnapped by a band of Indians?" he asked, but then interjected, "Just kidding. Sorry I didn't call, but I went on the spur of the moment."

"You know how Arren worries about you. Let him know, next time. Did he tell you what he wanted?"

Mark hesitated with the reply. "Oh, he was just wondering about my next article."

The conversation that followed was as dry as the French dip sandwiches they ate. He was relieved when Betty noticed it was time to return.

"I hope I didn't bore you," he said at the door to the brick building. "I was just thinking of the article. I'm still pretty far behind."

"I understand, but I enjoyed it. Maybe we can have lunch again, when you're finished with the article."

"That would be nice," he said to his reflection on the glass door. He was glad for the deadline, an excuse to sequester himself for a few days inside his home.

Chapter 11

*I*nspiration cannot be granted by a vacuum, but at times, a writer's search of it may resemble a pagan ritual. It was Mark's custom to set himself before the reference library, shelved in a full wall bookcase of his living room, and shuffle through the pages that recounted the story of man.

None of the reference books reported on the Cherokee, but he leafed through a historical account of the Sierra Nevada tribes. With the book opened to the section of interest, he read, as if for a mystical brew, of the Maidu tribe.

These were an aboriginal people of northeastern California, whose lives reminded him of the pine rooted on the granite perch. Their survival was in the balance of passion, desire, and outright tenacity. Ingredients he lacked. What was it like, he wondered, to be so vulnerable?

He wondered how their extinction happened. The subject was not dealt with in any article he had read, nor was their interaction with European culture. Mark rested in his recliner and considered. Miners from the United States, Europe, Mexico, Canada, and even China encroached upon the Maidu's ancestral lands. With the resources to dominate their environment, the miners eventually displaced the Maidu.

Mark sat at his laptop. The clutter on his desk remained otherwise untouched. As if reaching across the gap of time, he stretched his hands to type on the keyboard. It was his first tale of an aboriginal people in the Old West.

◆◆◆

Against a log wall, Sadie sat on a chair. The skirt of her dress was unfurled to below the knees. Her bare feet dangled over the earthen floor, and her fingers gripped the raw wood of the seat. Strands of her black hair were bound back from the face with a thin leather ribbon. She remained quiet, her eyes turned away from the sight and subdued sounds of a woman giving birth.

The room was dim, partly lit by the fire in the corner stove. In a lead kettle, water boiled. On a tulle mat in the middle of the floor, Sadie's grandmother knelt between the woman's legs and coaxed, with outstretched hands, the infant from the mother's womb.

A silence was followed by the shrill cry of the new-born child. Sadie turned to see her grandmother place the infant on the mother's naked abdomen. "It's a boy," she joyously proclaimed.

At her mother's hearty laugh, Sadie relaxed her grip of the seat and looked curiously at her brother. His black hair glistened with moisture. Patches of red coalesced with a thin mush that coated his skin.

The grandmother tied the fleshy cord that extended from her brother's belly and hid between her mother's legs. A gush of blood splattered when she cut the cord.

Her brother's loud cry abated as he suckled on her mother's breasts, wrapped in a rabbit skin blanket.

"Pour some water into that basin," the grandmother directed Sadie.

Quick to jump out of her chair, Sadie did as she was told. With both arms, she lifted the kettle off the stove and set it on the floor. She leaned over it with caution and poured the boiling water into the basin.

"Use the hide to wipe your brother clean," the grandmother added. She tugged at the cord, still hidden between the mother's legs. Sadie noted the concern in her grandmother's stare.

At the end of a stick, the rabbit's hide was dipped into the water. When the hide cooled, Sadie wiped off the thick film that coated her brother's skin. The olive color of her flesh contrasted with the light pink of her brother's.

"Push," her grandmother commanded her mother.

Her mother grunted in response. Sadie noticed her look of pain. The infant continued to suckle at the breast.

"Sadie, get the child to the bed," the grandmother shouted.

Blood had pooled at her grandmother's knees, and more continue to stream from between her mother's legs. It had the odor Sadie remembered from when her father had skinned a brown bear. She recalled the fright she had felt then. Sadie rushed to her brother and carried him to the bed.

The grandmother let the cord drop and washed her arms with the rabbit's hide. She buried her hand in the mother's womb. With her free hand, she tugged on the cord. The mother's muted cry blended with the grandmother's pleas to push. The child wailed from the bed.

Sadie did not recognize the silence that followed a burgundy mass pulled from the womb. The stream of blood ceased to flow. Beads of sweat on her mother's face shimmered in the fire's glow. She sat still on the edge of the bed, and waited for her grandmother's words.

"Evelyn?" the grandmother asked softly.

The stillness that followed shook Sadie's body. Her mother was pale, as she had never been before. The tulle mat at her grandmother's knees was lost in a solid redness that frightened her. The smell of blood nauseated her.

"Bring me your brother." Her mother's words echoed loudly in Sadie's ears.

The grandmother helped Evelyn sit, and Sadie handed her the infant to feed.

"Sadie, come help me." They folded the placenta in the mat. With the moistened hide, they washed her mother's body, wrapped her with a blanket, and then walked her to the bed. The child slept on his mother's breast.

Decorated with black and yellow bird feathers, the basket her grandmother had woven over the last month of the pregnancy was used to store the rolled mat. It would later be buried. Sadie slept at her mother's feet.

◆◆◆

Steam billowed from the covered kettle on the stove. The grandmother stoked the flames. Sadie awakened to cold on her face. It was, after all, late winter.

"Would you like tea?" asked her grandmother.

"Has mother taken any?" She took in a whiff of the manzanita scent.

"No, she is tired from the birth of your brother. She'll take some soon."

Her mother lay still in bed, but Sadie watched the slow rise of the blanket over her chest. Visible above the hem was a tuft of her brother's black hair. She listened to his whimper as he was fed.

Sadie scooted out of bed and spread her blanket over her mother's legs, then covered her own seven-year-old frame with the deerskin coat her father had made. The door was just her height.

The winter had not been harsh, but the ground was still spotted with a thin layer of snow. She preferred to walk barefoot, to feel the trail she could not see in the dim light of morning.

This was a new world for her family, but on her walk, she imagined it like when her father had been with them. Then, they had lived at the edge of the forest. Her mother tilled the flat land about their home. Her father fished and hunted in the woods.

At the end of spring, her father staggered out of the forest and fell into the vegetables her mother tended. Blood stained the skin of his chest. Four light-skinned men followed from the trees. Her mother screamed for her to hide in the forest.

Hidden in her father's sweathouse, Sadie waited.

When the sun rested below the crown of trees, her mother appeared with her face scratched and the dress torn from her breast.

Her grandmother soon followed. Behind her was the travois used to carry wood from the forest. On it was her father, his motionless chest red with blood. In the river that ran past the sweathouse, the three women washed his body. Her grandmother chanted a song Sadie had heard at the death of other villagers. She fought back the tears that filled her vision.

◆◆◆

The rise on the trail from the hut was Sadie's preferred spot to watch the sunrise. When daylight outlined the crest of the mountains to the east, the last star to the west was her father's. At night, his shined among her ancestors'.

Squatting behind a gooseberry shrub, Sadie listened to her urine fall on the hard ground and flow into the canyon below. That morning, Sadie waited until her father's star rested for the day.

On her return, Sadie whispered the song her grandmother had chanted at the burial of her father; it had called on the white man's spirit to guide his soul. She looked at the steeple of the Presbyterian Church that loomed high above their hut. Before her father's death, the family had taken up Christian ways; it was how they had obtained their names. After his death, when their food stores had been exhausted and the winter cold prevented replenishment, the minister and his family had given them shelter.

Sadie thought to get more fuel for the stove. Her mother and brother needed to be warm. Her father taught her to take for fuel only the branches that littered the forest. The townspeople simply cut down the trees. From the stack the minister had placed against the hut, she carried away an armful, and noted the forest on the opposite side of the canyon.

She stopped at the door and listened to the voices of

men in the distance. Her mother called them white-skins, but Sadie had noticed some with flesh the shade of hers, others as dark as cedar trees. Every day, a horse-drawn carriage took them to the mines deep inside the canyon.

Initially, she was frightened by so much that was new. There were those like her, with a slant to the eyes, but whom she didn't understand. Some had hair as yellow as the sun; others had eyes of sky blue. At the church school, she learned the language of the townspeople, and everyone became a friend. Writing, though, fascinated her most; she could carry a message and not have to speak a word.

◆◆◆

Her mother was still asleep when Sadie returned. It seemed she had not moved at all. Sadie dropped the lumber by the stove and went to the foot of the bed.

"Let her rest," the grandmother said. On her lap rested a basket, into which she wove colorful bird feathers. "Go get ready. Let Reverend Calhoun know your mother gave birth to a boy and won't be in today." The grandmother picked the nativity mat from the floor and forced it into the basket.

◆◆◆

The grandmother held the basket to her chest, carried it outside, and followed the trail Sadie had taken. She exulted that her prayers for a son were answered.

Not long after the arrival of the white man to their ancestral lands, births of village children slowed. Many of the villagers blamed the cloudy river waters that flowed from the white man's mines. On Reverend Calhoun's first visit to their village, when she was barren after four springtime's in marriage, he told a Christian tale of a virgin mother and a patient father. Not long after his tale, she bore a son and named him Joseph, the patient one. She took the name Margaret.

Eventually, the Christian villagers followed the reverend into town to work the mines. The non-believers left to where the water ran clear. After the death of her beloved husband, Margaret remained in the land of her ancestors to venerate his spirit. Joseph married Evelyn, and Sadie was their only child.

◆◆◆

Margaret stopped at a rise in the trail and viewed, from across the canyon, the forest in which her ancestors dwelled. She bent to the ground on which she stood, and with a sharpened cedar wood, dug a small burial site in the hard earth.

Life continued into death, she thought, but to burying her son had challenged her beliefs. Over his body, she had cried with the howl of a wolf, to prepare his spirit's journey. Christian prayers she had said, so that he would no longer suffer, but her own life had been emptied at her son's death.

After Joseph's death, Evelyn missed her monthly bleed and thought to destroy the white man's seed inside her. Margaret prayed her son's revenge would be the birth of a son and dissuaded Evelyn from suicide.

Margaret placed the basket she carried into the hole she dug. In it was the afterbirth, her son's manifested revenge. Over the gravel mound that covered the grave, she rolled the largest granite boulder she could push and prayed, "Brother stone, guard the seed of my people."

Sadie sat at the edge of the bed and held a cup of tea to her mother's lip. She smiled when her mother took a sip.

"You must go and clean for Mrs. Calhoun," Margaret said from the door. "I'll help your mother drink the tea."

Sadie went to the Calhoun home but wanted to write the announcement of her brother's birth. She could carry it throughout the day and thereby keep her mother company. The decree, though, slipped from her lips as soon as Mrs. Calhoun answered the knock on the door.

She rushed through her duties, but it only made for more idle time before school started. Throughout the day, she anticipated the bell's toll at the end of class; Mrs. Calhoun's lessons became difficult to follow.

"Sadie," shouted Mrs. Calhoun from the podium after the bell rang. Sadie stopped in mid-stride and waited for a scolding. "Let me come with you. I want to visit your mother."

◆◆◆

With a pull of the hand, Sadie led Mrs. Calhoun through the door of the hut. Her grandmother sat at the edge of the bed and cradled the infant in one arm. Margaret wiped the mother's forehead, which was drenched with pellets of sweat.

"Oh, my," Mrs. Calhoun said, and freed her hand from Sadie's tightened grip. At the head of the bed, she touched the mother's cheeks. "Oh, poor darling. She's with a bad fever. I must get the doctor."

The breeze that followed her out smelled of roses. Things will be better, Sadie thought, since roses grow only in spring. She sat on the chair and gripped the seat, waiting for Mrs. Calhoun's return.

The young doctor took charge after he followed the Calhouns into the hut. The grandmother stepped back from the bed, and he took seat.

"She's burning up," he said with his hand on the mother's forehead. He lifted her blanket above the waist and parted her legs.

"She's not bleeding," he said, more to himself. "I don't think it's a retained placenta."

The doctor felt the abdomen and noted her grimace, but the mother cried out in pain when he inserted his long white fingers into her womb.

"It's post-partum sepsis," he announced.

"What can we do?" the Calhouns asked.

"Pray. There's not much I can offer," he answered, then lifted from the floor a black purse he had carried in. "Her body will have to fight the infection. Give her this for the fever and this for pain." He handed the grandmother two labeled vials of white powder.

"She doesn't understand English," Mrs. Calhoun said when the grandmother hesitated. "I'll let Sadie instruct her on the directions."

"Good. Call me when the fever breaks." The doctor clipped the purse shut and walked out of the hut.

Sadie understood every word they had spoken, but not what they meant. She listened to Mr. Calhoun lead a short prayer she had heard before, on sad occasions.

"Amen," Sadie answered, willing her mother better.

"Sadie, tell your grandmother we must take the child with us. Your mother won't be able to feed him," Mrs. Calhoun said and reached for her brother, in Margaret's embrace. "Tom Lopes will lend us his nursing goat."

She may not have understood anything that had been said, but Margaret had watched the tone of their voices and the gloom in their faces. With complete trust in the spirits of her ancestors and the will of the Calhouns, she surrendered the last male of her people.

Margaret closed her eyes against the tears and prayed, "Brother stone, guard the seed of my people."

◆◆◆

Under the single cedar tree where she stood, the ground was flat, but her shoes seemed stiff. Sadie wished she had not worn them. She wanted to feel the pebbles beneath her feet. A warm sun shadowed her face, but a cold breeze drifted from the forest across the canyon. That morning, she had helped wash her mother's skin and draped her with a dress. It was fashioned from deerskin her father had hunted in spring. A beaded necklace, in the colors of butterflies, adorned her mother.

Wrapped in a white cotton blanket, her brother suckled noisily from a bottle. Her grandmother watched him, cradled in her arms; the sunlight gleamed in his eyes. Mrs. Calhoun stood behind them.

The reverend read from the scriptures—words to guide her mother's soul. Two dark-skinned men lowered the pine box in which her mother rested deep into the ground. Gravel was shoveled over it, to seal her into the earth for eternity.

◆◆◆

Sadie wanted to howl like a wolf, to call her mother's spirit into the forest. She wanted to hear her grand-mother's wail, as when they buried her father. She knew, though, that this was a different world, into which she would lead her brother. With the palm of her hand, she wiped away her tears.

◆◆◆

Mark sat back from the laptop, satisfied. On Monday, he would take it to Arren.

Chapter 12

He pulled away from the keyboard, glad to be finished. Strips of sunlight warmed his chest as he rested in the chair. Mark was satisfied Sadie would succeed in her journey; she, after all, was endowed with trust.

Writing granted its own rewards, but three days of isolated concentration was difficult. "Cut yourself some slack," he heard Arren say as he stared at the closed blinds.

"Hi, Kathy," Mark said into the phone. He sat at his desk. "Is Spencer Tate in?"

"Hi. Who's this?" Kathy asked.

"This is Mark Balcon."

"Oh, sure," she replied, somewhat hesitant. "Haven't seen you in a while. He's upstairs. Let me get him."

After a few minutes, Spencer came on the line, "Hey, bud. What's up?"

"Hi, Spencer. How are the war games?"

"Okay, I guess. I was actually on the 'net, trying to dominate the world."

"Just called to see if you were into a commando mission for tonight," Mark asked.

"Kathy and the kids are back. She won't let me go," Spencer answered. "By the way, how did it go with that babe?"

"What babe?" The term irritated him as much as being referred to as "bud" did.

"At the Seoul Lounge. I didn't think you were going to go with her," Spencer added.

It seemed so long ago, the tryst at the Seoul Lounge, but not the officer's warning he not bring pathogens to the neighborhood. Mark felt how sad Spencer judged his life to be. "Why did you leave?" Mark asked with indignation.

"Man, I wasn't going to stay while you got your jollies," Spencer replied. "I'm a married man—too much temptation for me to wait."

"How sad" was a simple phrase, but a fitting portrayal of unsated desire, as much as its disdain. After a period of numb conversation, Mark ended with "Call me."

Children's laughter personified for him the sounds of Sunday, and it was what distracted him to the window. Opening the blinds, glaring sunlight splashed into the den and briefly blinded him. His focus was the image of a wind chime locked in ice.

Two small girls about the age of five were at play in his neighbor's front lawn. One he recognized as from across the street; the red-haired one he assumed was the cop's daughter. Fredrickson was what his partner had called him.

"Don't go out on the street," Fredrickson said to the girls who had run to the curb. His voice was gentler than Mark recalled. He stood up from behind the new pickup and walked around to Mark's full view. With the slow spray from the water hose in hand, he squatted to scrub the rear wheel. The weather must be warm, Mark thought, since the cop wore only shorts and a T-shirt.

"Honey, here's your beer." An attractive woman walked out of the open garage carrying two beer cans. She wore jeans and a loose T-shirt.

Fredrickson stood and reached for his can and took a sip. A chance spray of water soaked her chest. "Oh, Christ," she said. Drenched, her breasts shown firm, round, and full. She either was lactating or had perfect implants.

"Oh, yeah," he responded, and stared at her breasts. "I know what I'd rather have."

With a seductive smile, she walked to him, her back arched to accentuate the objects of his attention. She brushed her breasts against his body and enticed him to reach for an embrace. With a quick pull of his shorts at the waist, she dumped her beer into his crotch. "Chill it, Eric. I got a baby to feed," she said with a laugh.

In the shadow of his window, Mark watched the couple playfully pull and grab at each other. Their Sunday was what he had hoped for himself when growing up. Now in middle age, he missed what he never had. He turned away from the window, and with a chuckle, longed to redeem his past.

Voices of the children in play resounded through his home. On the recliner in his living room, Mark awaited inspiration, as one would the toll of a bell. He picked up the phone and dialed.

"Is Betty in?"

"Hi, Mark," she answered, "Who else would it be?"

"I don't know. I was just surprised to find you at home. It's so beautiful outside; I would have expected you be out."

"It sure has been a beautiful day, but I had a few chores to take care of," she said. "I'm glad you called, but are you procrastinating, or taking a break?"

"Matter of fact, neither. I finished the story for my column in record time so I could call you."

"I should be flattered, but somehow I don't believe I was the mainspring," she replied.

"You doubt me?"

"Yes, I do," Betty replied in a more serious tone, "but only because you seem changed recently."

"Well, let me prove I am changed." He wondered if she referred to the frazzled state that the coffee shop waitress had observed. "I intend to never again ignore a beautiful woman. Let me take you out for dinner."

"Arren told me what he talked to you about," she simpered, "but I won't pass up an opportunity, no matter how much arm-twisting it takes to get it."

Arren described their age difference no greater than an older brother's, but with a four-day beard, he feared Betty would think "paternal" was a more fitting description. A shave, Rugby shirt, and pants achieved the transformation he hoped. The image of a cocky brother returned his glance in the vestibule mirror.

As if to pace his drive, he tapped on the steering wheel in time to the bebop jazz on the radio. He arrived as Betty stepped out of her car, just before sunset.

"I see your mother chose your wardrobe," she greeted him.

"Why?" he replied, disconcerted.

"You have that preppy look mothers like their sons to wear. I was kind of expecting the rough look of a cloistered writer."

"Just wanted to develop a smarter image." He looked her up and down. "Everyone thinks I'm a fool to have snubbed a beautiful woman like you." He took a step back. "You look fantastic."

Her auburn hair was twisted into loose temple braids joined in the back with a butterfly pin. A red embroidered silk blouse graced her trim figure, and a long, dusty lilac skirt enhanced her lean legs. Mark fixed his gaze on the provocative side slit of her dress and the gleam of her flesh.

"You said I looked good in red," she said, walking into the restaurant. "So here you have it," she added and pirouetted.

Surprised by the abrupt turn, Mark reached, as if to catch her. With his hands on her waist, he said, "Are we in the mood for dancing?"

"A table for two," Mark requested of the hostess who greeted them. They were led into the non-smoking section, but it didn't seem to matter, as none of the few diners seated in the restaurant smoked.

A large Boston fern screened their view of the parking lot. A floodlight on the plant's underside directed their focus to its finger-like projections.

"That's one of my favorite plants," Mark said.

"Sexually self-sufficient," she added.

"Oh, really?" Mark felt the warmth of a blush on his forehead and a snippet from his subconscious. *Love without grace.* "I didn't mean for that reason."

"I'm sorry," she laughed. "It just popped into my mind when I noticed the spores."

He picked up the menu and glanced beyond the selections. "I am envious it can be so easily satisfied."

Betty was likewise silent as she reviewed the menu, until a college-age waitress came for their order. "I'll take the salmon," she requested.

"That sounds good," Mark said. "How is it prepared?"

"It's marinated in garlic and wine, and then broiled, wrapped in foil," the waitress replied.

"That sounds tasty." He glanced at Betty and lifted his eyebrows, relieved by the change in subject. "I'll take it."

"That's twice we've ordered the same meal," she commented. In a more lively tone, with arms folded at the edge of the table, she had a new thought, "What is your article about?"

"Vulnerability and trust," he answered.

Taken aback, she asked, "Like Roy Rogers and Trigger? Aren't your articles always about miners and cowboys?"

"Actually, now that I think about it, vulnerability is the primary fault of all my characters, and trust, or the lack thereof, the handle by which they deal with the plot."

"When did this insight come to you?" Betty sat back on her chair, and as if to assuage a brewing suspicion, added, "In Lake Tahoe?"

"I suppose so." With his focus on the table, Mark fiddled with the silverware and tried to mirror Bullwinkle's grin. "What is 'Love without grace'?" he asked, without looking up.

"Love without grace," she repeated slowly, as if to search for meaning between the letters. She took a sip of water and concluded, "I don't think I know. Does it have to do with being vulnerable and trusting?"

"It could well be," he answered. "As far as I know, it's a riddle, or maybe poetic prose to challenge one's mettle."

"I suppose it depends on the poet," she said.

Mark appreciated the distraction of the salads' arrivals and the waitress' query, "Anything else?"

"Some white wine would be nice," he suggested.

"A Riesling would go well with the salmon," Betty added.

To break the silence while they ate the salad, Mark took the glass of wine the waitress had returned with and lifted it for a toast. "A poet's riddle is this man's reproach."

"At least it's not a rebuke," Betty countered, and took a drink of the wine.

"Sounds like an admonition," he said.

"Maybe." She hesitated to take a drink and held the glass against her lips, but then added, "You've been different since returning from Lake Tahoe."

"How so?" he asked defensively, and reached for the fork resting on the empty salad dish.

"I don't know," she answered timidly. "You just seem—delightfully vulnerable."

"What?" he responded with a chuckle, "You mean like a preppy kid wearing the clothes his mother laid out for him?"

"Maybe more like the preppy kid waiting for his mother's approval." It was Betty's turn to blush.

Mark wanted to count the sighs that shook his body, and ward away the feeling of when blackness had replaced Emilia in his rear view mirror. But he had nothing to grip, except the salmon sautéed in garlic butter.

He recalled watching salmon swim upstream, along a channel built to the side of a dam in Seattle. Their instinct drove their passion against the torrent. He felt, though, he needed more than that—a handle to stay the tide.

◆ ◆ ◆

"I had a good time, thank you," Betty said as they stood by her car. Mark held the door open as she sat into the driver's seat. Pulling at the door handle, she wistfully looked at Mark. "You need to go back to the poet and ask what *love without grace* means."

Chapter 13

*S*teel bars guarded the front windows of the small medical building, and similar shields highlighted other facades in the neighborhood. The demise of downtown had been rapid, as the changes hadn't been present on his last visit. The process of urban decay, Mark thought, was similar to that which had resulted in mining ghost towns; he felt the same forlornness.

Passing graffiti-painted boards that sealed the emptiness of the adjoining structures, he tentatively walked into the medical building. An electric chime announced his entry.

It had been over five years since he had last seen Dr. Chen, and he could not remember what had prompted that morning's appointment, scheduled two weeks before. But it was opportune, for the wound on his knee had seemed to heal slowly. Better have a doctor check it, he had decided.

American Colonial cherry wood furniture cluttered the waiting area, every chair set on the same spot as his last visit. Only the Chinese porcelain lamp at the side of a reading chair and a Persian rug in the center of the room were new. Probably travel mementos.

Dr. Chen's California family roots were as deep as the gold mines' need for labor. Mark supposed the Oriental decor celebrated some ancestral bond. As soon as the thought came to mind, he tried to recant the supposition as a harbinger of prejudice. Considering Sadie's tale, also written on a presumption, he dispelled the assumption of arrogance; it had been written from his heart. He intended to submit it to Arren later that day.

The glazed glass of a small service window slid open on the wall opposite the entrance. Mark was startled.

"Are you Mark Balcon?" asked a young woman.

"Yes," he replied.

"Since you haven't been here for a few years, we'll need you to update your file," her voice commanded. An arm displaced her face and stretched through the window with a clipboard. Before the arm was withdrawn, Mark grasped the board, fearing he had no other option.

He sat on the leather of the reading chair. Dim light from the adjacent porcelain lamp sprayed upon the sheet he held at arm's length for a clearer view. He examined his answers. The only symptoms he conjured were the slow-healing wound in his knee and the occasional chill.

Behind cardboard boxes, he had sought shelter from a chill that then spurred him to travel to Lake Tahoe; a wound on his knee had stirred his last episode, when he ran into the lake to stop the bleeding. Do we make our destiny, he recalled Emilia asking, or do we become what we are destined?

Coincidence, he concluded, was not a medical condition, and he briskly erased his answer on the sheet.

"Excuse me." He rapped the pencil on the glass and watched a profile of a woman swell behind the glaze. The window slid open. "I finished."

"Thank you." The arm projected towards him and, as swiftly, withdrew the clipboard. The young face reappeared. "Please have a seat. Mrs. Wright will be with you shortly."

In a somber corner of the room, he sat back in the reading chair. From the shadows, Mark contrived gothic images, including Edgar Allan Poe. Deep in a gloomy recital of *The Raven*, Mark was bolted to his feet by a bellow from behind him.

"Good morning, I'm Mrs. Wright." A corpulent woman with a contralto voice greeted him at the rear door, which she held open with her broad buttocks. White teeth filled her smile. "I am your nurse. Follow me."

The antiseptic white of her uniform contrasted sharply with the ebony of her skin. A brilliant gold cross hung from her neck, suspended in the deep cleavage of her voluminous breasts. Framed by sterile white walls, she led him down a short corridor to a balance scale.

"Take your shoes off," she directed, then added, "Stand against the bar."

Mrs. Wright balanced the weights and extended the bar to the crown of his head. She called out, "One hundred and eighty pounds, six feet," as if at auction.

Yo, I'll take the barter, he thought to say, but remained motionless. He drew in his girth for her to wrap a tape around his waist.

"Thirty-two inches," she continued, but added with a smile, "That's with an inch sucked in."

Mark followed barefoot, shoes at hand, into a small side room. A leather exam bed rested against a windowless back wall. An aluminum washbasin projected from the wall adjacent the door.

"Undress fully, except for the underwear, and put this on." She handed him a paper gown and closed the door on her exit.

He let his clothes drop to the floor and clipped the gown onto his body. Mark bent to pick his clothes up. A chill seeped through the posterior gap of the frock's paper flaps.

"Honey, that sure is a fine view, but you'll have to show me better to excite me," Mrs. Wright said from the opened door. "Clip the gown to cover your behind, and then sit on the table for your vitals."

She took his blood pressure and inserted a thermometer into his mouth. "You're awful quiet. Scared of doctors?"

"It's hard to talk from inside a paper bag—and now you have a rod in my mouth," he mumbled in response, the thermometer under his tongue.

"Son, be glad it ain't up your butt," she chortled, amused. "Now, lay back and let me take an EKG."

The examining table was as hard and frigid as a butcher's slab. He felt sympathy for beef after all the prodding and number calling he had suffered.

She pulled back his gown and adjusted the electrocardiogram cables. "Honey, I be blessed! You ain't got hairs on your chest." She adhered aluminum strips to his chest.

"What are those?" He bent forward at the neck for a view. The strips pulled at the few hairs he wanted.

"Those, my boy, are wanna-be's. Now stay still so I can record the rhythm of your heart. You Spanish boys got rhythm, don't you?" Her breasts jiggled with her laughter.

"Mrs. Wright," he said without moving, afraid of verbal retribution. "I think you are trying to make fun of me."

"There, got it. You can move now." She stared at the squiggles on the recording paper. "It looks like your ticker is still prime meat."

She removed the cables from his chest. The strips pulled some hairs. "Oops," she said, "now you've got even less. Don't get me wrong, baby. I'm just an old dog that likes a good tease. Now stick your arm out."

"What's that for?" he asked of the syringe she handled.

"It's supper time," she said, and tightened a tourniquet around his upper arm. With a gloved finger, she dabbed at the blue cord that filled under the skin at his elbow. There was no hesitation when she pricked it with a needle; blood rushed into the syringe. "Kind of thin, ain't it?"

"All of this, just to have my wound checked?" He faced away from the gush of blood.

"My paper says you're here for a mid-life physical," she pointed to a clipboard on a writing table against the wall. "That's a complete work-up. You ain't going to go chicken, are you?"

Mid-life carried with it more drama than the *middle age* he had applied to himself. Mid-life was a crisis, whereas middle age was an epoch. There is absoluteness to a *life half-lived,* that there wasn't to a *period in transition*. Mid-life, he concluded, was terminal, with no recourse but submission to the fate of aging.

Mark had not considered himself in a state of inevitability. Age was retrievable. It was why he worked out—to improve his physique—and applied Minoxidil. Viagra was under consideration, and he thought to discuss it with his doctor.

124

"Dr. Revels will be in shortly," Mrs. Wright said from the door, but he continued to stare at the mirror across the room.

"Who is Dr. Revels?" he asked as the door shut behind her.

He felt the room compress around the mirror above the washbasin. He wished to compare a photo of himself to his reflection, at ten years younger. *Age was an incessant artist,* he thought, *each wrinkle an indelible stroke of its brush.*

His skin felt rough, but he thought it due more to sun exposure, and the wisp of white hair at his temples added a polish to his features. We make our destiny, he concluded, and persevered at middle age.

"Hello, I am Dr. Danielle Revels," an attractive woman said, opening the door. Mark stood still, in front of the mirror, his index finger fixed at the wrinkles in the corner of his eye. "Seems Kathleen has been at it again. Please call me Danielle."

"Hello, Dr. Danielle." He turned back to the exam table. "Was just brushing something from my eye."

"By chance, was it age?" she asked from the writing table, where Mrs. Wright had left the clipboard and EKG tracing.

The doctor's white coat was open at the front. A fuchsia tunic dress was noticeable between the flaps. She was thin, but under her smock, it was difficult to judge her shape. Long brunette hair was draped over her left shoulder in a ponytail. Mark thought she seemed too young to be a doctor.

"Where is Dr. Chen?" he stammered.

"I bought into his practice two years ago, and he recently retired." Danielle reviewed the data on the clipboard. "I hope you don't mind. I am fully boarded in internal medicine."

"No, no. It's fine. I've just never had a woman doctor."

"Well, good. Then please have a seat on the table." Without glancing away from the questionnaire, she continued the review. "So you are a writer?"

"Yes." He thought of Viagra and decided it was not a topic for discussion.

"What do you write?"

"Articles for a specialty magazine, also short stories."

"You've never been married." She looked up from the clipboard to him. "Are you insecure? Or are you gay?"

"I hope you can offer me more options," he retorted. "Not much tact in your questions. Would you accept that it is more convenient?"

Convenience seemed to govern the course of his life. It was no wonder that destiny would play such a factor in interpreting life's events. But he had not previously considered the state of his loneliness within this spectrum, until he realized the comfort it offered him.

"I am sorry, but sometimes tact mystifies the issue, and a person's sexuality is of medical significance." She stood up and prepared to examine him. "Your only medical concern today is the wound on your knee?"

"Yes. Actually, I had forgotten I made this appointment." He cleared his throat to abrogate the 'mid-life' modifier.

He sat at the edge of the exam table and parted his legs to make room for her approach. The gentle probe of her fingers in his scalp soothed him.

"That is what our records show; it's time you undergo a mid-life evaluation, physical and emotional."

Relaxed by her fingers rubbing his neck, he wondered what they were in search of, but did not heed her verbal note. "A small peri-auricular node on the right."

She peered into his ears and nose with a hand-held light, which she then turned on his throat. Was every orifice to be explored? he fretted.

Through a lit pinhole, she approached his face and flashed his eyes. A wanton curl slipped from her forehead and brushed the tip of his nose. He tried to slow the pulse pounding inside his chest, but knew it could not be concealed from the stethoscope she placed over his breast.

He took a deep breath, as directed, and with it came the fragrance of her perfume. Distracted by the tender tap of her fingers on his abdomen, he turned away.

"I'm sorry," he said to the inadvertent slap of her hand. "I'm very ticklish."

"Please stand on the step and pull your underwear down," she directed, uninterrupted by the apology.

To play for time against his arousal, Mark sat on the step and removed his socks, along with his underwear.

"You don't have to remove everything. I'm just checking for hernias." From an adjacent table, she reached for latex gloves.

Made flaccid by modesty, he stood naked, as if to confront an inquisition. Danielle grasped his testes and inserted her gloved finger deep into the inguinal canal. In the open palm of her hand, she lifted his penis, but his body twinged when she retracted the foreskin.

"Turn around and bend over the table." With a gloved hand on his shoulder, Danielle assisted his motion. "No, no, don't put your underwear back on."

"What are you going to do to me?" he asked and assumed the directed position.

"It's just a rectal exam," she said with a nonchalance he hoped was not irreverence. "From now on, you should have this done about once a year; don't worry, I clipped my fingernails earlier."

The muscles of his body tensed, as if to expel her finger. He gritted his teeth to prevent a groan of discomfort. After the finger was withdrawn, Mark recovered his underwear and sat on the firm leather table. With knees drawn together, he assumed the protected posture of a schoolgirl.

"I hope it was as good for you as it was for me." He hoped the cliché would ease his awkwardness. "You still haven't looked at my wound."

"I'm afraid to," she answered from the writing table, the EKG at hand. "It looks like you haven't changed the dressing."

"Once. Actually, I removed it to take a look, but I didn't have any bandages to replace it."

"How did it happen?" She was at the knee and cut the dressing before he could reply. "This is going to hurt."

"Whoa!" he shouted as the flash of her hand ripped away the encrusted bandage. "I thought medicine was practiced with finesse."

"Did Leonardo wait for Mona Lisa to finish her smile?" she asked. "Sometimes an artist has to do what is most expedient."

"I don't think I am going to get any sympathy around here."

"Oscar Wilde suggested that the less said of life's tribulations, the better. Rather, one should sympathize with the color, the beauty, and the joy of life. I say 'Cry watercolors.'" She evaluated the wound and concluded, "It actually looks pretty good."

He dabbed with the ripped bandage at small drops of blood seeping from the wound edges. "Cry watercolors," he repeated to himself, and then openly added, "To master a human complexity through metaphor."

"It is, after all, the human condition," she replied, matter-of-factly. "Keep it clean, and change the bandage daily. It won't need to be covered after three days." She applied a new dressing to the wound and washed her hands at the basin. "It'll heal just fine. Go ahead and get dressed."

He did as he was told while she was bent over her notes at the writing table. He leaned over the examining table and asked, "Well, Doc, how long do I have to live?"

"We'll just keep an eye on that node, but otherwise, your physical exam is very good, and your wound is healing well." She grabbed the EKG from the clipboard and turned to him. With a serious stare, she added, "But the tracings of your EKG suggest a recent heartbreak."

"You're kidding. An EKG can tell you that?"

"Well, why not? If a fortune teller can judge the spirit of a man from tea leaves, palms, and tarot cards, I should think the tracings of a man's heart more accurate." She chuckled. "That, my friend, is the art of medicine."

"And I had trust in you."

"But seriously," she continued, "mid-life can be a new beginning. It is an opportunity to take knowledge from your past and follow the wisdom of your heart, rather than the passion of your mind. To cry watercolors and enjoy the composition."

128

"Are those your closing remarks on every mid-life physical?"

"No, just for those Kathleen stirs to pull at their wrinkles." She waited at the door, as if for further discussion. Mark remained silent. "I wish you good fortune," she added and stepped out of the room.

◆◆◆

Many voices he had not heard previously preceded Kathleen. "I forgot to collect some urine," she said on her return to the room.

Mark instinctively shielded his groin with his hands. "Show me to the bathroom, and I will give you some naturally."

He returned to the front desk with a clear glass of urine at hand. Many patients were waiting in the reception area.

"It sure got crowded all of a sudden," he said to the secretary.

"First hour is reserved for new insured patients and complicated cases. The rest of the morning is a free community clinic," she answered, and then handed him an appointment reminder for a review of the laboratory results in one week's time.

Chapter 14

he interlaced fibers of a spider's snare were tethered to his hiking boots. Desiccated insects decayed in its trap. A butterfly wing jutted from it—still life of flight. Spiders spin their webs in man's indifference.

On the return from his physical exam, Mark sat out in the garage on a storage shelf, pondering the spider's web. Its intricacy was in the simplicity by which each fiber wove about another. The miracle was the spider's fulfillment of function, to snare food.

He reached for the boots, as if to an estranged appendage, and wished he had worn them on the hike through the peninsular park. Neglect dismissed virtue; generations of spiders had been sheltered within the leather boots. It had been a long time since he had worn them. He plucked the butterfly wing from its bed, but the cobweb he left intact. The boots were the spider's rightful claim.

Between his two fingers, Mark pinched the wing and carried it to eye level. The black outline of its veins, through which once flowed nutrients, traversed an amber field. It was the composition, he thought, that created the butterfly; even in its demise, it remained beautiful.

He had woven the tapestry of his life with the passion of his mind, to ensnare the critical adulation he could not grant himself. All he wrote was weighed by this measure. But the wisdom of his heart remained in disregard.

"Cry watercolors" was a metaphor for a human complexity he had not mastered, and, at that moment, he ached to be with Emilia.

"Arren Sheffer's office, this is Betty. May I help you?"

"You have already," he said into the phone.

"Mark, I was just thinking of you. I had a very good time last night. I hope I didn't ramble on too much about Venice."

"Not at all." He was ashamed he had not paid much attention to the tale of her romance. "I wish we had talked more about it. It'll make a good storyline. What if we made it into a spaghetti western?"

"Don't embarrass me," she said.

"Why didn't you ever contact Estefan again?"

Silence carries its own tales, and that which followed suggested the question had provoked pain. He wished to retract it.

"Too much time has passed," she said, "and it's too impractical, considering how far we are from each other."

"The *passion of the mind*," he said in a low voice.

"What was that?"

"Nothing. I think I've been overwhelmed by poetic prose."

"Seems like the Tahoe poet bared some raw nerves."

"Matter of fact, that is why I called." He raised the palm of his hand on which he held the butterfly wing. The plans for the composition he was out to enjoy were developed as he spoke. "I'm doing what you suggested and asking the poet directly."

"There is no other way. You have to find out what could become or what could have been. I am glad for you."

"Is Arren in?"

"So it's not me you're calling for?" Betty pretended resentment.

"Truth be told, I would rather talk to you all day, but since Arren is our boss, I should give him some attention."

"Arren had advised me to be patient, that you were just shy." She laughed, "But in fact, you are sly as a fox. You were just in waiting for the rooster to roost."

"Don't know about that. I may be more foxy than a fox."

"That you are," she said. "Hold on. I'll transfer you."

"Mark, good to hear from you," Arren said. "Betty told me you two went out to dinner last night. How was it? Isn't she a great gal?"

"That she is. We had a good conversation." He hesitated, but then added, "I'll be going out of town for a while."

"What do you mean? How long is a while?"

"I'll be at Lake Tahoe; but I'm not sure how long it will be for." He stared at the wing. "I have a life to make up for."

"Oh, geez, Mark. Did you kill someone?"

"What are you talking about?" Allegorically himself, he thought.

"Running away to make up a life. If that's not cryptic for having murdered someone—" Arren began.

"Arren, you've been editing crime articles too long. I'm just going to do what you suggested and remove my blinders."

"It's a mid-life crisis, Mark. All men go through it. You don't have to go off the deep end." Arren sounded hurried, as if to stop a train. "Wait a minute. This is about a chick, right?"

"Well, not one that hatches."

"Oh, god. How am I going to break it to Betty? She really is a good woman."

"I know she is. Just tell her I went for a poetry lesson."

"What kind of lame-brain excuse is that?" Arren shouted into the phone.

"She'll understand."

"Oh, geez, Mark. All right, all right, after forty-one years of marriage, I'll think of a better excuse. Now, how about your article?"

"I'll fax you the latest one. But Arren, it's different than anything I've written in the past."

"Ah, shit! Okay, okay, I'll judge later. Just get it to me."

"I'm sure it'll work out." Mark said it more for himself than to assure Arren. "I'll keep you posted on other articles."

◆◆◆

The winter lawn crinkled with each step as Mark crossed the front yard. Its mustard color was tinted with sprouts of green. With the warmth of the afternoon sun and the spray of an automatic sprinkler, it would not be long before the grass was lush.

Flowers bloomed in a large planter to the side of Fredrickson's front door. He rang the doorbell three times before a latch slid open. The cop's wife guarded the gap of the partly opened door, one foot wedged behind it.

"Can I help you?" she asked.

"Hi. Sorry to bother you. I'm Mark, your next door neighbor." He pointed towards his home. "I'll be out of town for about two weeks, and I was hoping you would keep an eye on the house while I was away."

"Oh, yes. I'm sorry. Didn't recognize you." Her hand let go of the inside handle and combed back her hair. The door slipped open wider. "We don't see much of you."

"I'm pretty much a recluse. I suppose many writers are."

"So you're a writer, interesting," she said with a tone of un-sated curiosity. "My husband is a cop, but you know that. We'll certainly keep a watch." She turned her face to the cry of a newborn from inside her home. She grasped the casing of the door. "I'm Rose, and that's my four-week-old Andrew you hear calling, just like his dad."

"Congratulations. I won't keep you any longer, and I do appreciate you watching the house."

"No problem. I'm glad we finally got to meet. Maybe we can have you over when you return." She held the edge of the door and motioned to close it.

"That would be nice," he said as the door shut.

On the walk back, Mark glanced at the neighborhood. The cul-de-sac was quiet; no one was outside. By its neglect, his lawn stood out from all the rest. Mark thought to call a gardener before he left. The sun was bright, but the report was for rain later in the day. He hoped the snow had melted at Lake Tahoe.

◆ ◆ ◆

How does one pack for a lifetime? With clothes laid out about the room, he considered it from the foot of his bed. *Certainly without hiking boots.* He laughed at the thought.

Preparing for the journey generated an excitement that overwhelmed the trepidation. Two large garment bags bulged with as much as he could pack; he was afraid to do without. He paid the bills two weeks before their due and arranged a gardener for weekly care of the lawn. Out of the pants stuffed into the luggage fell the doctor's reminder, which he gathered with the rest of the rubbish.

Mark approached the fax machine with the release with which a man writes a suicide note. He faxed Sadie's Tale, as if it outlined where he had failed. With it, he attached a note for Betty that read, "I've gone for a poetry lesson." He was determined there would be no retreat to his past.

◆◆◆

The luggage waited in the garage as he reclined on the sofa, gathering his thoughts. It was late evening when the voices of neighborhood children parried their parents' summons. The last one at play was called the harshest, and the slam of a wooden door was the final exclamation. He listened to the sounds fade into the chirp of a cricket.

Emilia's note was safeguarded in his breast pocket, but crinkled loudly in the grip of his hand. A calm, moist breeze drifted through the open window as Mark re-read the words. With the flare in her writing, she invited him to call.

Chapter 15

A moist breeze drifted through the open window and carried the muted sound of rainfall on the dormant lawn. In the living room, the chill awakened Mark. At the window, he inhaled the fragrance of moistened soil and glanced at the sapphire gray of an overcast sky. The clouds seemed fissured with the colors of dawn on the horizon. He hoped it did not warn of snowfall on the Sierra Nevada range.

With no time to outrun the rain clouds over the mountain pass, the sea of wrinkles that billowed the clothes he had slept in was dispiriting. Yet, with all he intended to wear packed tight in the luggage, Mark decided well-enough would have to suffice, and reverted to a tried and true bachelor's trick. While he showered, the wrinkled clothes were pressed under the weight of his mattress. Thank goodness for permanent press, he thought as he pleated the pants with his fingers.

◆ ◆ ◆

The highway from San Jose to the Lake Tahoe basin was the route with the least distraction; but given the geometry of Mark's emotion, the incidental distance between the two points merited limited attention. His focus was on the end-point.

A shiny gleam of moisture on the asphalt and a fine mist off the slower cars he passed were all that remained of the earlier rainfall. Ahead of him, over the flatlands, was a pale blue sky he hoped would continue easterly, where smoke-gray clouds showed the aft of the storm. Expecting to arrive behind the worst of the weather, Mark paced the speed of his car to the rhythmic swipe of the wiper, which seemed to score the minutes of his travel.

Lightning flashed in the mountain ridges as he ascended Donner Pass, but rain did not fall until he reached the Lake Tahoe basin. Sandy grime, remnants of the melted winter snow, coated the road through town. Like rock-studded white ribbons, the ski runs ahead of him appeared to stream from the summit's misted forest, as rivulets of rainwater cascaded in the gullies on the side of the road up to his home.

Indoors was a respite from the deluge that followed him, but the frenzy of emotion compelled him to the phone. His desire did not balk at the monotone voice that took the first call, nor on the subsequent many redials. Its request to leave a message only prompted him to drop the handset into its cradle. There were no words he could gather to express either his contrition, or his petition to be with her again, at least not until he heard her voice.

A man obsessed is one without much else to do, so Mark unpacked the luggage and re-organized the closet. By early afternoon, he was overcome by impatience. He grabbed the keys from the kitchen counter and marched to town.

He held the storm door from slamming behind him and hung his wet jacket on the coat-rack. The Maidu Cafe appeared empty. With no one at the counter, Mark slipped into its first seat.

"Hi. Would you like a menu?" a young waitress asked, and placed a glass of water with the silverware.

"Yes, please." She was not one he had seen previously, nor did he recognize the name on her tag. "Karen. Hmm. You must be new."

"No, not really. I've been here for ten months, ever since I graduated from high-school." She wiped the counter in front of Mark. "I mostly work the afternoon shift."

Karen had the built of a skier, lean and tall, with strong, long legs, firm buttocks, and adolescent breasts. Her black hair was plaited in a single braid to the back of her head and hung to her waist. At the service window, she picked up a tray with hamburger and fries. He watched her carry it to the only other diner in the cafe.

Victor sat at a table by the front window. Sheets of rain continued to fall on the parking lot beyond the glass. He appeared in deep thought, until his attention was commanded by Karen's arrival. She placed the food on the table in front of him and engaged in a short conversation. His smile was followed by her giggle, which seemed to launch her back to the counter.

"Ready to order?" she asked Mark.

"I'm sorry. Let me look at your specials." He hesitated, but as she turned away, he quickly interjected, "Is Emilia working today?"

"No." Karen answered from the basin, where she poured old coffee from a glass urn. "I believe she's out of town."

"Oh, I see." But *I feel* was more appropriate phrasing, as the moisture on the palm of his hands dried, and the beat of his heart calmed. He took a sip of water and ended his breadth with a sigh. "Do you know where she went?"

"No, but I'm sure she'll be here tomorrow." She replaced the urn on a metal burner and left it to fill. He watched her walk into the kitchen, and the brewing coffee drip into the pot. The aroma seemed to form the aura around what she had said.

Tomorrow, he thought, *was a cheap overture from those without a cause, but for one who is driven, patience becomes anguish.* A flash of light heralded the roar of thunder, and a curtain of water descended across the front window. Faith, replied the query, would grant better weather for Emilia's safe return.

***

Victor's pensive stare continued out the window. "How are you, Victor?"

"Hey, guy. What's up?" he replied nonchalantly.

"We met at Steamer's," Mark answered Victor's puzzled gaze. "I came with Emilia."

"Emilia came with Norma," he interjected. "Didn't she?"

"That's right. Emilia invited me to meet the group."

"Yeah, I remember you." Victor took a bite of the sandwich. "She's a fine lady. Always kind to stray cats."

And dirty dogs, Mark wanted to counter.

"I suppose you're here to see her, too."

"Karen says she's out of town."

"Yeah, man. Hey, sit down." Victor pointed to the seat across from him. "She goes to Berkeley for some religious thing."

"That's right, she mentioned that." Mark sat down. "Native American prayers."

"I guess it was a good day to get out of town. This weather sucks." Victor looked at the rain out the window.

"Thought you left." Karen approached their table. "Ready to order?" she asked Mark.

"I think I'll just have a diet coke," he answered.

"Victor, anything else you want?" she asked.

"No, thanks. You're all I can handle," he replied. Karen giggled and returned to behind the counter. "She's a great kid," Victor added, "but she's also my boss' daughter. Totally out of bounds for me." He sipped his drink and glanced in her direction. "She sure filled in nicely, though."

Karen returned with Mark's drink and set it on the table. Turned to Victor, she winked at his stare. "The Rodeo Dance is at the Elk's Club on Friday."

"Can't wait to see you in those tight jeans," Victor said.

"They're yours when you want them," she answered with forced sensuality in her voice. A smile preceded the exaggerated swivel of her hips on her return to the service area.

"Ride'm cowgirl," Victor whooped in response.

"Out-of-bounds seems to have no limitations," Mark said.

"It's just horseplay. But hell," he said with a wink to Mark, "you got to keep a woman moistened. You never know when you'll need a ride."

"And I suppose you keep the spurs at the ready."

"I never seem to take them off." He leaned forward and dropped his arms to his lap. As if recalling an occasion, his body then tensed to add, "But the gun has got to be loaded."

Forethought, Mark realized, was as titillating as foreplay—one's prowess engorged by imagination. It was no wonder that a man could be spent even before the act. Sexually self-sufficient

140

seemed to apply to his own bravado, Mark reproached his response.

"Aren't you tired?" he asked, "of always being at the ready?"

"On a day like today? You got it, man." Victor slumped back from the table. "Got nothing to do but come here to horseplay with a high-school kid."

"Why not settle down?"

"Emilia is a fine woman. I'd considered settling down for her, but she says I lack grace." He raised his head and looked at Mark. His face contorted into a bout of laughter. "I guess she didn't like me burping at the table."

"No, I wouldn't think she did," Mark laughed as well, but when Victor's eyes had dried and his merriment sputtered, Mark asked more soberly, "What do you think she meant by that? Ah, forget it. It doesn't matter."

"Women are like that. They play along with your jokes, and tolerate your gases, but when they want something that you can't guess at, they blame your graces," Victor commented. "Don't tell me she got you with it, too? What did you do? Come with the wind and leave with a fart?" He snorted through his nose, and tears gathered in the corners of his eyes.

Conspiracy, Mark thought, was to respond in like. Betrayal was to feed the frenzy. Support was to stand up and walk away. But strength was to accept Emilia's own will, and she considered Victor her friend. Mark watched the wrinkles of laughter sharpen Victor's handsome features, but a shallow smugness masked his lonely mood. Mark leaned over the edge of the table onto his elbows, and with his hands, covered the smile on his own face.

Chapter 16

*L*ike a swarm of locusts on the shingles of his roof, rain continued to fall. Drawn into a trance, he stared at the cathedral ceiling of his living room. Reclined on the sofa, cuddled with the throw pillows against the cold, he shuffled words of redemption in his mind. But their Biblical references troubled him and to expunge the thoughts, he took refuge in sleep.

Waning sunlight greeted him when he wakened, and the sound of departing rain comforted. At the window, he watched the lake's silver shimmer fade and the sun set among retreating storm clouds.

With no words prepared, Mark dialed from the crinkled paper. "Hello, Emilia," he answered the monotone message at the end of the line. "I've called to apologize, but I know there is no forgiveness for what I did." He hesitated, and after a deep breath, added, "Call me when you get back."

◆ ◆ ◆

The clamor of sound he thought was thunder awakened him, but the second ring led his hand to the phone.

"Hello." He attempted to sound alert.

"I hope I didn't wake you."

Jolted by her voice, he sat up to the edge of the bed. "Emilia," he exclaimed. "It's okay. I was hoping you'd call."

"It's good to hear from you. I just got your message."

"I'm so glad to hear you. Are you home?"

"Yes, I just got in. I was in Berkeley for the last three days. I had to wait out the rain before driving up."

"I'm glad you waited. It was a bad storm."

"Are you all right?" she asked.

"Me? Yes, of course. I've been indoors all day. Are you?"

"I'm just tired, and I have to get up in a few hours to go into work."

"I missed you so much. I'm sorry I abandoned you. I've been a coward." The contrived glossary for redemption crumbled on his lips. "I want to see you."

"And I want to see you," Emilia responded.

"I know you're tired, and you still have to work this morning. How about after work? I'll prepare you that bachelor dinner I promised."

"I would love that. I have nothing in the cupboards."

"Great. It works out, then. I'll take care of dinner tomorrow, or is it today already?" He glanced at the bedside clock. "It's three. I guess it's today already. You better get some sleep. I'll pick you up at six this evening."

"Don't worry. I'll drive up. Male cooks can be finicky. I wouldn't want to disrupt your momentum. I'll be there by six-thirty; I have a few things I've got to take care of before then." Her voice was solemn when she added, "I can't wait to see you."

"Neither can I," he said and wished her a goodnight. As if the electricity in the intertwined fibers of the phone could heighten hearing, he continued to grip the handset to listen for Emilia resting in bed. Long after her voice had gone, and not until the phone buzzed, he closed the line.

To entice sleep, Mark worked in his mind the revolving queue of Disney characters Emilia had said she would not eat. Gradually, slumber overcame the task of pairing these to the meats condemned to his skillet.

He wondered whether it was the sun's glare or the droop of his eyes that veiled the recipes he read that morning. No matter—he had never being good at following instructions. The cunning of literature was his forte. Mark decided on a familiar recipe: a dash of this or that to whatever was in the refrigerator.

Maidu Café was the epicenter of his travels, for everywhere he went that day, it seemed to be just down the street. One block from it was the market, and on his way for groceries, he noticed the cafe parking lot was not crowded. Mark was tempted to stop briefly to wish Emilia a good day.

He held the storm door open, but hesitated to enter. Three tables were occupied with diners, and one sat at the counter. Emilia's back was turned to him; she stood at the service window, waiting for an order. The momentum of his heart's flutter propelled him in her direction. The door shut with a thump. Emilia turned to the sound.

"Mark," she said, surprised, and froze where she stood.

He rushed to the counter and reached over it to kiss her. "I'm sorry," he offered, when they recovered their breath. "I had to stop and see you."

She wiped her lipstick off his face, but then repeated the kiss. "I'm so glad you came."

"Order up," the cook shouted from the kitchen.

"The breakfast is going to get cold," Laura cautioned on her pass behind Emilia.

"Stay here. Have a seat," she said to Mark. "I'll be right back." She retrieved the plates and rushed them to the couple at a front table; their stare led the way.

Mark was partly seated on the chair, undecided whether to leave. "I'm holding you up. I better get going," he said on her return.

"How about breakfast?" she offered.

"My belly is full, thinking what food to feed you. I was actually on my way to the market."

"I'll walk you to the car. Laura won't mind." She reached back to untie her apron.

"That's okay. You're busy. I'm afraid I would abduct you. What would Laura say then?"

"She wouldn't care, as long as I was with a man. She worries about me. All right, but you have to tell me what we're having for dinner. I can't wait." Emilia brushed her finger through his hair.

"Moroccan road-kill and Loch Ness eel."

She pulled her hand back as if from a sting. "Interesting, but not very romantic."

"It's all I could come up with that Disney has not made a movie of." Mark stood up from the chair and held her hand. "You know an artist reveals his work only upon its completion." He kissed her hand and walked backward to the door. "I'll miss you."

Emilia responded with a kiss of a finger that she flicked in his direction.

◆ ◆ ◆

Bewitched by her parting smile, Mark soared on a magic carpet to a Marrakech bazaar. He imagined the exotic smells and vibrant colors of the produce and wares. From each shop rang the banter of a chandler hawking his treasured curios. Emilia, he thought, would be enchanted.

Reality, though, landed him in the parking lot of the town's monster-market. Inside, neat aisles of vegetables were aligned in military order, their freshness preserved by mechanical spray. The fruits were sorted, as if for a designer's paint swatch, and the scents of spice were sealed in beveled glass.

To bring Emilia the enchantment he imagined, Mark composed a rainbow of assorted items. He gauged the leafy green lettuce against the stout green spinach; pale tan potatoes to the maroon of onions; carrot orange to turnip white; and squash yellow with apple red.

Determined to balance the rainbow of produce, Mark sniffed up and down the shelves of beveled glass jars of herbs and spices. In their aroma would be revealed character and utility. Chili and paprika were desert dry, but culinary basics. Cinnamon was hearth warm, but fastidious. Nutmeg and thyme were bitter and discriminatory. Cumin and curry bore oriental mystique. Cloves intimidated. Ginger was High Mass at the cathedral, and pastoral mustard was color's majesty.

At the checkout line, he reviewed his bounty and realized he was missing wine. Though it seemed cliché to include it, he wanted to assure the meal did not lack occasion for romance. He ran to the aisle of colored glass and selected a Moroccan Chardonnay.

◆◆◆

Bewildered by the array of colorful produce, Mark sat back to consider his meal plans, as much as his chance for romance. Safeguarded as he was by a temperance for passion, he hedged his ability to explore the wisdom of his heart, as the doctor had ordered. He recalled her advice *to cry watercolors and enjoy the composition.*

With the determination of Van Gogh, he returned to the kitchen and ripped open a bag of black beans. Rudimentary, rather than a delicacy, these were the color of the most fertile soil. It was where he began.

With a dab of salt and a hearty sprinkle of paprika, he slowly boiled the beans. Diced cilantro was more than a favorite condiment; it was his mother's culinary signature, a family tradition. Rice, in purest white, was their natural companion. Mark considered it God's favorite starch: so many world civilizations depended on it as primary energy food.

He laid romaine lettuce out like green plumes on a dish, and then overlaid diced scallions, carrots, tomatoes, and avocado on the leafy green bed, and capped it with slivers of Swiss cheese.

The grandfather clock on the living room wall chimed the half hour before Emilia was to arrive. He sprinkled garlic and diced red onions, and let drop two chicken breasts, wrapped with bacon strips, into a buttered pan to simmer. For garnish, he added sweet red pepper, black mushrooms, and parsley. The meal waited in low heat for the table setting.

Startled by the doorbell, Mark inspected the kitchen one last time. Satisfied that all the used dishes had been washed and stored away, he rushed to the door before it sounded a second time.

"Welcome to front row center on paradise," he said on opening the door. "Dinner will soon be served." Emilia stood with an armful of red roses and a boxed chocolate cake on the palm of her hand. "Oh, gee. I forgot the flowers and dessert," he said.

"That was my duty." Emilia handed him the roses.

"I've never been given roses." He reached for the flowers as he leaned towards her for a kiss. "Thank you. But I wish I had remembered to get you some."

"I think we shall need to transcend 'never,'" she said, and embraced him with her free arm. "Also, to recognize a 'wish' as the failure of our will."

More enticing than the cake was her eager kiss. "Wow! I love the way you punctuate. Okay, I will get you flowers next time," he said as he raised them for a whiff. "Thank you again for the roses."

Emilia wore a long, emerald green coat, buttoned against the cold. "The food smells so good," she remarked from outside the door.

"I'm sorry. Come in. The food must be ready." Mark held the roses to his chest.

"Just show me where the kitchen is." She took back the cake box. "You need to find a place for those roses before you crush them."

He directed her to the kitchen and followed her in. As if to preserve the pleasure of their kiss, he inhaled the fragrance of the roses and placed them on the glass top coffee table in the living room.

"Mark!" she said from the kitchen. "I didn't mean for you to kill them. They need to be in water. Is there a vase in here?"

He took the flowers into the kitchen, where she removed the coat to reveal a lilac column dress that tapered at her slim waist. Its print of sierra flowers blended with the roses she recovered from Mark.

"You look beautiful," he said, standing back. "And yes, if I think it so, it means I wish—excuse me—I seek for more."

"So you did listen to me at the lake." She raised the lid over the chicken. "It smells delicious."

"And does being delicious make you want more?"

"Of course. I'm starving."

He opened a cabinet door by her legs. "You've got nice, muscular calves. Is that due to all the skiing, or is it genetic?" He reached for a glass pitcher. "Will this do?" he asked from his crouched position.

"You better be satisfied with only a wish." Emilia smiled and took the pitcher. She stepped back from him and filled it with

148

water. "Right now, all the will I have is to eat that meal you've prepared." She set the pitcher on the bar and arranged the roses.

"It's a nice arrangement for the dining table," he said, and counted the roses. "That's interesting. There are seven of them."

"A dozen is a ritual, but so is a single rose. Half a dozen is a wish, but seven is a promise." She carried them to the table and rested the pitcher off-center, away from the place settings.

"You are puzzling, with subtleties you impart to what would otherwise be trivial. So tell me—a promise for what?" he asked from behind her.

"To give you more." Emilia straightened from over the table, and turned to him, lightly touching the side of his face.

Mark took a deep breath, as if to enhance the shiver that spread throughout his body, and shirked the urge to shut his eyes. He didn't want to lose sight of the gleam in her face; it mirrored what he felt.

The tick-tock of the clock was all that sounded, as if the span of its arms dutifully created time. He wanted it silenced, as in that moment, he was granted a reprieve from his guilt.

"What can I help you with?" she asked, and turned to judge what was absent from the table. "You have everything set up so neat and orderly. Even the kitchen is clean. I'm impressed."

He recounted the seven roses, in unison with the tick of the second hand, and brought himself from a daze. "You're not an oracle," he said. "You are a fairy, a Cherokee fairy. Everything you say and do fascinates me."

"I am just a simple waitress." She turned to go to the kitchen, "and since you cooked, I will serve the dinner."

"No, no," he interjected, and held her hand to stay her from the kitchen. "Tonight is my turn to try to charm you. There will be no drip of egg yolk on my shirt and no haphazard fall in the snow. I will serve you dinner with grace and glory. Please have a seat, and tell me if you would like some music."

"To be pampered is always nice. I can get used to that." She sat in the chair Mark held out for her. "Some music would be nice."

"Do you mind country-western?"

"It's my favorite. There's nothing better than regular folks' melodrama played to a tune."

"Good, because I broke my ghetto blaster's antenna about three years ago, and it's the only music I get up here. One of these days, I'm going to remember to get some CDs," he said from the living room. "I don't entertain much, but I suppose you assumed that already."

"What makes you say that?" Emilia asked.

"Because of how introverted I've been." He raised the volume of the radio. "This song is about me." He returned to the kitchen and brought the salad to the table. "I am the 'Desperado.'"

"I don't understand," she replied.

He returned with the wine bottle and opened it. "Would you like some Chardonnay?"

"Yes, please." She raised the wine glass.

"Shall we toast?" Mark took the seat beside her and filled his glass for the toast.

"Of course, go ahead."

"To fairy tale wishes, for there you'll be." The crystal chimed on contact. They both took a sip.

"That was cute," she said, and began to eat the salad. "Why are you like 'Desperado'?"

"Well, like the song says, I had to come to my senses and let someone love me before it's too late." Mark returned the fork to the table and paused. He sipped the wine before he continued. "I hurt you when I left, and I can't forgive myself. But you are my fairy tale, and I had to gamble that you would give me a second chance."

"It's not that I wasn't hurt, or that I understood why you left, but I hoped you would return. There is no second chance. I never let go of what we were creating."

Mark held Emilia's hand and felt the softness of her skin. Her fingernails were glossed, and she wore no rings. He traced the contour of her veins and embraced their course to her heart. He leaned to her, and she to him, and in their kiss, 'never' was overcome.

It was difficult to break away, but the sound of steam spurred him to jump out of the chair and rush to the alarm.

"Our meal wants to join us," he said from the kitchen.

"Well, bring it on. I'm starving," she replied.

"It's not gourmet," he said on his return to the table, with a dish of food in either hand. "But it's this cowboy's melodrama, served to you on a plate." He laid the meal before them.

"It's beautiful. Love the colors." She stared into the meal. White rice ridged the plate on one side, and black beans on the opposite. In the center of the plate was a brawny chicken breast wrapped with bacon strips that oozed flavor. Mahogany mushroom and red sweet pepper adorned the meat. "It smells so good," she said with fork in hand.

"I hope you enjoy it." Mark waited for her response. "In the Old West, chicken was expensive," he added, as if to bribe her for vigorous appreciation. "It was difficult to raise chickens in large numbers."

A chef's fulfillment was granted Mark with her display of satisfaction: closed eyes, slow chewing, fork gripped in silence.

The radio accompanied them throughout the meal, but their conversation was the only melody they heard. On their emptied dinner plates, a colorful collage of dried juices formed while they talked, and the clearing of the table was only a provisional diversion.

Mark swigged the last of the wine as he watched Emilia stand at the window. Her arms were folded to her chest, and a quiet stare looked on the blackness of night. He approached her, and their reflection showed in the glass.

"It's a beautiful view," she said.

"It's even more spectacular in daylight."

"I can imagine," she replied.

"Would you like to go out on the deck?" Mark reached for an afghan from the closet and handed it to her.

Emilia went out to the deck without replying. She stood at the banister, the afghan wrapped around her shoulders. "It's magnificent how black and endless everything appears," she said.

Mark sat on a lounge chair and looked in the direction of her stare. Black shadows filled the view. Except for themselves and the shimmer of stars, the universe was a void. Like flakes in a snowstorm, constellations spiraled into the abyss. Emilia seemed to stand among them.

Silence beyond their voices stalked the rustle of a gentle breeze among the trees. Were it not for the flicker of lights on the south shore, he could imagine they were alone on earth.

"There are a billion stars in that sky," she said.

"Can you be sure of that?" he replied.

"Yes," she said, and with a finger dipped into the void, she began to count. "There's Taurus and Orion. Ah, let's see how many other constellations I can make out."

"When did you study the constellations?"

"When I told fortunes." Emilia turned, but in the darkness, she followed only his voice.

"You were a fortune teller?" he asked in disbelief.

"Not really. But in my religious studies, I attempted to apply Greek philosophical corollaries of the zodiac to contemporary events." Emilia set herself on Mark's lounge chair; he dropped his legs to either side to make room.

"Whatever that means. It sounds more complicated than fortune telling." He wrapped his arms around her.

"It only means I spent a lot of time and proved nothing," she said as he pressed her back against his chest. "You're hands are freezing." She raised the afghan above their heads, and cast it around them both.

"Oh, that feels much better," he said. "What do you think of fortune telling? Is there anything to it?" He remembered the fortune his doctor read from his EKG.

"The Greeks and other ancient cultures believed that human pathos interplay with the constellations and are influenced by these celestial groupings. I believe we are products of the environment and our will. Some aspect of destiny, though, seems to be involved." She turned her head to glance at him. "I'm not a fatalist. Fortune telling is more wish than will."

"And what factors influenced our chance meeting?" Mark kissed her forehead. "Was it destiny, the environment, or was it will? It couldn't have been the egg yolk on my shirt?"

"No. It was diehard patience on my part." She laughed.

"What do you mean?"

"It took you so long to respond."

"And that will be my eternal remorse," Mark replied soberly, but then added, "Hey, my doctor read my fortune from an EKG."

"Well, why not? I would think it may be more accurate than tea leaves."

"That's exactly what she said."

"And what was your fortune?" she asked.

"Actually, she went through a ritual before reading the EKG. I'll spare you the gory particulars, but through my electrical energies was revealed the need to seek out the wisdom of my heart, more so than the passion of the mind."

"Interesting concept," she said.

"But I think that with you, Miss Emilia, I need to have both wisdom and passion. My heart and mind are fascinated by you."

Emilia let the afghan fall from her grip and turned to him. Her legs draped over his thigh, and her body swiveled to caress him. With her lips to his ear, she whispered, "Desperado, let me love you, before it's too late."

The scent of buttered garlic greeted their return indoors. Mark cradled Emilia in his arms. The radio's music followed the wake of their passion. It was dark down the steps to his bedroom, but he continued without fault; desire lit their path. On the bed, they sat in an embrace.

"Be still," Emilia said, with her lips upon his, "and let me make love to you tonight."

She stood away, keeping her hands on his chest that he might not move. One by one, she released each button. The shirt dropped to the carpeted floor. With her lips, she warmed the skin of his chest. Mark loosened the buttons of her dress and felt the softness of her flesh. He nudged his face into her breasts. Her hands pressed his shoulders.

The window blinds were open, but in the darkness, the forest was their only witness. The fabric of her dress brushed the inside of his legs when it slipped from her body to the floor. She stood naked, embraced in his arms and legs. In the night light, she seemed to glow.

Emilia bent forward, and slowly let her weight propel them to the bed. Her breath was in him, and he wanted never to exhale. The mist of her breath was on his tongue, and Mark drank. As she lay on him, her fingers clutched at his hair and the nerve fibers of his body imprinted her weight. Without sight, he saw her beauty. Mark became firm with desire, and reached to unclip his belt.

"Shh," she appealed, and pushed his hand away from the buckle. Her fingers unzipped his pants and slid them to his feet.

Her body seemed to glide on the sweat of their passion. A sensual touch of her tongue to his toes radiated through his body. Mark yearned to reciprocate and moved his arms to embrace her. "Shh," she whispered into the hollow of his ear. He succumbed to her touch on his nipples, the clasp of her hand, and the feel of her flesh. He submitted to her favor and was motionless in a storm of arousal.

His eyes closed, her image was superimposed on his senses. The rapture that swelled within knew no temperance. With her straddling him, he yielded to her sway. Her hand guided him inside her, and Mark sat up to her embrace. Their bodies trembled; his mouth coveted hers. His cry of pleasure became her own.

Chapter 17

Green ponderosa pine needles dazzled in the reflected morning sun. A blue jay assumed a perch on the roughened wood of the deck. Patches of snow remained only on the shadowed, craggy hillside of the forest. Mark's life had changed as quickly as winter had become spring.

Emilia still slept on his arm. Her closed eyelids flittered, and Mark rejoiced to the feel of her naked flesh upon his own, warmed under a quilted comforter. Curls of her hair lay unfurled on the pillow. Her perfume suffused the air he breathed. He remained motionless, afraid to shatter his dream.

Mark watched as her eyes squinted against the light. "Good morning," he said, and brushed a wanton curl from her forehead.

"Good morning," she answered, and rubbed her eyes with a finger. She tried to focus on him. "Have you been awake long?"

"I think I'm still dreaming," he said.

She turned her body and raised herself partly over him. "I know ways to find out that are better than a pinch," she said, with her lips on his.

Mark was aroused while embraced in her kiss. "You're right. It never felt this good in a dream."

"I can make you breakfast, if you like," she offered.

"I like everything you do."

"Karen switched with me this morning. I won't have to go in

'til early in the afternoon." Emilia rested her head on his chest. "I wanted last night to happen."

"So did I. Thank you for being patient." He brushed his fingers through her hair. After a pause, he added, "You make me feel so good. Is this what being alive is like?"

They remained in bed, not wanting to move, as if time would likewise stand still. The sun lifted shadows into the room warning the passing of time.

"I suppose I better get ready and make you breakfast." She cast off the comforter before Mark replied, then moved away from the bed toward the bathroom. "Would you like to join me?" she asked from the door.

No one was more beautiful to Mark. With her brunette hair lifted between her fingers, Emilia gazed at him with a coy smile. Her hazel eyes shimmered in the sun, and her soft skin held a light tan. Round and full, her breasts graced her naked body. Mark remained uncovered on the bed, unabashedly aroused.

"The water feels great," she shouted from the shower. Mark ran to her.

She was lathered in white, foamy soap when he stepped into the water's spray. He pressed his body against hers and wiggled to attain a soapy film of his own. With primordial fascination, they touched and stroked each other's bodies. Their lips and mouths sensually sated fantasy and curiosity. Mark wanted her more than he wanted life. His joy was in her pleasure and the feel of himself inside of her. In the warm rain of the shower, they shared their love.

◆◆◆

Water dripped from his hair to his skin. Mark sat at the edge of the bed and watched Emilia dress. Motionless, he stared, as if at a museum display. He envied the column dress that covered her skin and the shoes that supported her step. The full-length mirrors on the sliding closet doors reflected her image, and his thoughts would reflect on her when she was gone. Silence had once been without pity. But this silence was like a companion, for all the thoughts of her it allowed to cross his mind.

"Aren't you getting dressed?" she asked.

"I was waiting to get into the closet after you finished."

"You should've told me. I could have moved."

"As much as I should stop my heart," he said, and embraced her from behind. "You are beautiful."

"You are an animal." She pulled away. "Get ready, while I make your breakfast."

Summits along the mountain range seemed like spires of ancient cathedrals, rising above the mist that shadowed the lake at the south shore. It was late morning when they sat at the table for breakfast.

"Two eggs, over easy, home fries, two whole-wheat toasts, and a cup of coffee," She set the meal before Mark. "Did I forget something?"

"No, you've got it all."

"Mark Balcon, you are a man of habit." She sat at the table and poured milk into her bowl of cereal.

"And what have you thought about that?" he asked, and dipped the toast into the yolk.

"About what?"

"A man of habit."

"We pattern our lives for comfort when we are most afraid of its challenges," Emilia answered.

"Is that what you see in me?" He placed the fork on the table and looked at Emilia.

"I've seen so much, yet so little, of you, and what I've seen has led me here." She reached for his hand. "For two years, I've wanted to be with you."

"Isn't it a sorrowful man who hides from life's challenges? Was it pity that kept you interested?"

"Only pity for myself." She sat back and stared out the window. "Look at all the beautiful things around us, and most of the time we can only admire them by the virtue of their being. Our lives, though, are enriched through knowledge of them. Without being with you, without touching you, and without cooking your breakfast, I could not know you." She paused and smiled at Mark. "I could only admire your eccentricities."

He took the fork, scooped it into the potatoes, and held it before his mouth. "Well, as long as it's not me you pity." He smiled and bit into the potatoes. "I can live with that."

The water kettle whined with a shrill cry. "I thought I turned it off," Emilia said on her way to the kitchen. "Would you like more coffee?"

"I'm fine, thanks. You know, I often let that kettle whine, even long after I finished the coffee. It seemed as if I could carry a conversation with it." He looked at Emilia, who sat back down. "And now it's only an interruption."

Emilia glanced away from the conversation, seemingly impressed with the daytime panorama. In the glare of the noon sun, though, she became aware of the time. "Oh, my word. I'm going to be late." She stood to clear the dishes.

"I'll take care of them," he said.

"Thanks. I appreciate it." She gathered her coat and purse from the living room sofa. "This is the first time Karen let me switch. Don't want to discourage her; we may need her favor again." She winked.

"I'll drive you in," he offered.

"Don't worry, I better drive myself. I may need the truck."

"Will you come back tonight?" he asked, with a rhetorical overtone.

Emilia touched the side of his face and reached for his lips. In the fervor of their kiss, she avowed her return. "You may eventually prefer the whine of the kettle," she said with a laugh.

Against the cool breeze, he put his hands in his pockets and shivered in his short sleeves. Mark walked her to the truck and waited until she drove past the turn at the bottom of the hill.

Like an old friend, silence greeted him inside the house. Inspired by thoughts of Emilia, he cleared the table. A rose petal fell when he wiped against the pitcher; its softness was that of her skin. The bouquet was in full bloom; the clusters of petals had broadened since the night.

Seven roses Mark counted again; one more than a wish—and plenty of promises before it was a ritual. *Fragile promises,* he thought, as the petals plunged with each swipe of his hand. Was his lonely life as fragile, that Emilia should enter and tumble its defenses?

◆ ◆ ◆

Huddled with a book on a living room sofa, Mark framed the words he read to force comprehension. Pleasurable thoughts were difficult to distract.

A thump against a side window startled him. Looking out from inside, he noticed the moisture stains on the splintered wooden floor of the deck. It was all that remained of an icicle's silent cascade.

Outside, on the floor below the frame of the window, he found a dark-eyed Oregon junco in a struggle for its life. The bird lay turned on its side. Hooded with black feathers, its head was still. Only with its somber eyes did it express an appeal.

The bird filled the cup of Mark's hand. The buff feathers of its chest quivered, and from its pink bill, spastic breaths of air flitted against his thumb. Charcoal wings, edged with white, were drawn against its body, and its legs flexed, as if stilled in flight. It remained immobile until a cough of blood preceded a wild flap of the wings. Motionless thereafter, the eyes were partly sealed, its breath ceased.

"We pattern our lives for comfort when we are most afraid of its challenges," he recalled Emilia's words. *And nature enriches all living things with the challenges it bestows*, Mark thought.

At the side of his home, the hill sloped away from a single Jeffrey pine tree. Under its canopy, with a chisel fashioned from a fallen branch, Mark dug a shallow grave into the rocky ground. With loosened dirt and gravel, he covered the bird in the hollow.

A blue jay rested on a boulder. With its bishop's crown, it sounded a scolding High Mass. Mark imagined it a burial rite. Other birds beckoned Mark into the forest, and he considered what Emilia had said. "Look at all the beautiful things around us, and most of these we can only admire by the virtue of their being."

The forest ground was littered with kindling. Fluorescent moss dressed fallen branches. In clearings, seedlings sprouted on springtime's promise. Among them leaped a grasshopper's cousin, a tenth its size. While in flight, it seemed to chirp with castanets. The undersides of its wings were the yellow of sun-flowers, and the borders were brown, like the ground on which it came to rest. With wings folded, it mimicked a dry leaf.

Much like a chickadee, a squirrel's call belatedly warned of the dropped pinecone that fell at Mark's feet. Deeper into the forest, the slope steepened into a ravine, and the forest thinned on the rocky walls. Inside the canyon, unfiltered sunlight was bright. He climbed down to the stream, crags his only foothold.

Black oak and maple were harbored in the gorge, water cascaded to the distant lake, and yellow stream violets were strewn along its banks. From a five-foot waterfall, a fine mist drizzled on orange wallflowers that bloomed on the granite palisade. Mark lay back on a large boulder at the summit and rested under the sun's rays.

He looked at all the beautiful things around him. In the budding leaves, he saw the glow of anticipation. The cool breeze carried the thrill of an impulse, and softened by the sound of water's flow, was nature's challenge. To this world, Mark thought, his life had led; the love of Emilia was its culmination.

Chapter 18

Recent winters had been harsh, and the effect of windblown snow showed in the frayed varnish of the front door. The wood surfaces throughout the home had long appeared neglected. It was not like Mark to undertake home maintenance. It had only been luck that the house was durable, though no longer as attractive.

With his fingers, he skimmed the surface of the door, as over a crystal ball. As if stirred by an apparition, he quickly pulled his hand away. The door, he decided, would have to be sanded soon. Emilia might get a splinter from it.

Time was an illusion, he thought. *Created by the span of the second's hand and catalogued in memories.* It was strange that in the seven years he had owned the house, only thoughts of Emilia filled its inside spaces. On the dining table, where he had written many short stories, only her gesture of gustatory content seemed to matter. Countless seasons had colored the vista where he sat to write; these were merged with the abyss in which she had dipped her finger.

The phone clattered, shaking his thoughts. "Hello," he answered, hoping it would be Emilia.

"Mr. Balcon?" He recognized the sonata voice of Dr. Revels' nurse.

"Yes," he answered, cautioned by the seriousness of her voice.

"Dr. Revels has been trying to reach you all day. We called your home and left a message. We finally were able to get in contact with your secretary, who gave us this number." It sounded like a rebuke. "Dr. Revels had an emergency at the hospital, but she wanted me to set up an appointment for to-morrow at three."

"Wait a minute," he said to the storm stirring inside of him. "What does she want me for?"

"She only said that it was important you come in. She didn't say much else." Her voice was forgiving, but he wanted it apologetic. Her request was intrusive. "What time would you prefer?"

"I can't come in at all. I'm in Lake Tahoe. It's at least a six-hour drive back." He felt for the wound on his right knee. It was healing well. There was no reason to make the trip. "Just tell her to call me when she returns."

"We need you to come in," Kathleen persisted. "She works a half-day on Saturday. We'll make it for then."

"No." He wanted to end their quibble and free up the phone. Emilia may want to call before she drove up from work. "I'll talk to Dr. Revels on the phone, and that's all."

"All right," Kathleen said, not surrendering. "I'll have her call. But you have to come in."

As if it had burned him, he dropped the phone on the hum of a disconnected line. *What,* he wondered, *could be the urgency?* His wound was healing well, and he felt better than he ever had. Dr. Revels had confirmed his good health.

Three o'clock had been the nurse's first offer for an appointment. He recalled the secretary's mention they conducted a free clinic after the insured patients in the morning. It must be, he decided, that the insurance claim was rejected. He turned the answering machine on, so as not miss the call.

Shadowed by an easterly sun, it was not long before Emilia was to leave from work. Fearful the disorder of the house would distract her, he rapidly gathered the breakfast dishes into the dishwasher, arranged the throw pillows neatly on the living room sofa, and centered the pitcher of roses on the glass coffee table. He forwent vacuuming; whisking away only what was visible.

The master bedroom in the lower level was the only one ever used, and it heartened him to notice its disorder. There was the set of wrinkles on the bottom sheet, on which lingered the scent of Emilia's perfume, a rumpled comforter thrown to the side, which he placed on the bed with its underside up, garments strewn about the room, each seemingly with a tale on how it made its journey. He was amused at the strength of Emilia's arm.

The sweet smell of maple entered the room with a mild wind that rushed the blinds. From the deck, through the distant gaps of the forest, the road from town was visible. He waited for dusk to mask his view, and the tires of her truck to grind the gravel in front of his home. The gentle patter of steps quickened toward the front door and then the doorbell pealed. Barefooted, on the second ring, he opened the door. "I've missed you."

Emilia dropped the clothes she carried and embraced him. Her fingers in his hair, she pulled him to her lips. He wrapped his arms around her and held her tight, raising her to the tip of her toes. Mark leaned to the jamb; her body pressed against his, and he felt the moisture of her tongue deep inside him.

To keep the warmth of her breath and the taste of her lips, he would persist, pinned to the splintered door. Were it not for a honk of a passing car, they would have remained at the doorway.

"I suppose this is the right house," she said, and slipped from his embrace to collect her clothes.

"No. I think it's two doors up, but you might do an old man in with your greeting." He was afraid to move with the splinters pricking his back.

"Well, then, you'll just have to do." Emilia walked past him, her arms draped with clothes. "I brought a few things, in case what I'm wearing gets ripped." She wore the cafe uniform.

"I meant to ask you—do you play baseball?" He cautiously wiggled himself free of the door. "Oh, that's better."

"No, only volleyball in high school. Why?"

"You have a mean arm." He took what she carried and set them on the stair banister. "My clothes were thrown a pretty good distance from where you stripped me."

"Me?" She laughed. "Someone else was too willing."

"So, you prefer some resistance?" Mark sat on the sofa and faced the fireplace.

"Passion can not be granted, taken, nor borrowed. It blossoms with love." Emilia sat to his side and rested against his chest.

"A mandate of silent emotions," he said. "Listen to me; I'm speaking your lingo."

"Aphorisms," she replied, "are romantic ways to epitomize beliefs. Don't be ashamed to play with them."

"Romance," he continued to play on the theme, "is a nice way to spend the night. Wouldn't it be romantic to have a wood fire? If I wasn't so comfortable, I would start one."

"I'll do it," she offered and stood up from the sofa.

"But wait a minute. Now I'm not so comfortable, just lazy."

"Who's the whiner?" Emilia placed two small logs in the hearth and wagged a lighted match over the wood. "I'm going to cheat and use the gas." She turned the valve of a narrow spigot, and fire surged toward the logs. Twigs burst into flames, and it was not long before the logs were on fire.

Emilia stood in the shadow of the flames and stoked the fire. A gust of heated air completed her satisfaction. Back on the sofa where he reclined, one foot planted on the floor, she lay cradled between his legs. Her head rested on his chest.

"How was your day?" Mark asked.

"I thought it would never end. I kept thinking of you. I called a few times, but there was no answer. The last time I just got a busy signal."

"I'm sorry. I went out for a while."

"Why didn't you stop and say hello?"

"No, no," he said as he gently massaged her head. "A bird crashed into the window and died. I thought you would want me to return it to its ancestral spirits. So I buried it, and followed the cry of birds calling from the forest. I saw many beautiful things, and I guess I stayed out too long." He disregarded the urgency of the nurse's call.

"Ancestral spirits? You're sounding native. Are you getting off your John Wayne horse to smoke the pipe?" She touched his hand.

"I have found my inspiration," he replied and held her hand to kiss. "I will trek on no horse when my squaw walks the earth."

164

"Then we shall see the sunrise together."

"Is that a Cherokee proverb?"

"No, I don't think so. My grandmother often said it, mostly to cheer me. She meant there was no reason to be sad when so much was good. I've made some adaptations to it."

"Like 'cry watercolors,'" Mark added.

"I don't know. Is that a Conquistador proverb?"

"I suppose it's about the same as your grandmother's. My doctor used it," he hesitated and looked back at a message light on the answering machine. "She wanted to stop my self-pity."

"Self-pity can be a matter of comfort, but eventually it becomes destructive. Was this your medical doctor?"

"Why do you want to know? Having suspicions about my mental health?"

"I overcame those suspicions last night," she replied with a snicker. "Your doctor cured the self-pity."

"Why do I want you so much?" He hoped the doctor would not call. "I know you so little."

"Because a lonely man cries."

"There you go with another riddle."

"It's not really a riddle. It's just that some questions can't be answered with a simple response. Instead of an answer, I'd rather provoke thoughts about the question. More insight is gained that way. I suppose you can blame my religious studies."

"All right, but will you explain why a lonely man cries?"

"Beware; I can make it into a doctoral dissertation."

"Let's keep it simple. Consider your audience."

"Simply, when we hurt, we seek to make it better. When you are alone, you search for company," she said.

"Don't you think there's more to why I want you than just being lonely?" he asked with disbelief.

"You asked me to be simple. We could discuss chapter 12, which is destiny, or chapter 15, which is relevancy and mutualism, or chapter 9, which is vulnerability. Better yet, we could forget all those issues and see the sunrise together."

"You're right. But wait. Before the sun rises, answer me this. Why do you want me?"

"Because you invited me to share this moment of our lives."

"But if all it took was an invitation—" Mark hesitated for a deep breath. "Why not a man like Victor?"

He felt a chill as the flames subsided. At the fireplace, Emilia added two more logs and stirred the cinders to provoke the fire. Sparks flared into the spiral of an updraft and disappeared into the flue. Gradually the fire intensified, and warmth was restored. She returned to the sofa and lay prone on Mark, the side of her face resting on his chest. He smelled the balsam fragrance of campfire in her hair.

As one would for a sleeping infant, he watched for her chest to rise, and hoped her silence was discontent rather than detachment. But if he knew anything of Emilia, retreat was not in her character. He rubbed the muscles of her back and waited for a response.

"He told me you met at Maidu," she said.

"Yeah." He pretended nonchalance. There was honor in affection, as much as honor in friendship. He wondered whether, in his complacency of Victor's mockery, he had transgressed either. Was he guilty of love without grace?

"Victor is a wonderful man, but he hides his emotional shortcomings in his physical attributes. With him, there is nothing a good fuck will not heal."

With Bullwinkle's demonic grin, Mark was purged by laughter. "I would have never imagined you ever using that word."

"I told you, we will transgress 'never.'" She raised her head onto her overlapped hands.

He returned her stare, animated by the press of her body. He was aroused. "There may be value in what he thinks."

"What he thinks is not what he does."

"I want to know everything about you: what you think, what you do, where you're from." His finger swept the curve of her eyes and glided on the slope of her nose. The din of his emotions overwhelmed their silence, and he said, "I'm jealous of your memories."

"And if lust is the driver, 'it will sate itself,'" she said, as if to prompt further inquiry.

"Is that another of your grandmother's proverbs?"

"No, it's from Hamlet. It's an inference for wanting more beautiful things."

"Do you think I lust for you?"

"If you do, we have made progress in our relationship."

"Your prose, is it mostly influenced by Cherokee culture? It's difficult to think religion had such a romantic effect."

"I never really thought it one way or the other. It just happened." He waited for a proverb during her pause. "Do you see Native Americans through 'Hallmark' images?"

"What do you mean?"

"We're often depicted as an aboriginal culture grounded by an earthly poetic wisdom, which is epitomized in two to four sentence platitudes inscribed on postcards."

"You have to excuse me then. I did grow up with *Rin-Tin-Tin* and *The Lone Ranger*. I can't deny my ignorance. But isn't that better than vicious stereotypes?"

"Unmerited innocence, as much as shame, is just as harmful," she replied. "I struggle to gain respect on my capacity to transcend 'never.'"

"Please, never doubt my respect for you." He shuffled on the sofa to assert a better posture. "Don't exclude me from your struggles. 'We' are to transcend never."

"There are no differences between the general reference of 'me' and 'we.' From Mother Earth we are raised, and to Mother Earth we succumb. From one to the other, we follow trails our ancestors trekked, which we preserve for our children." She smiled and added, "That is an Emiliasm."

"I can well see you on a picture card." Mark laughed to think of it oil stained and hanging on Trapper Garza's coffee shop wall. "You would be an angel, with wings wide open, aloft over the clear waters of Lake Tahoe."

"And what would be its inscription?" she asked.

"You're better at it than me," he countered.

"But it's your imagery. I wouldn't want to interfere."

"All right, I'll give it a try." He chuckled as he recollected phrases from the past.

Inspiration on a half tank of gas,
but a mile up the road
fog obscured the view.
Winding curves ahead
threatened to intercede,
but an angel aloft
set my spirit soaring.

"That's nice, but not a platitude. Sounds very personal."

"I suppose it describes where I was heading with my life." He brushed his fingers gently through her hair. "An old man summed it up for me when he said he stayed where his folks wanted him to be, rather than go beyond where half a tank of gas would take him. That is, until I came upon you, my angel. Now I feel like soaring above my limitations."

"I'm far from being an angel."

"You must have been once," he said. "What did you do to be cast from the ranks?"

"I was never among them." In the glow of embers, her attention seemed remote. The crackles from the hearth deepened their quiet. "William Boatwright would probably think that," she said, after a delay.

Mark waited for further details, but none followed. "Who is William Boatwright?"

"I called him Billy." The tone in her voice was cheerier when she continued, "My grandmother often told us tales of the ancient Cherokee, which Billy and I would play out in the forest around our home. He was my closest friend in Georgia."

"Was he also Cherokee?"

"We thought it didn't matter to the ancient Cherokee, since he considered himself one. My father, though, called him the 'black boy from down the street,'" she said with remorse.

"I guess he didn't like Billy," he said.

"It wasn't a matter of liking. My father didn't know him beyond his skin color."

"You would think coming from an Indian reservation would make him more tolerant," he said.

"There's never an excuse for prejudice, but I believe it is in all of us, and color is the most vivid capitulation of judgment. Also, this was Georgia in the seventies, a period of monumental transition in the South. My father was an English teacher in a small Christian college. His survival was dependent on adapting by adopting. He, like the rest of America, has changed since then."

"Were you close to your father?"

"My father was too involved with the torment of my mother's death to be close to anyone," she answered. "Actually, my sister and I were cared for by our grandmother, and since my sister was six years older, I was pretty much left alone. It wasn't until the fourth grade that I had a best friend—that was Billy. He was my companion in the world of my grandmother's ancestral spirits."

"Sounds like the making of a Tom Sawyer story," he joked.

"Pretty much so, but we'll call it 'Pocahontas meets Tom.'"

An occasional spark was all that remained of the embers. A dim lamp in the hall faintly illuminated the living room. She remained prone, the side of her face resting on his chest. Mark felt detached.

"Why would Billy not consider you an angel?" he asked.

Deep sighs accompanied painful thoughts, as if she needed to breathe in life before she could continue. Mark caressed her, wishing to be where her thoughts were.

"You know," she began, "I thought my mother's spirit was among those my grandmother told us about, so the forest became my favorite place to play. Billy and I spent a lot of time in the woods. We thought it would always be our playground."

Mark recalled the prickly blades of grass he lay on to watch the parade of animal clouds on his childhood Sundays.

"Things don't always stay like you wished they would, and a child's game is not so innocent at fifteen. I can't remember why we took a hike that day, but it had been a while since we had last gone into the forest.

"We preferred to hike along the riverbed, since we were more likely to see wildlife along it. It was a beautiful spring day—that is, until a thunderstorm came on us."

"Those can be fun, though," he interjected, fearful to be left out as she reminisced.

"Sure they can, as well as test your mettle, especially when the storm arrives as rapidly as deer dodged our imaginary spears. But the weather wasn't unusual, and storms often passed quickly. So we tried to wait it out in an abandoned lair. We were more afraid of the coyote returning to its home than we were of the storm."

"Sounds like you're building suspense." He regretted his effort to be jovial when she continued with a slight tremor in her voice.

"Our clothes were soaked through before we got inside the small shelter. Billy's T-shirt clung to him, and I saw him as I had not seen him before. He seemed more muscular, more attractive. I glanced at myself and saw my body exposed through my wet clothes. For the first time, I felt embarrassed with Billy. I sat on the ground, with my legs folded to my chest, and hoped he hadn't noticed. Billy crouched next to me.

"The thunder was loud, and the rain heavy, but we were well protected. I wasn't afraid, except for the feelings that stirred within me. We remained silent, since there was not much reason to shout over the noise of the storm. He stared at the lightning, as if to force his thoughts from where mine had roamed. I wanted him to hold me."

Jealousy and self-pity, he realized, were well entwined; but Mark was free of either feeling, for he began to feel her pain.

"My grandmother had often warned that a man's eyes lead him to desire. I became limp when he turned his gaze on me. Billy embraced me firmly, and we lay on the dirt ground. My lips seemed so slender against his full ones. The breath from his broad nose warmed me, and I wondered if mine was too narrow. The color of my skin was white against the stout black of his. His muscles felt hard against the suppleness of mine. I envied him our differences, but it was why I wanted him.

"He touched me where I hadn't imagined I could be touched, and I touched him where I never had thought to touch. I don't know if it was pain, or if I didn't want it to hurt, but I cried when he thrust himself against my pelvis. Billy stopped and brushed away my tears. We remained embraced on the floor, not knowing what would follow. I only knew I didn't want him to let me go."

Emilia paused, and slightly shifted her hip before she continued, "I raised my hand from where I had felt a trickle on my thigh, and my fingers were stained with the redness of blood. He sat up, and mirrored my fright. Billy rolled up his white T-shirt, and helped insert it inside of me. The blood stopped flowing, but he sat away from me, farther than we had ever been."

In the impotence of the confessional, Mark learned the delusion of comforting the bereaved and guilty. With Emilia, he realized that love granted its own absolution, and the will to live beyond the pain. Mark held her tight against himself, not so much to comfort her, but with a wish to have been with her then.

"After he walked me home, I never saw Billy again."

Implicit in the tenderness of her voice was an untold story. Her subsequent silence ripped through Mark, like a pull of the blinds on a voyeur. "What became of Billy?" Mark heard himself ask.

"We stayed away from wherever we knew the other would be." She hesitated before she continued, "Late in the summer, my father rushed to tell me 'Billy boy must have gotten himself into trouble.' Police and an ambulance were at his home when I got down the block. I didn't see him or the family." Her body trembled, and her voice quivered. "The following day, I read in the paper that Billy went into his closet and shot himself in the head." Emilia looked at Mark and cupped his hand over her lips. After she kissed his palm, she cried. "He never even left a note."

I'm sorry...I'm sorry
Mark said to himself
I'm sorry...I'm sorry
He held her tight
I'm sorry...I'm sorry
Mark also cried

Chapter 19

Sunrise never seemed to happen over the mountain peaks that rose five thousand feet above his eastern view. As well, the thicket of the forest dimmed the light if it ever did occur. He, therefore, had never found reason to greet the dawn. But then, he was on a quest to transcend never.

With each breath, he felt Emilia's naked flesh brush against his own. He remained motionless and watched her sleep. But for fulfilling her grandmother's proverb, he hated to make a stir.

A strip of light fell across her face and roused her. "Good morning," she said and strained to open her eyes. "You didn't leave me?"

"Why would you think that?" They had not made physical love that night, but he felt just as gratified. There was nowhere else in the world he preferred to be. "Actually, I haven't moved from where you kissed me, before you fell asleep."

"Well, I hope you got some sleep."

"I just wanted to stay up all night and watch over you." He lifted her hair away form her face when she rolled toward him.

"Good," she replied and moved closer. "I've needed a guardian angel."

"That would be a full time job; but if that's what you need, then it's what I'll be."

Emilia reached for his kiss. "What time is it?" she asked, as if to the light coming through the open blinds.

"About six."

"The first angelic order," she said, and threw the comforter away from her, "is to get me out of bed on time. You're going to get me fired." She rushed to the bathroom.

"Me?"

"You should have woken me earlier," she called from the bathroom, her voice followed by the sound of the shower's spray.

"You didn't tell me what time you were going in." He recovered the comforter from the foot of the bed. "Actually, I was hoping you would sleep away the rest of the morning."

Her arms crossed to cover her breasts, she stood naked at the door to the bathroom and asked, "Would you scrub my back?"

The glow of her smile imparted warmth he felt when she dropped her arms to her side. She quickly turned and walked back to the shower.

A man's eyes lead him to desire, he heard her grandmother warn, but he was no exception. Mark jumped from under the covers and followed her.

The contagion of her giggle belied the complexity of her prose. Her smile was gratification, and a temptation. *Desire,* he thought then, *was to want more of what is beautiful.* And that she was, with the sheen of water that dripped from her flesh. *I envy her our differences,* he rephrased her words, *but it is why I want her more.*

In front of the mirrors, she dressed and brushed her hair. He dried with her towel and then, gilded with her fragrance, said, "I thought you were going to be late."

"You have to give me credit for planning," she laughed. "I told Laura I was going to be an hour late."

"Didn't she wonder why?" he asked. He dressed in shorts and a T-shirt.

"I told you she doesn't mind if it's because of a man."

"I hope it's not just any man." He hugged her from behind and whispered into her ear, "I want to be the only one with whom you see the sunrise." Emilia turned to him within the embrace, and with her hands cradled his face, drawing him in for a kiss.

174

"There will be no other," she answered. Stepping back, she asked, "What does that say on your shirt?"

"Orale," he read from the reflection on the mirror. "The accent is on the le. It's an exclamation of pleasure, approval, elation, or victory. Chicano slang for something like 'hurray.'"

Patches of moisture showed on his shirt. He retrieved the towel, and as he finished drying, Emilia lifted the shirt to lick at the beads of water on his chest. "Orale," he exclaimed, his eyes closed with pleasure, approval, and elation. *Victory*, he thought, *can be pursued later.*

She pushed him flat on the bed. "That's just a teaser," she said. "You'll have to wait 'til tonight. I've got to get to work."

"How about breakfast before you leave? I'll make it while you finish getting ready."

"Maybe some coffee. I don't have much time."

Mark whistled on his way to the kitchen. *A child's game is not so innocent at fifteen*, he thought while he prepared coffee, *but it sure can be more fun.*

He noticed the red flash of the answering machine and watched; it seemed to issue a dare. But startled by the kettle's incessant shrill, he turned away and lowered the heat. Flushed by the steam of the water he poured into the cups, he decided to retrieve the message after Emilia had left.

In the whirlpool of the coffee he stirred, he envisioned Emilia's hazel eyes. Gleefully, he pledged to write a poem and serve her with a romantic adjective.

"'My mistress' eyes are nothing like the sun,'" he said to himself. "'Coral is far more red than her lips' red.'"

"What did you say?" she asked from the top of the stairs.

When he turned to her voice, the hot coffee sloshed from the cup he carried. "I was just seeking inspiration from Shakespeare's words, and more wisdom on lust."

"My tease was effective then?" She entered the kitchen. "There is no greater overture of love than poetry."

"Oh, that hurt," he said and quickly handed her the cup. Under a cold stream of water, he cooled his burned hand. "What greater inspiration is there than pain? Especially for a poem on romance. Let's see if a muse has come my way." He worked the muscles of his face, pretending troubled thoughts. After a deep breath, with closed eyes, he continued:

"My flesh,
seared and impassioned,
flushed in your presence,
bereaved when you are away."

"It has potential," she said with a laugh. "Maybe you can work on it the rest of the day." She took a few sips and left the cup on the counter. "I better get going."

"Do you really have to go?" he asked on their way to the door. "Can't you call and say you've been kidnapped?"

"I did ask for a week off." Emilia stopped at the door. "My boss is supposed to let me know today. But it's kind of iffy on short notice."

At that moment, sunlight burst through the opened door. He was stunned to a halt, two steps behind her. "One week?" he asked. "Just you and me? Emilia, that would be great." He embraced her.

"Let's not get too excited. I don't think he'll be able to give me the time just yet."

"We can start making plans, though," he said. "We can go somewhere that's not so cold, where we can lay nude on the beach."

"A quiet time together would be nice. But let's hold off planning until I know for sure."

"I suppose I can be patient. We'll do anything you want. An entire week together." His voiced was subdued when he added, "I hope I won't bore you."

"My grandmother has a saying—'the chestnut grows best where the tree blooms full.'"

"Your grandmother is going to think I'm a fool. I can't seem to understand her sayings. What does she mean by it?"

"Simply, what nurtured the tree will nurture the seed. In our case, passion is that seed. It will flourish nearest from whence it came—you, and me. There's no way we would get bored."

He leaned against the door. "Would your grandmother have a saying for the fool a man becomes when he lives his life alone?" he said, with a stare at his feet. "How would I know to share when I've not had to?"

"Take a note of your friend, Shakespeare, who wrote, 'the hearts upon our sleeves.'" Emilia cuddled to him; her hands slipped under his shirt. "What is pleasure for you is pleasure for me. It takes no skill to do what you feel, just the courage to know it's right. When I get bored, I'll just have my way with you." Her body pressed against his, and they laughed into a kiss.

From the door, Mark returned her wave as she drove by. He remained outside to think about a poem. *Which would work better as premise for a poetic metaphor,* he wondered, *a chestnut, or a heart on the sleeve?* He had a bountiful selection from the proverbs he had been told, but decided he'd better work on one of his own.

The distant ring of the phone evoked his attention; but only his taped voice, inviting a message, was heard, followed by the click of a terminated call.

As if transfixed at a railroad crossing, Mark stood by the phone and stared at the red flash of a message, still waiting to be heard. He felt sure it was Dr. Revels, yet hesitated to listen. He would not submit to persuasion. He would not leave Emilia.

Startled by the phone's clamor, he impulsively took the receiver. "Hello?" he asked with apprehension.

"Mark?" a female voice asked. "Did I wake you up?"

"Oh, no, no," he stuttered, like a weighted train out of the station.

"This is Betty," she answered. "You couldn't have forgotten us already. Or are you busy?"

"Betty. I'm sorry. My mind was off on another tangent."

"Is everything okay? Arren and I—we have been worried. He said something about you going up there to cover up a murder."

"You're kidding." He enjoyed the relief of laughter. "He didn't really say that, did he?"

"He was only joking, but I can tell he's worried."

"I'm here to reclaim a life," he said. "My life, that is. Just as you suggested, I came to find the answers directly from the poet." His mind wandered to Emilia's abstractions, and he thought himself incapable of writing a loving poem. "I'm glad you called. How is everything in the publishing business?"

"Well, we are still using ink to get the message out. It hasn't been that long for anything to have changed," she replied. "Arren loved your short story, but is already worrying about you getting the next one in on time. Leave it to Arren to worry about something. By the way, your doctor's office called yesterday. The nurse said they had to get a hold of you right away. I gave them your number." A more serious voice followed her pause. "Have you any idea what it's about?"

"Gee, Betty. You sound like you expect them to give me a death sentence. It's more probable the insurance forms didn't go through." He glanced at the red flash.

"Yeah, that's probably true. I suppose the doctor would consider it a death sentence if he didn't get his money. Would they take a kidney back if you didn't pay for the transplant?" Betty chuckled. "I better get going. Arren will dock me for being late. Let me know how it goes with the poet and the doctor."

"Sure will. Thanks, Betty, for caring. I appreciate it. Tell Arren the body has decomposed and is in the trunk of his car."

"Oh, he'll love that," Betty said and hung up.

With his stare on the railroad cross light and the dial tone bellowing into his ear, Mark hesitated to make the call. But Betty's concern prodded him to press the numbers.

"Internal Medicine," responded a voice on the other end.

"Dr. Revels, please," Mark requested, the tone of his voice suggesting a demand.

"Who's calling?"

He recalled the secretary's name. "Nancy, this is Mark Balcon. She left a message for me to call."

"Yes, please hold," Nancy directed.

Before the musical note had carried a tune, a second person came on the line. "Mr. Balcon, we've been trying to reach you. We need you come in today." It was Dr. Revels.

Had their request been repeated too often, or had he played it in his mind too many times? In either case, it irritated him. "Did my insurance not accept the claim?" he asked, somewhat hostile.

"It has nothing to do with your insurance," she replied cordially. "I have to review some of the lab results with you."

"Can we do it over the phone? I won't be able to go in for a while." He imagined Emilia's hand under his shirt and an uninterrupted week at her side. "I'm in Lake Tahoe, and I can't leave just yet."

"Mr. Balcon—" She accented her requests with formalities. "Some of your results are critical. I can only discuss them with you in person, and it cannot wait."

"It's just going to have to wait until I get back to San Jose." They battered him with their demands.

"When will that be?"

Not until forever, he hoped. "I don't know. One or two weeks, I think."

"Mr. Balcon," she continued, "I wish we had time to wait." Her voice trailed as if into a thought. After a tedious pause, she added, "I took the liberty of having your blood smears reviewed by two pathologists. They both agreed that there is the strong probability that you have acute myelogenous leukemia."

He heard nothing else the doctor said, but it had to do with further tests and investigations, about doctors to see and treatments to be considered. They were words without feelings, and the only word he could clearly recall was *leukemia*. There was nothing said about his wanting to be with Emilia.

He had promised her to transcend never, to enjoy their future. But a trap was laid: never was intertwined with the future. Could one be overcome, he wondered, without severing the other? On the phone, the doctor tried to explain—only he did not want to understand.

The red flash of the railroad cross sounded an alarm, *But where was the immediacy?* he thought, but never asked.

"Let me call you back." He hung up the phone.

Chapter 20

*W*ords are engendered with ideals, Confucius taught, which their namesakes should be made to suit. Human beings should live up to the ideals built into their language. Through it, man can attempt to understand and affect his world. To care for language is to care for that world. In his writings, Mark had gone beyond the bounds of language. He had mastered his world.

The finality of Dr. Revels' words revealed a betrayal that threatened his life. They transcended ideals, to the loneliness of a life without Emilia, of a futile destiny the cool moisture of his palms would not wash away, a wish to cry no tears would indulge, an absolute emptiness within his chest that his pounding heart could not fill. These words were an abstraction, a metaphor he would become.

◆ ◆ ◆

Even after a vigorous pull, the door didn't open. Neither did it respond to a push. Someone's finger, though, rasped on the window and directed his attention to the sign that noted the library did not open until ten in the morning. *It'll only be a thirty-minute wait,* he thought, and stepped back a few feet, but he stared at the glass door, as if to call its bluff.

Stacks of books were visible inside. They seemed like old friends; but he sought their betrayal.

A wind shook the bristles of the pine trees and swept the cotton fibers of his T-shirt. *Orale*, he thought, and supposed Emilia's fingers the stream of the breeze.

The stone under his bare feet did not distract his stare as Mark considered the reflection on the glass door:

It appeared like the image of a ghost, all in white. Perched on his head was a black ten-gallon hat; a rattler skin formed the ribbon on the inside of its brim. Readied pistols were holstered at his sides, while eager fingers edged the ivory handles. As he walked the dirt street, his hips carried his feet. He gradually neared, then stopped in a wide stance, recognizing the features of the opponent he knew as "Leukemia." Glacier blue eyes pierced the distance. His hairless face, drawn to a squared chin, bore only the shadow of the hat. His broad shoulders projected beyond the barrels of the pistols. He was hauntingly handsome. As they stood before each other, there was no doubt of their intent. Mark reached for his empty pockets as a metallic bang sounded.

"Good morning," said the librarian and flung Mark's foe to the dirt when she swung open the library door. "Isn't it a lovely morning? But aren't you cold?" She gazed at his T-shirt, shorts, and bare feet. He continued, without reply, to the inside.

Rows of shelves were laden with books, radiating from either side of the central lobby. The librarian's counter was just to the side of the entrance. Inside, the hall was bright, lit by the sun, which shone through the large windows on all four walls. Mark was instantly drawn to the reference section, opposite to the librarian's counter.

Footsteps that had followed him in dispersed among the other aisles. He stood alone among the reference books. Mark studied their titles and wondered where to begin. There was demographic data, economic statistics and literary annotations, but he was at a loss for medical references.

He couldn't recall if he had ever done such research; the characters he wrote about were more likely to die from common ailments—the bullet inflicted in conflict, and a scorned lover's vengeful stab. Who would not turn the page if ahead lay the threat of a cave-in at the silver mines, or an avalanche in the high Sierras? In the Old West he wrote about, no one died of acute myelogenous leukemia. "Or did they?" he asked aloud.

"Did you need some help?" asked the librarian from behind the desk counter, where she shuffled through returned books.

Mark turned toward her. Except for the finger that had rasped the window, or the voice that had welcomed him in, he had not noticed her. With hair fastidiously combed, a plain dress buttoned at the collar, and a plaid woolen scarf wrapped about one shoulder, she seemed maternal. A June Cleaver to sort out one's troubles.

"Thank you." He forced a polite monotone, afraid his voice would fail. "Where are your medical references?"

"Let me show you," she said and walked toward him. At the small reference section, she added, "I'm sorry we don't have much of a medical reference, but I think it will be a good start-ing point."

Stowed beyond literary references, before economic vital sta-tistics, was a small pack of medical books. As she selected a thick paperback, he contemplated on the logic for the sequenc-ing of the subjects, but could not think of any.

"This one might have what you're looking for," she said, and coaxed the book into his hand. "What, in particular, are you re-searching?"

Typical wounds in marital discontent, he would have pre-ferred to have said and aroused the librarian's romantic interest. Leukemia would only incite pity. Instead, he blurted, "I'm not sure yet." He balanced the heavy book on the palm of his hand. "But I'm sure I'll find what I need in here."

"If I can be of any help, you know where I'll be." She re-turned to the counter to shuffle through the stack of books.

Mark scanned the index while he carried the book to the reading table. "Acute myelogenous leukemia," he silently read. Seated at the far end of the table, Mark stared at the words and repeated each for its own merit. "Acute" was innocent, and "leu-kemia" feminine. These seemed agreeable. "Myelogenous," though, was villainous, and if the company kept determines character, he decided the doctor's suspicion was evil.

He skimmed through the laborious medical discussion and wondered if a threat existed in an adversary that required only three pages of deliberation. It didn't even have its own chapter. He recognized no implications with signs and symptoms, but dismissed the thought he was delusional.

The details of its pathology were fogged by medical terms he had to read many times over to understand. It was a foreign language. But the English seemed to inflict a growing sense of vulnerability. In untreated cases, there was complete fatality; in treated cases, there was a twenty percent cure beyond three years.

He snapped the book shut and threw it to the edge of the table. His eyes moistened as he stared away. He was betrayed.

"Then we'll see the sunrise together," he heard Emilia say in his thoughts. With no tears streaming down his cheek, only resting in his muted eyes, he peered beyond the window to the crown of trees outside, and listened for her to continue, "No reason to be sad when so much else is good."

He returned his vision to the room, and his attention to what he read. There were no alternative treatments. Discussed was how to improve quality of life, its depreciation resulting from the treatment's side effects. His thoughts focused on the apparent contradiction.

Should life not be quality? he wondered, and snickered that he be the judge. Yet to the acrimony of the echoes that resonated from the fronting shelves, he answered with thoughts of Emilia.

Settled back in the chair, his hands folded over his lap, Mark contrasted his life of cloistered emotions and his passion with Emilia. There was no contradiction, he decided. Life was quality of its own accord. With a loosely fisted hand, he brushed away a single tear. "There are no alternatives," he said.

From the clock on the wall, he counted three hours until Emilia would finish her shift. It was not news he wanted to share, but because she was part of him, it was news he had to tell. The three hours would be difficult, but he would wait until they were alone.

Captivated with thoughts of Emilia, he felt restless. He marveled at how love accorded anticipation, whereas loneliness required resignation. Acknowledging an impulse, he stood. The chair screeched loudly on the concrete floor. Mark turned to the librarian, who responded with a tender smile to his grimace of apology.

The pages sounded hollow when he pressed the book back into the shelf. Noticing how its hardcover neighbors gripped it, he hoped to exact revenge for the treachery within, and walked away with vigor in his stride. The wisdom of his heart was now his only duty.

"Did you find everything you needed?" asked the librarian as he walked by her counter toward the door.

"Yes, thank you, very much," he answered, and waved his hand.

With the sun at midday, high above the forest, the asphalt felt warm beneath his feet. He turned to the sound of a metal clang when the door closed behind him. The reflection of his prior menace, he noticed, had vanished from the glass.

Idleness with imagination is froth with temptation to think on better times. He sat inside his truck, captivated by the veins that coursed the back of his hands, as thick as shoelaces.

He placed his palms against the windshield and felt the warmth of sunlight coming through the glass. A cool, gentle breeze drifted through the gap of the side window and whisked through his hair. If only it was as simple, he thought, to conjure the moisture of her lips and the softness of her breasts.

◆ ◆ ◆

He drove through town to the beach. All he could recall was the moment he opened the truck's door at the waterfront park. It was the perfect place to wait, as the cool of spring kept visitors away, and the unobstructed sunshine warmed the sand. In the higher altitudes, where white still trimmed the mountain peaks, cold persisted.

He strolled along the water's edge as frigid alpine water lapped at his feet. Shielded from the road by a row of trees,

Mark sat on the warm sand and listened to the rhythm of gentle waves, which harmonized the ripple of a sporadic breeze.

He removed his T-shirt and felt the strength of the sun. It was the right occasion for a first-time nap in the nude. Naked, he shaped a sand angel, into which he set himself spread-eagle. The rhythm of the water lulled him to sleep.

A throat-clearing sound startled him. Mark focused his eyes on the clear blue sky, but remained still within his imprint on the sand. The stinging flush on the skin of his chest suggested he had overslept.

"Excuse me, sir," a masculine voice announced from beyond his field of vision. "But what do you think you're doing?"

Mark bolted up and turned to the voice. A forest ranger stood a few feet away. "Just celebrating my birthday," he blurted and shielded his eyes to the sun. The face of the ranger was familiar. "You're the guy at the gym," he exclaimed.

"But now I'm the ranger on this beach, and nude bathing is not allowed. I would appreciate it if you celebrate your birthday like all other middle-age men and put your shorts on," he replied.

Shadowed by a flat-brimmed hat that seemed borrowed from a Yogi Bear cartoon, his face was guileless. His muscular arms were less daunting when covered by long sleeves. The ranger didn't appear the demigod of their first encounter.

"Aren't you supposed to be protecting the birds and bears in the forest?" Mark asked in defiance. There was no one else on the beach. Why did his nakedness matter?

"My job is to enforce the laws that protect them." The ranger's voice softened.

"And how does being naked threaten your bears?" he asked. "All I want to do is tan my penis. I've not done it before, and I think it's about time I do."

"I don't think that's going to happen," the ranger snickered.

"And I suppose you're going to handcuff me." Mark was annoyed at the challenge.

"That won't be necessary," the ranger answered, and

glanced at Mark's groin. He added with a laugh, "It's shriveled up into its hood, where it's well protected."

Mark looked at himself and covered up. Rapidly he stepped into his shorts, but then joined the ranger in laughter. "So, you won't use force, but will revert to insults."

"I'm sorry, man. I couldn't help but notice." The ranger's face relaxed into a smile. With an extended hand, he added, "Congratulations on your birthday."

"Thank you." Mark shook the ranger's hand. "But it's not my birthday."

"I thought you said it was."

"No. I am just celebrating my birth." The breeze felt like it scraped the burnt skin of his chest. He partly stuffed the shirt he retrieved from the sand into his pants' pocket. He thought it would chafe the burn. "My name is Mark," he said, and walked to the picnic table the ranger had sat on.

"I'm Shannon," the ranger responded. "Thanks for covering up. If I were a betting man, I would wager this was an act of love."

"Why would you think so?"

"Only lovers seem to do foolish things," Shannon said.

"Like go naked on a cold spring day celebrating their birth?" Mark took a seat across the picnic table from Shannon.

"Not so much that," Shannon replied. He leaned forward and gripped his hands between clasped thighs. "But wanting to tan your penis? Ouch! Now, that is insanity. Only a woman can make a man think to do something like that."

Mark responded with a broad smile, and considered how sunburn on his penis would feel. *So this was love,* he thought. *The confidence to be foolish and not care for the consequences.* If that is the case, Emilia will not be bored. There was a boundless repertoire of activities to explore.

"Your thoughts are so heavy, I can almost see her," Shannon remarked.

"I'm sorry. You have good observation skills. You suppose it's from watching out for those bears?"

"Maybe, but more likely from watching lovers approach each other in the forest. It's like lifting a veil of indiscretion."

"You're right in my case. I wouldn't have considered going nude on a public beach, otherwise," Mark said. "You might know the cause of my folly—Emilia Locklear."

"Emilia, the waitress at Maidu?" The incredulity in his voice irked Mark.

"Yes, sir," he replied.

A gentle breeze rippled across his chest; he imagined her fingers upon his flesh. "Orale," he countered, and stared into Shannon's eyes, as if into the reflection of the lake. He hoped she would soon be home.

"You know, I was just there at Maidu's for lunch. It was pretty slow. She was thinking about leaving early. Do you want me to call her to meet you here?"

"Yeah, that would be nice." Mark turned and raised one leg to straddle the bench. He stared away. A shadow of a single cloud darkened the distant lake. Waves on the open waters warned of the wind's surge. Yet, on the beach where he sat, the afternoon sun was radiant with pleasant warmth. *Was there ever a best time for confession*, Mark thought, *and could it be accompanied with a proclamation of love?*

"I have a crazed man lying naked on the beach, aiming to be arrested, unless a responsible party can guarantee his safeguard," Shannon said into the cellular phone on the return from his vehicle. "He has identified you as the source of his delusions."

If delusions bore a motive, Mark thought, it was to grant happiness. That being the case, Shannon's appeal to Emilia was befitting.

When the call was completed, the ranger rested his booted foot on the adjoined bench. In the comfort of the subsequent silence, they shared the view.

"Buddy, there are no answers out there," Shannon offered, as if to read Mark's thoughts. "They are all in here." He pointed a finger to his chest over the heart.

Solomon, in Ecclesiastes, concluded that all of life was vanity. In another time, Mark would have agreed. But at that moment, he heard the muted sound of rubber tires on gravel, and the thud of a shut door. With the gentle steps leading to where they sat, Mark felt his life's worth.

"He just wanted to tan his penis," Shannon said to welcome Emilia. "Do you know this man?"

"You might have to line him up with other naked men for me to be sure," she answered. Mark remained on the bench, a smile on his face. She proceeded around the table and sat on the bench by him. Leaned back on the table, she stretched her legs out to the sand. "So, you are the lunatic stirring up the forest so much, a ranger had to restrain you to restore order."

"Since he finally agreed to put his pants back on, I'll be able to release him to your custody."

"But, officer," Emilia interjected. "I won't be able to guarantee his safety later tonight."

"As long as whatever happens does not occur in the forest, it is not my jurisdiction," Shannon said and walked toward the parking lot. "Have a good day."

Mark continued to smile at Emilia and held her hand in his lap. He leaned forward to stroke her hair and drew her closer. Greedily, he kissed her.

Her hand rested against his chest, and she slowly withdrew. "Wow," she said. "That's a mouth-to-mouth resuscitation for a working woman."

"Will you go with me?" he asked.

"Anywhere you want," she replied and returned his gaze. "Where are you taking me?"

"Fort Hamilton, Nevada."

"What?" she blurted, and then rested her hands on his lap. "What's in Fort Hamilton?"

"I borrowed a life from an epitaph, and I want to return it," he answered without hesitation.

"You think Shannon was right—you are delusional?" she joked. "Isn't Hamilton a ghost town?"

"Yes, it is." He raised her hands from his lap. "I have my own life now, and I don't need a ghost trailing us."

"You're serious." She looked at him as he held her hands to his lips. "Why so somber, Mark? Is everything all right?"

His body shivered when the breeze picked up strength. He glanced away to the louder crash of waves onto the shore.

"You better put your shirt back on. You have goose bumps all over you," she said.

"There's just not enough time." He continued to look, as if to an audience beyond her. After he put the T-shirt on, he returned his gaze to Emilia and said, "But when I'm with you, I feel eternal."

"I suppose it's my turn to get lost in riddles. I don't under-stand what you're talking about."

The quizzical look on her face flustered him. His voice stammered. "My doctor called this morning." He hesitated. *A truth left unsaid cannot exist,* he thought, *but is it then a lie? Does it challenge the integrity of his love?* He was exasperated. "I don't know how to say it."

"Say what, Mark?"

"The doctor said I may have a cute form of leukemia and wants me to return to San Jose for more tests and treatment." He took a deep breath to relieve his agitation.

"Oh, Mark." She reached for his hands and looked into his eyes. After a pause, she said, "I'll go with you to San Jose. They gave me the week off. I can always extend it."

"I hope you can understand," he said, and turned his gaze away from her.

"Understand what?" In her voice, he felt her discontent, and the urge to shake out the feelings that had failed to accompany his plea.

"I can't go through with any of it—the tests or the treatments." To accentuate his resolve, he looked up. "If the treatments are unlikely to succeed, why bother with the testing?"

"Mark." She held his hands with a firm grip. A mist settled in her eyes. "There are no options. I may be a coffee shop wait-ress, but I know there are no 'cute forms of leukemia.' Without treatment, they are all killers. You have to be tested. It may not be leukemia, but we have to find out. Then we can discuss treatments."

The muscles of his face loosened with thoughts of the high-noon encounter. He smiled at the image of the black-hatted villain, knocked to a cloud of dust when the librarian swung open the glass door. If only his imagination wielded such power.

Emilia turned away, as if incensed by his introspection. He lunged from his seat and knelt at her feet. With his hand on her chin, he directed her stare. "Emilia, you have to understand why I can't go through with it."

"I can't allow you to die." Her eyes glistened with tears. "I can't deal with any more guilt."

"There is no guilt to be had." He wiped a tear that cascaded on her cheek. "You have given me a life I never considered having, Emilia. Billy took his own life because he surrendered to his pain, but it was pleasure he most feared, and that is life. It requires responsibility to be sustained, which a pained heart is not capable of. It's how I've lived my life until now—afraid to take the risk of pleasure for fear of being hurt."

"I survived by borrowing the life of a ghost." He sat back on his heels and rested his hands on the bend of his knees. After a pause to brush away his own tear, he said, "It was the life of a dead man—one who could never be vulnerable, whose life was fully narrated on a wooden tombstone. It simply read, 'Born April 7, 1891; died November 29, 1913.'"

Silence carries its own memory, and the loneliness of that day in the cemetery recurred to him. Mark felt the distance his thoughts imposed between them.

"He was only 22 years old, the same age I was then." He propped himself up with his arms behind him and stretched his legs between her feet. With the resolve of a storyteller, he continued, "I stood before his grave for a long while and imagined what his life must've been like. But the more I thought about him buried below my feet, the more exaggerated I made the particulars. Eventually, I grew jealous."

"Why be jealous of a dead man?" She leaned forward. Elbows bent on her knees, she steepled her hands to support her chin.

"Until then, I had isolated my life by guilt. The ghost, though, had lived carefree, with adventure. His life seemed more appealing than mine, and so I determined to assume his character." Mark chuckled. "It's ironic that now it seems his life was just as ordinary. There was no passion portrayed on the epitaph I read; his name was not given, nor was there mention of a family to pray for his eternal rest. There wasn't even an angel carved on the wood to guard his mortal repose. He was probably buried by a bureaucrat."

"What did he die of?" she asked.

"I don't know for a fact, but that didn't stop me from given him a cause. When I stood over his grave, I actually heard the gun battle at the saloon where he sustained the fatal wound, as well as the cry of the chorus girl he fought over." They both laughed. "He probably died of something less romantic, like consumption."

"What is that?"

"I think it's tuberculosis."

"Imagination can sure be a double-edged sword," she said.

Quiet, laden with anticipation, settled between them. She gazed at him as he glanced at the margins of the forest and lake.

"This forest has been my refuge for many years," he said. "Like the pine box the dead man was buried in." He motioned his arms to the expanse of the forest, as if to gather the view into his words. "But what a casket I have had."

As quick as his arms dropped to his lap, his voice changed to scorn. "How incidental my life has been." He reached for her hands, and she tightly grasped his. "Your flesh upon mine, your breath I want so much to be my own, your sorrow I intend to make amends for. These have made me beyond incidental. I mattered; you granted me a life."

He pulled her to him, and they sat on the sand, embracing. "You are part of me, as I wish to be of you, and as we are of this life. I beg you to understand why I can't hide away in a twenty-percent chance of survival. To kill time with treatment is to kill eternity. I'll take life on its own accord, even if the ultimate is death."

Chapter 21

$\mathcal{A}$ mirror of still life was their imprints on the sand, framed in the shadows cast by the waning sun. It was their pleasure memorialized.

They strolled barefoot toward the parking lot, but then Emilia made a sudden turn and ran back. In the momentum of her spin, Mark was whirled in her direction. He stood still and watched what she would do.

In each hand, she held a shoe, and with a lifted foot, she scraped the sandy reflection of themselves. After the shadows resembled other small knolls on the beach, she returned to his side.

"You didn't want ghosts trailing us." A relaxed smile adorned her face. More than the act of their love, the words avowed her intent to follow.

"How will you ever manage with me?" He caressed her firm against his chest, the fibers of his T-shirt their only distance.

"I don't know," she replied. With her arm around his waist, she led him to their trucks. "Let's go find out."

From the parking lot, Emilia glanced back to the trail their staggered feet had shaped. "Do you think Shannon would have objected?"

"Oh, I'm pretty sure he knew what would happen when he got you out here," he said, and held her truck's door open. "But I don't think he cared, as long as no underage bear was watching."

Clouds loomed over the western range behind them, and in their relative altitudes, appeared to travel faster than from sea level. Darkness approached rapidly as she followed his truck up the hill. But through the rear view mirror, he felt as if he was at her side.

If only time would slow in the cloud's wake, Mark thought, *like the whorl of dust that tailed the truck*. He looked back, as if to recapture the time he had lost. Emilia followed.

◆◆◆

Mark had not wanted to sleep—not that night, or ever again. If the wind blows, he thought, the dust never settles. But he was exhausted when he lay back on the bed and was asleep before Emilia had changed.

That morning, his first glance was at the wrinkled sheet at his side. His arm wrapped around her pillow, he inhaled her fragrance. There was no need to rush. From the footsteps above, he knew she was preparing breakfast.

"Have you ever fallen asleep while making love?" he asked from the kitchen's doorway. He watched her scurry about the counter opposite to him.

"What?" She turned to him, her mouth half open in surprise.

"I've been admiring you for the last three minutes, and it dawned on me how little I know of you." His arms, folded at his chest, dropped to his sides. "I want to know everything about you."

The egg flew across the kitchen, and Mark was late to dodge. "Oh, my god! I'm so sorry," she said. "I didn't mean to hit you. You were supposed to catch it. Oh, god, I'm sorry!"

"Well, now I know for sure what a deadly throw you have." The yolk dripped from his forehead. "Not only do you have a good arm, but quite a temper." He wiped his brow and added, "But it only makes me want you more!"

"What? Were you fooled by my sunny disposition?" She carried a dishtowel and walked to where he stood. "I just wanted to make breakfast. Aren't you the man of habit who always has his eggs over and easy?" She cleaned the wall behind him. With each swipe, her body swayed against his. "It can't get easier than this."

"No, it certainly can't. You did manage to get it all over me." He wrapped his arms around her from behind. "I think you aim to fry it with my own heat." He kissed the nape of her neck and felt the warmth of her flesh. His breath quickened, and she turned in his embrace.

She licked the yolk on his eyebrow. "Easy," she said softly, her lips on his. "Let me churn the fire."

Emilia untied the sash of his bathrobe, and brushed her hands through the egg on his head. "Over and easy. It's how you want it," she said and arched back. With her pelvis pressed against his, she let the slime of egg white ooze from her palms as she massaged it into his chest.

"Breakfast has never been served like this." He dropped the bathrobe and gently lowered her on it. With an outstretched arm supporting his weight, he ripped open her blouse, but paused, as if surprised by a gift. "You are part of me, as I am of you, and as we are of this life," he said. "I want to love you with all my soul."

◆ ◆ ◆

"What about the country potatoes?" He stepped out of the shower and into the towel that she held open around her. "They're actually my favorite part of breakfast."

"Oh, I didn't finish." She rushed into the bedroom. Mark remained naked under the heat lamp.

Spiced with cilantro and bacon bits, she served the country potatoes with two eggs. "I am in heaven," he said as he dipped buttered sourdough toast into the yolk. "Who would have thought—two fine breakfasts in one day."

She stopped his hand from reaching for the napkin and leaned toward him. With a swipe of her tongue, she licked the breadcrumbs from his mustache, and a bead of yolk on his lip.

"I can't wait 'til lunch," he said, his eyes closed as if to retain the pleasure. "It'll be my turn to cook, and be warned—revenge is sweet."

With her elbows bent on the table, she rested her cheek on her clasped hands and maintained her stare. "Life was simple," she said, "when I had all the answers."

"Don't tell me you don't." He sat back in his chair, appreciating the interruption. "I was hoping to get them cheaply."

"I thought that I could judge your character by the way you eat." She sat back in capitulation. "But looking at you now, I have to second-guess everything I considered."

"Uh-oh," he said. "I make love without grace?"

"Don't get me wrong. It's almost poetry watching you enjoy breakfast, even if the syntax never varies." She shuffled in her chair. "I just have to remind myself that, no matter what we ex- perience together, we offer only a glimpse of our capacity."

"To transcend never is what you're saying?" he asked.

Swiftly, she stood up from her chair and said, "Come with me. I have some things I have to pick up from my house."

A loud screech of the chair on the wooden floor sounded when he stood away from the table. "Don't regret this invita- tion," Mark said as he followed her to the door. "You'll never shake me off."

◆ ◆ ◆

The wind through the driver's window was all that stirred the scene of the lake. It was like indigo glass fallen from the sky. Only the sun seemed to have ambition. At the lakeshore park, the snow melted, and the granite boulders continued their timeless march. The road rose above the shore, and Mark stretched to see, through the crystalline surface, how deep the water was.

She turned into a wooded valley and drove among ever- greens that rose tall from redwood stalks. Budding leaves were bountiful on the aspens and cottonwoods. In a distant meadow, glimmering in filtered sunshine, two deer strolled among the grasses. It was springtime after a winter rest.

"It's all so beautiful, like a Snow White fairytale," Mark said. "That's right; you are her, and I'm the dwarf Happy."

"You've confused the fairytales again. It's Hansel and Gretel," she responded.

"Oh yes," he said, but added in a sober tone, "Is Hansel still over the fireplace mantle?"

"Of course," she answered, and stopped the truck in front of the rock-faced cabin. "Come with me, little boy. I have some candies I am sure you will enjoy."

Unfettered in the warmth of spring, the wind chime pealed as he chased Emilia through the front door. In the living room, he reached for her from behind and said, "I don't need an oven to be fired up, or a candy to be enticed. Touching you is enough to arouse my desire."

"Ooh!" she exclaimed, and turned to him. "You are a poet and a bit of a cad."

Stretched on her toes to reach for his lips, she returned his caress. As if to safeguard their intimacy, he closed his eyes when they kissed. In the slit of his vision appeared the effigy of Bullwinkle, hung on his pulpit above the mantle. "Oops," he uttered, and then let his arms drop.

"What happened?" she asked.

"I'm sorry," he answered, and feigned a chuckle. "I was spooked by your Bullwinkle friend."

"Hansel," she corrected. "Isn't he the cutest? Maybe I should take him with me."

Mark turned away from the fireplace and walked to the bookcase on the opposite wall. He pretended to browse through a book of native art. "So what are we really taking from your treasure chest?" he asked.

Without a word, Emilia walked past him into the bedroom. He snapped shut the book and waited for a summons, but none followed. Bullwinkle's grin filled his glance. "Not this time," Mark snarled in response.

"What did you say?" she called from the room.

"I like your wind chime," he improvised.

"I got it from the Catskills," she replied. "It keeps me alert to the spirits in the forest."

"That could be scary, when you're here alone and in the dark," he said, watching her rummage through undergarments in the lower drawer of a bedside armoire.

She looked up to where he stood at the doorway. "Have a seat," she offered with a motion to the bed. "There's no reason to be afraid of spirits. They exist everywhere, if we care to pay them heed."

He sat at the corner of the bed, and dropped back on the mattress with an exaggerated bounce. Turned on his side, he watched as Emilia held up a bra. "Will you be modeling those?" he asked playfully, but more earnestly added, "I would still be spooked, being here alone and thinking of ghosts."

"Like you were of Hansel?"

"Well, no. He just annoys me, but to know there are spirits of the dead watching me—that would scare me."

"I suppose it's just how one sees death." Emilia sat back against the side of the bed, with the negligee she had inspected grasped against her breast. He rolled back on the mattress and glanced at the ceiling. Their silence sounded the confession of emotions concealed.

"I'll make sure no ghost trails us," she said with a conciliatory tone in her voice.

Mark could not think of something to say to make everything all right; but he listened to her breath, into which she seemed to dispel her thoughts. His death was not what he wanted to discuss.

"Do you think Shakespeare lived passionately?" he asked, matter-of-factly.

"Mark!" she cried out in surprise. "The questions that come out of you. I swear!"

He reached for the bra she had set on the bed and spun it with his finger. "I need to know. It's important, because if great poetry comes from desire, more so than from an experienced pleasure, I'd better settle for writing you a mediocre poem."

On his overture, she rose from the floor and lay next to him. "Your passion is poetry enough," she said.

Silence bound their embrace, and time cradled their thoughts. In their impassioned universe, they were the earth and the moon.

Framed photographs hung on all walls of her bedroom. In the dim daylight, he focused his attention on them. "Emilia, why do you live alone?"

"I've been waiting for you."

"But I mean—" He released his arm from their embrace and

pointed the walls. "These are of your family. You seem to treasure their memories. Why aren't you with them, in Georgia or Oklahoma?"

"Where would we be then?" she replied.

A deep sigh seemed to propel her to sit up on the side of the bed. She leaned toward a framed photograph that rested on the night table. Mark remained on his flank, but shifted to wrap around her from behind. He looked in the direction of her attention, to the black-and-white image of a young couple. The yellow tint of an aged photograph, or the gray light that sifted through the window, made it difficult to discern the particulars of their semblance.

"They seem much in love," he said, more so to explore her apparent gloom. "Are they your parents?"

She reached for the lamp behind the photograph. The soft light revealed the likeness of her in the couple. "Yes, they are; and, yes, they were much in love."

The past tense of their love offered a supposition. "Did they get divorced?" he asked.

Half-straddling the edge of the bed, she leaned into Mark. With her chin on her folded hands, she rested on his shoulder and continued to stare at the photo.

"They were young and very much in love," she said. "Looking at it now, though, they seem more a euphemism for what eventually happened. It wasn't long after that picture that their dreams were shattered."

Words are engendered with ideals, he recalled, which we should live up to, in order to understand and affect our world. But he wanted to protect her from the pain of what she had said. He turned flat on the bed and supported her weight with his chest. Gently, he brushed her hair and remembered this, their posture for confession.

"You've talked of borrowing a life from an epitaph," she began again, then gestured to the photos on the walls. "These lent me a past. I suppose we both have ghosts to bury?"

"But these are real. They are your family," Mark said. "They are who you are. You can't bury their memories."

"No, I can't, but I can carry them with me. It is that one second of life they portray, in which everything was right, that I cherish. But there is sorrow in their hearts, hidden in their smiles; that is the ghost I've not yet come to terms with."

It is from vulnerability that we seek love, he thought, *and from our sorrow that we gain strength*. But a riddle was a safe haven in which to displace unsettled emotion. An answer would be a shortcoming. He held her closely, because it was all he could do.

"How sad." Spencer Tate's decrying of his loneliness, and the inability to write about romance, stirred Mark. In response to the recollection, he imagined the vulnerable child who gripped the wooden chair, the determined child who promised the world to the infant brother cradled in her arms. What was sad, he decided, was to have denied his own compassion. He remained silent, and awaited the torrent of her emotion.

"I didn't keep the newspaper clippings that reported 'Indian woman kills self,'" she said.

"I am so sorry!" he replied, and at once felt its futility.

"How can someone be truly sorry and not accept guilt?" she asked, as if prompted by his sympathy. "And if one accepts guilt, should punishment not follow?"

"I didn't mean to—" Mark attempted a defense.

"What?" He had interrupted her deliberation, but she continued unaffected. "My grandmother, in her Christian way, would often tell me that there's no love where anger lingers." To a photo of an older woman clad in colorful folkloric dress, she answered the apparent homily, "It is only because of deepest love that anger can be perpetuated."

"With whom are you angry?" he asked, surprised that she bore such sentiment.

"When I was sixteen, Billy committed suicide, never telling anyone why. I was devastated. My father, who had not embraced me since my mother's death, held me then. He still called Billy 'the black boy from down the block,' but he told me he understood my desperation and guilt," She paused; her hands felt tense on his chest. "He said that when my mother had driven

200

the car off the road into the tree, she took his life along with hers. It was his guilt to be alive.

"I had not known until then that she had committed suicide." Her hand tightened to a fist and wiped a tear from her eye. "He said that since my birth, things had been difficult for my mother; she'd suffered bouts of hysteria and withdrawal."

Her brief pause suggested resignation. "All I could say then was that I was sorry. It is all I have ever said to him about her death."

"So, with being sorry you accepted guilt, not only for your mother's suicide, but also Billy's. Was running away from your family the punishment?"

As she stirred and arched back into outstretched arms, she looked at Mark. "You know, I majored in psychology to find an answer. But I didn't, not among the formulas and postulates. What did become clear, though, was that science is man's arrogance. I turned to religion, thinking it to be his humility. But in faith, I only found complacency. That is where I find myself now." She laid her head on his chest and stared at the photograph. "What has the intellect to do with emotion, anyway?"

He lifted her head with a finger at her chin. Her hazel eyes returned his gaze. "Emotion is our response to how intellect interprets life's events," he answered.

Where Emilia had borrowed a life from the images of those she loved, he had buried everything of his past. In her eyes, he saw no anger, only a desire for reconciliation. In him was the emptiness that his fear of love had granted.

Emilia deserved his unburdened love, and he was committed to provide that. He had promised to amend her sorrow, but recalled Bullwinkle's skeptical grin. As if to vindicate himself of their first encounter, he determined to retrieve his past.

◆ ◆ ◆

Mark watched the filtered light from the corner lamp glow on her moistened lips. Her hair, brunette fibers, a veil on her head, rippled like gentle waves to her shoulders. Her skin, tinted by the shadows, drifted to the fullness of her breasts. Her legs, which sloped from the curve of her hips, hung over the side of the bed. He relished the feel of her body.

He wavered with sublimated indulgence, until he noticed in her eyes the reflection of his desire. He held her close, to feel the warmth of her breath, and taste her mouth. With his tongue, he moistened a path to her nipples and felt the softness of her breasts. She tore his clothes and bore her fingers into the muscles of his back. Pressed against him, she took into herself the firmness of his pleasure, and arched her back for a shared surge of delight. In the tremor of her body, he felt his pulse. *Cry in my arms*, he offered, but knew no sorrow to prod the tears. *How does one forgive?* he asked, *when no wrong was committed? How does one take*, he considered, *when all is given?* He loved her completely, and in their love were answers. Her flesh upon his. Her moisture with his scent. Her breath that became his.

In the walls on which hung the photographs, and the forest in which the spirits dwelled, their rapture reconciled the past. They were eternal. The world ended as it began, in each other's arms.

Chapter 22

How does one wake up in another's bed? he thought, and felt for himself under the covers. "Naked," he answered with satisfaction. Turned to Emilia, asleep at his side, Mark considered—revealed, exposed, and vulnerable, but very much in love.

His eyes were wide open, but he couldn't tell in the darkness of the room. In the void of his vision, he searched for a focus and came to a stream of light cast at the foot of their bed. He followed it to the window above their heads, and beyond to the shroud of forest that muted the sun's glow. Emilia's grandmother would, without doubt, bless their sunrise union.

Shadows in the room quickened in the flare of sunlight. Were these the spirits about which Emilia had talked? Or of his own? Mark listened for the chime that remained silent. Prodded by anticipation, he slithered out of bed, so as not to awaken Emilia. From the door, he watched the gentle flicker of her closed lids and hoped she dreamed of him.

In the living room, he followed a cool breeze to the fireplace, as darkness waned with the morning light. Above the mantle, he noticed the Bullwinkle, discolored in shades of gray. With a fisted hand, Mark reformed its sneering grin.

"I found the grace in love," he retorted, and then shadow boxed and feigned a few more jabs. "Take that, Victor," he added, pleased with Hansel's crimped grin.

On the bar table rested a binder packed with loose white paper. A pen rose from it, like a sword in its scabbard. As if it were the hand of an old friend, he gripped it. *Ah, Shakespeare's passion*, he thought.

"'The sword within the scabbard keep, and let mankind agree,'" he recited to himself. "I've chosen my weapon," he rebutted Shakespeare's quotation, "and it is my passion." Mark flailed the pen in the air, and sat down to write. "And beware, sir, that into an ancient tomb it will not keep."

Words flowed from his hand, and ink bled from the pen. In the dim light, Mark felt what would be read, scribed on paper; it was, after all, the poem he wanted for Emilia.

"What are you writing?" she asked from behind him. The pen flew across the kitchen floor, and Mark jerked back into the stool. "Sorry. I didn't mean to scare you."

"It's nothing." He leaned forward to shield the paper, and folded it into a closed hand.

"You're acting awfully suspicious for it being nothing." She combed the back of his head with her fingers.

"It's just a poem." He swiveled the seat around to face her. "But you can't have it until I'm finished."

"You were serious, about writing me a poem?"

He felt the gentle brush of her fingers on his face. With his arms wrapped around her waist, he drew her close. The cotton fibers of her nightgown could not stifle the smell of their love, still on her breasts. "Didn't you say my passion was poetry enough?"

"You are a quick learner." She pressed her thighs against his erection. "But are we creating a monster?"

"I hope so." Mark grabbed the band around her waist with his teeth and loosened the single knot. The gown dropped. He buried his face in the cleavage of her breasts and eased her to the floor. Straddled over her, he leaned forward for a kiss.

"Oh, my god. What happened to Hansel?" Emilia's shriek pierced his ear. Mark fell limp to her side.

"Do you think my penis would grow if I told a lie? Let's see— it was an accident?" Mark kept his face to the floor, while her hand searched for the truth.

"Mark?" she chuckled. "I can't believe you're jealous of that hairball."

"I'll fix it." He stood up and walked to the mantle. The Georgia Tech cap was straightened on its head, but Hansel's snout could not be remolded. A breeze from the fireplace spotlighted his nakedness, and himself, still flaccid. "It was an accident," he repeated, but didn't turn to face her.

"You better go put something on, before I'm tempted to look for more lies."

As if spurned from the Garden of Eden, with the weight of Adam's guilt, Mark attempted one last try. "I tell you the truth," he laughed. "Were it not for the sweetness of your flesh, and the pleasure it has granted, I would still walk contented and naked in the absence of temptation."

"Oh, give me a break. Go get dressed." A thrown pillow accentuated her mocked exasperation. "I'll make some coffee. Maybe that'll speed the blood to your head. On second thought, maybe I shouldn't."

◆ ◆ ◆

The buttons of his shirt were torn off, and the zipper of his pants was ripped. What amused him most was her bra hanging from the lampshade above her parent's photo. How was it that Shannon had described lovers in the forest? "Like lifting a veil from indiscretion."

"You left me nothing to wear," he shouted from the bedroom to Emilia in the kitchen.

"What do you mean?" she shouted back.

"You've torn everything I had to wear."

"I did no such thing." With feigned indignation, she stood at the door. "Take a shower, and I'll get you something to wear."

"Not too much lace at the collar. It gives me a rash."

He lowered his head to pass through the narrow doorway of the bathroom. It seemed the size of a linen closet, probably designed as an afterthought. The original, most likely, had been an outhouse, which he was grateful no longer existed.

He swung his fisted hand in defense against the jolt of cold water from the showerhead. "Wow," he screamed.

"You have to let the water warm for two minutes. Sorry," she called from the room. "I left some things on the bed. I think they'll fit."

A younger man could possibly contort his body to enjoy company in the shower stall, but he had second thoughts that even alone he would fit. "Ah, but what does age matter when love is eternity?" he sang to the spray. The warm water soothed his reservations.

Mark was startled when he stepped out of the shower. He was reflected in the full-length mirror, but in the cloud of steam that filled the room, he conjured an apparition. "A little touchy are we?" He wiped the mist from the glass.

Water dripped from his hair, and a blush reddened the skin of his chest. He outlined its margins to the nipples and felt the imagined flick of Emilia's tongue. His hands coursed over the gentle ripple of muscles in his lower abdomen, and in a tuft of hair, his penis hardened. All lies were absolved. There were no regrets for any second of his life that led to that moment.

◆ ◆ ◆

At the foot of the bed were laid a red flannel shirt and well-worn jeans. "Whose were these? Johnny Appleseed or Paul Bunyan?" he asked Emilia, who was still in the kitchen.

"Whichever you prefer," she answered.

Mark stepped into the jeans and buttoned the shirt. "Must have been Paul Bunyan. I prefer his mystical deeds. These fit perfectly."

"Maybe not when you exhale." Emilia smiled from the door.

"You think they are tight?"

"A little more than when Victor wore them."

"Victor?" He dropped to the corner of the bed. "I thought the two of you were just friends."

"There's that look of jealousy I missed earlier. Now don't go taking it out on Hansel again."

"You did wash them?" His hands rubbed the thighs.

She sat next to him. "He left a few things with me when he moved to a smaller apartment. I think he meant to take those to Goodwill." She turned him. "Good thing, though. My men have found them handy. That is, after I ripped their clothes off." He reciprocated her laugh with a kiss.

◆ ◆ ◆

At the bar table, Emilia replaced the binder with a place mat and served him a plate of eggs and potatoes, "I thought you were just going to make coffee," he said.

"I felt guilty about your clothes, and I thought it would be better to make up for it by fixing breakfast." She prepared a smaller plate and brought it to the mat across from him. "Why were you up so early?"

His eyes didn't waver from her glance. "I thought I heard the wind chime."

She sipped at the coffee, and over the brim of her cup, her hazel eyes shifted slightly from her focus. "But I know it didn't sound."

"It has been rather quiet. I suppose there's no wind."

"I put it away last night," she said, replacing the cup on the table.

Her fingers encircled the cup's edge, and her eyes stared into the black coffee. His own breath hastened and the muscles of his chest tightened. He grasped her hands from across the table. "Will you go with me to Fort Hamilton?"

She pulled away from his hold and carried the cup to the sink. To the morning light outside the window, she replied, "I said I will go anywhere with you."

There was no crime for her guilt, but plenty of punishment. In the expression of her body, turned to him, leaning on the sink she gripped behind her, he saw her pain.

"Let the guilt go," is all he said in their embrace.

Chapter 23

US Highway 50 traverses ranges and desert basins in the heart of Nevada. Its designation as the loneliest road in America is well deserved. No other vehicle had come their way for more than forty minutes. In the flat road ahead, none was anticipated.

Unfurled onto the valley, the late morning sun glittered on the sagebrush. The monotony of recurrent rents on the yellow median carried Mark's thoughts beyond the black asphalt, to the stripe of highway that continued unbent ahead of them. It seemed as straight as the ruler Sister Eugene had whacked across his head to distract his attention from Lillian, a third-grade classmate. With chagrin, he recalled the note for his mother the nun had pinned to his shirt pocket. It was not the slap with the ruler, nor the maternal spank of his buttock that had evoked remorse, but his mother's frown of disappointment. He had then determined to not ever bear such public shame.

To the imagined feel of the pin on his shirt, Mark brought his hand to his chest. Inside the shirt pocket, the paper on which he had dueled Shakespeare crinkled with his touch. He had finished the poem that morning, but had left it unread. The sullen look on Emilia's face had unsettled his determination. He had stowed it for later; then was not the occasion.

In days, it was not much time, but the last four made Mark feel he'd lived a lifetime. In the kitchen, he had held Emilia. "Let the guilt go," he had advised, but except for her grip on the sink behind her, she remained impassive.

It did not take long to transport to his home a week's wardrobe and her toiletries, but it seemed to Mark that something had been left behind. That night, they shared childhood stories, but only to keep each other company.

"We don't have to go," he told her in bed.

"It's something you feel you have to do," she answered. "I'll get over it." Her breadth in his ear was deep; her fingers on his chest were moist.

The phone rang at five, and she went in to work that morning. For two days that were to be vacation, she pledged to work.

"They're short-staffed," Emilia explained, and kissed him on her run out of the darkened bedroom.

Waste is what a meal becomes when it is not eaten. It was what Mark felt the night after her second shift. He told her the dinner he prepared was to retrieve her distant spirit.

"If I could surrender my guilt as casually as you have your life," she replied at the table, "I would have no hesitation to walk you to a sacrificial altar."

Tears are for sorrow, and solitude for despair, but he had no response to what Emilia had said. With the ache of his shattered heart, Mark simply stared away.

She cleared the dishes, and proposed to follow him to bed. Mark lay on the mattress and waited in the darkness, but it was hours before he heard the stairs creak with her footstep.

His back was turned, but he saw Emilia's shadow from the hall light enter the door. He kept his eyes closed in pretended slumber and heard her clothes drop at the foot of the bed. A draft lapped his skin when she lifted the comforter and a gale when she lay down next to him.

"Let's leave in the morning," she said.

◆ ◆ ◆

A guitar carried the tune of a train on track, and a harmonica was at the whistle. "Let's make this a night we'll never forget," Emilia sang along with Suzy Boggus on the radio. "There's time for one more; one more for the road."

In the middle of the Nevada Great Basin, a country western station was the only selection with good reception, and it was

210

just as well. With her eyes closed, Emilia continued to sing, as if the journey she sang about was her own. Her hair streamed through the slit of the window and tousled by the wind outside the truck. He tapped his fingers on the steering wheel, in rhythm with the music.

It was early when they had awakened that morning, and he felt as if he had not slept at all. He hoped Emilia's quiet when they packed was weariness and not a change of mind.

"We should take my camping gear," she said, with it already at hand. "It's pretty comfortable for two people."

There was not much room left in the back of the truck when he loaded what she thought they might need. He joked it was good to have a woman as traveling companion, for there was nothing they would lack. That is, until it had to be carried. She seemed not to hear.

Emilia sat on the front passenger seat, the map opened on her lap. "Maybe we can have breakfast outside Carson."

The silence on the drive down the Sierra Nevada seemed to languor, but it was not until Silver Springs that they stopped. He needed coffee to keep his eyes open.

"I think we'll make good time," she said after the waitress took their order.

Mark remembered the Harley Davidson couple at Topaz Lake, who traveled on schedule toward Las Vegas. The love they shared was tattooed on their arms and seemed to have survived their cruel banter. Why, then, would his own love feel threatened by silence?

"We are not on our way to a funeral," he answered aloud his thought. "I only meant it metaphorically."

A drop of water dripped on the side of her glass. "What?" she asked, confused.

"Returning to the ghost town. Reclaiming my life."

"And under what pretense," she replied, "do you reclaim a life by relinquishing it to a challenge?"

He strained in her glance. "Leukemia is more than a challenge. I know. I researched it. It is, in fact, the consumption of a life."

"You're being melodramatic. You don't even know if that's what you have." She rested back in the chair.

"What I do have is what you have given me." He folded his hands and leaned forward to the table. "The pleasure of being a man. The joy of your love, and of loving you. That, I don't want to put on hold, nor compromise, as I've done all my life."

"Remember what you said about why Billy killed himself?" she asked. "He was afraid of the consequences of pleasure, and the responsibility to sustain it. All I want is for you to realize your responsibility for the metaphor you seek."

To confront his own guilt, he needed to understand the accusation, and that had eluded him. Love, he had thought, was the resolution, the confidence to be foolish and not care of the consequence. But what Emilia proposed was that his own absolution was not in love, but in his will to sustain it, as well as to endure the consequence.

◆◆◆

Blue, steel cold pierced the distance and recognized the features he knew were leukemia's. Mark cringed and awakened his thoughts to the clear sky ahead.

"Given more time to laugh and dance," Emilia sang with Vince Gill, "Given more time to have the chance, to show you this is where I want to be—Lord, I wish I was given more time for you and me." She returned Mark's gaze, and Vince continued on the radio, unattended.

"I love it when you smile," he said, and reached for the hand she placed on his lap.

Emilia slid toward the middle of the seat and rested her head on his shoulder; staring at the distant range. "Getting tired?"

"A little, but I don't think we have much more to go."

In the rear view mirror, he noticed mushroom clouds rising above the crest of the mountain ranges, which threatened rain. Ahead of them was the perennial thirst he used to describe the lackluster desert. Other than the shadows from the heavens, the colors of the panorama never seemed to vary. Only tan rocks on sandy soil, cropped by sagebrush, appeared to reflect the radiance of the sun.

"Do you think it'll rain?" he asked.

"The weather report was for it to be clear and dry, at least through tomorrow," she answered.

"Let's hope those clouds following us drop their load beyond our camp. I want to count the stars while we share a sleeping bag."

"That sounds nice," she replied. "We can wake up for the sunrise."

We pattern our lives for comfort when we are most afraid of its challenges. Mark recalled Emilia elaborating on himself as a man of habit. *Under what pretense do you reclaim a life by relinquishing it to a challenge?*

"I thought they would have paved it by now," he said about the turnoff gravel road from US 50. "I hope it's not like this the entire way to Hamilton."

"How long ago was it since you were here last?" Emilia sat back into the seat. "It looks kind of rough."

A lifetime, he thought to say, but answered, "Twenty years."

"Maybe we should set up camp first." She pointed to a campground and the "No Services" sign at the entrance to Humboldt National Forest.

"I'd just as well go on, before it gets dark."

Dry rivulets furrowed across the road and formed deep clefts in the decline of the steep hill. Granite boulders held sentry at each turn, as the sagebrush of the basin yielded to pine on the higher altitudes.

"Thank god for four-wheel drive," he said. "I suppose they haven't gotten around to repairing the road since winter."

Emilia looked at the mountain ahead of them. "There's still quite a bit of snow at the top. You think we should go on?"

"It looks like it's only above the tree line. Hamilton should be well below that."

◆ ◆ ◆

The road became level at the timberline, and just beyond the forest, a small wooden shelter stood to the side. A mound of snow lingered in the shade of its ramshackle porch. Mark pulled at the locked bolt on the wooden door and read the sign. Tourists were required to deposit a five-dollar entry fee into an adjacent secure box.

"From the look of the place, it doesn't seem a ranger will be by in the near future." Emilia called from her seat in the truck.

"Well, then, we'll save the five dollars." He slipped the bill back into the pocket of his jeans.

The valley and skeleton foundations of Hamilton were less than a mile from the station. In the shadow of Treasure Hill, they seemed a trough of shattered dreams, Mark's own among them. He stopped the truck at two weathered brick posts, vestiges of the courthouse.

"There's not much left." She stretched outside the truck.

"There never were, only the illusions for which so many lives were spent," he replied.

A sullen gust of wind tumbled sagebrush away from their feet and stole the hollow sound of the truck doors closing. Vacant brick stairs, molded by the step of wind and water, channeled the trail they followed. Wooden studs without walls, like a forest after a fire, rose from the ground. Shrubs reclaimed concrete slabs. They walked along Main Street.

"Are we fools to be led by dreams?" he asked.

"Are we fools to do otherwise?" she answered.

◆ ◆ ◆

Prosperity had bypassed most of the townspeople by the time of their death. Instead of marble, the headstone they read at the entrance to the cemetery was hand carved on granite rock. Its inscription was a farewell to a beloved wife, dead at childbirth. It stood alone.

"Do you think the child lived on?" Emilia asked.

"Epitaphs are unfair. They tease our curiosity and entice the voyeur to imagine what is left untold." He walked through the brush, and glanced at every tombstone. "No wonder I was trapped by my imagination. But I can't remember where it was."

Most of the epitaphs were difficult to read. Rain and snow had withered the wood on which many had been written, and windborne gravel had pelted the inscriptions. At the outskirts of the cemetery, hidden in foliage, partly buried by soil, Mark found the wooden marker for which he searched.

"Died 1873," he read aloud. "It once read Mark, age 22, but this has to be the one."

Mark stood still, his stare fixed to the earth. Emilia knelt and cleared the space of brush with her hands.

"He should be in there," he said.

In his introspection, he searched, but found no envy to dispel, or anger to feel. It was only dirt and stone under the soles of his feet.

"There never was a life to borrow, only an excuse." Solace accompanied his words.

A golden band striped the cherry-rose fluffs of clouds that drifted over the western ridges. A swift breeze tumbled the mustard-colored sage Emilia had cleared toward the town below the cemetery. Mark knelt where she had stopped to listen.

"It's been easier to blame what I could not control than to gamble and endure the consequences." He held her hands. "If to die is to be without you, I will endure whatever it be to live forever."

Pebbles, smoothed by the drift of snow and glide of wind, rasped on the weight of their love. Commitment is not words of duty, but assent to passion. He submitted to their intimacy, indiscreetly, and with lust.

"Let's go to San Jose," Emilia said when they rested.

◆ ◆ ◆

Darkness came to the eastern slopes earlier than Mark had anticipated. But the cloud cover that had developed over the town gave time a false pretense. It was seven when they returned to the truck.

Emilia strapped her seat belt on. "I guess we won't be able to see the stars tonight."

"We might as well head back. Eureka is about a three-hour drive. We could spend the night in a motel." He felt the chill of damp air and stepped into the driver's seat. "It's probably going to rain."

"So much for weather reports," she added. "I just hope it doesn't snow. It would be rough on that road out of here."

Past the ranger station that, in the darkness, appeared like an outcropping from the forest, the rain began to fall. Sounding like pellets on the truck's metal, sheets of water curtained the windshield. In intervals, the wiper ripped at his visual field. The road illuminated by their headlights, they continued heading down the mountain.

Flashes of lightning, reflected from the walls of granite, silhouetted the forest on either side of the hill. Water filled the rivulets, and the truck tires gripped the gravel with four-wheel traction. Mark was confident of their safety.

With the crash of thunder and a reflected flash of lightning, a boulder smashed into the front of the truck. Mark struggled to control the spin of the steering wheel.

As the truck rolled, the windshield burst into shattered glass, and the metal frame crumbled. When the dashboard jammed into his left flank, he released the seatbelt and turned to shield Emilia. His pain was concealed by fear that she would be hurt.

Metal scraped against rock on every roll of the truck. Mud oozed through the dented doors, and shrubs slapped at either side. The din inside their chamber cast its own dimension, and the unremitting rattle suspended time.

Silence erupted, as if the world had ended. He sat still and held Emilia tight. Counting the drops of rain that sounded on the ceiling, he knew the storm had passed. A brief spill of gravel disrupted the quiet, and he expected their tumble to resume. But the truck remained lodged against the bark of a tree.

Fate grants no terms and accepts no bargains, he thought, but the courage he awaited was granted when he felt her stir in his arms.

"Are you all right?" Emilia asked.

Mark pulled away from the dashboard that pressed against his side. Pain surged from his flank on the turn. He held back the scream swelling within his lungs and remained motionless, waiting for the pain to subside.

"Mark, are you okay?"

"Yes," he said and noticed her touch dripped with moisture that smelled of blood. He fastened his glance towards her voice, but only the gloss of her hair was apparent in the dark. "Oh, god, are you all right?"

"Yes, I'm okay. What happened?"

"I think we were hit by a rock slide." He looked ahead, through the soiled slime that screened the broken windshield. A single beam from a headlight illuminated a mound of rock and mud, in which the truck was partly buried. A thin cropping of trees stood on a forty-five degree incline.

"Can you tell how far from the road we've fallen?" she asked. Her side window was intact, but covered under a heap of debris. "At least we've landed right-side up."

The driver's door was caved in and jammed against a tree. There was only blackness everywhere he turned. The inside lamp worked.

"Mark," she said. "There's blood on your chest."

Deep abrasions on his left side oozed blood. It hurt when he raised his arm to lift the shirt. "It looks like only scrapes," he assured Emilia.

"I have a first-aid kit." She motioned toward the disarray of their gear and added, "Somewhere back there."

The luggage was strewn onto the downhill side of the truck. A clearing led to the rear door, which had burst open.

"Let's get some of this stuff out, and I can get you bandaged up." She climbed over the seat and out the rear door.

"Oh," he moaned when he made the effort to climb out.

"Mark, are you sure you're all right?" Emilia returned with a towel. "Here, hold this against the cuts while I look for the kit."

He pressed the towel against the wounds and watched the blood seep through to drip between his fingers; *kind of thin ain't it,* he recalled the nurse's observation.

"I think I broke a rib." He felt pain with the pressure of his hand.

Emilia returned and applied a bulky dressing. "Sit up," she said and wound an Ace wrap around his chest, applying pressure at the wounds.

"Have you got a silver bullet?" he asked through gritted teeth. "Didn't it all begin like this—you nursing me?"

"No, it all began with a bit of yolk on your lip."

She stared at the bandage she had wrapped and waited for seepage of blood. Her eyes seemed solemn, without the hazel tint of when she first glanced at him over the corrugated edges of the newspaper, a lifetime ago at the cafe counter.

"I think the bandage will hold. I don't see fresh bleeding." Emilia carried the kit to the backpack she had left outside and returned with his down jacket. "It's pretty cold outside. You better put this on."

His side hurt when he moved the arms, but he managed to put the jacket on. Emilia helped him climb over the seat and out through the back of the truck.

"It's a bit of a hike up to the road," she said. "You go on up. I'll put everything we need into one pack and carry it with me."

"I can carry it," he said, but fell with pain when he reached for it. "All right, so I won't." He carried the two sleeping bags, after Emilia helped him stand.

Fatigue, out of proportion to their altitude, overwhelmed him on the road. He sat on a fallen rock and panted to catch his breath, his back to Emilia, who followed.

"Mark, what's the matter?" she asked and let drop the backpack. She knelt in front of him to look at his face. "You're so pale. It's got to be more than a broken rib."

He could not reply and only wished they were in bed, to feel the softness of her flesh.

She unzipped his jacket and raised the shirt. The bandage was still dry. "I'll set up the tent here and walk to the highway to get some help. You rest."

"No." He did not mean to shout, but he was afraid it would not have come out.

Tears flowed from her eyes. "You need help. I've got to get you to a doctor." Emilia walked to the pack and strapped it on her back.

Wolves don't howl to the sunrise, he thought, and looked up to the crowded canopy of trees. There would not be much to see of the sky from where they stood. The ranger station was at the edge of the forest and faced east. It was a much better place, he thought, for them to set camp.

"We're less than a mile from the ranger station," he strained to say. "It'll take you a day to walk to the highway."

"But we need to get you to a hospital."

"A ranger will come before you can even reach the highway." He stood up slowly, with the sleeping bags held to brace his chest, and walked toward Hamilton. "He'll stop at the station."

The drag of his step on the gravel sounded a rhythm. He timed an iambic pentameter. "There is no greater overture of love than through poetry," he reminded Emilia, but could not muster the breath to recite the poem in his pocket.

"The chestnut grows best where the tree blooms full," she said at his side.

"Passion flourishes nearest from whence it came—you and me," he replied.

◆ ◆ ◆

Scattered clouds glided in a black sky glittering with stars. A mist seemed suspended above the chaparral in the flat valley at the end of the uphill road. That they had seen it in the sunlight allowed them to find the cabin in the moonless night. Mark rested on the porch.

"There may be a phone inside." She attempted to pry open the door with a knife, but it broke. A small gap, though, was left, against which she heaved with her shoulder. The door burst open. "Pretty good for religious studies, isn't it?"

Even in the dark, the heavy cloud of dust discharged inside, reflecting the scant light outside. She waited for the particles to settle.

"Come inside. It feels a little warmer," she called out to Mark. Just to the side of the door she found a lantern. The kerosene within the copper reservoir sloshed when she lifted it. "Good thing I brought some matches."

The wick burned dim, to last throughout the night, and the lantern was set on a side table she centered in the room. A small desk, a layer of dust on its flat top, was opposite the door.

Stored inside an adjacent steel cabinet were only the droppings of rodents. Against the sidewall rested a cot, most of its springs broken off and a rolled-up mattress that sagged through them to the floor. At a back corner was a cast-iron wood burner, but its chimney pipe lacked a segment to the roof. Nothing in the room was twentieth century.

She dusted off the mattress and turned to the window in which Mark's reflection entered the room. He slouched into a wooden chair on entering.

"I'll roll it out on the floor." Tears streaked a trail on her soot-covered cheeks when she carried the mattress to him. "It'll be more comfortable."

"You've been crying," he said.

Emilia sat at his feet, her chest against his legs. She rubbed his hands to relieve the cold and looked up at him.

He tried to respond, but could barely hold his eyes to return her gaze. He forced a smile, but felt his lips only quiver. "You are beautiful," he said and tried to grip her hand. After a pause, he asked, "I did come further than half a tank of gas, didn't I?"

"Why are you talking like this?" She straightened, and then spread the mattress on the floor. "Lie down and get some rest. The ranger should be here in the morning."

"I think it'll be a beautiful sunrise," he said and leaned forward on the chair to look out the door. "Let's put the sleeping bags together outside."

◆◆◆

Sage rustled beyond the platform of the porch. From the lantern, a dim flicker of light was reflected on the ceiling. She placed the mattress horizontally on the wooden planks, to cushion their upper bodies. Inside the sleeping bags, they were warm as a cold breeze fanned their exposed faces. He watched her hand reach among a billion stars and her finger dip into the void. Embraced with Emilia the rest of the night, he kept a watch for the last star on the horizon.

Biography:

Carlos Alvarado grew up in California and now lives in Florida. **Cry WaterColors** is his first book, and he is working on his second novel, **Tujunga**, a romantic medical adventure. He is a practicing physician.